VIOLET

THE PALMER SISTERS BOOK 6

KAYT MILLER

CONTENTS

Also by Kayt Miller   vii
Content Warning   xi

Chapter 1   1
Chapter 2   8
Chapter 3   18
Chapter 4   26
Chapter 5   32
Chapter 6   36
Chapter 7   40
Chapter 8   45
Chapter 9   47
Chapter 10   55
Chapter 11   60
Chapter 12   63
Chapter 13   68
Chapter 14   74
Chapter 15   80
Chapter 16   87
Chapter 17   106
Chapter 18   110
Chapter 19   120
Chapter 20   124
Chapter 21   128
Chapter 22   134
Chapter 23   137
Chapter 24   144
Chapter 25   152
Chapter 26   156
Chapter 27   157
Chapter 28   167

Chapter 29   171
Chapter 30   178
Chapter 31   181
Chapter 32   188
Chapter 33   195
Chapter 34   202
Chapter 35   207
Chapter 36   212
Chapter 37   215
Chapter 38   222
Chapter 39   226
Chapter 40   234
Chapter 41   237
Chapter 42   241
Chapter 43   243
Epilogue   248

Help   257
Acknowledgments   259
Also by Kayt Miller   261
About the Author   263
Thank you!   265
Sneak Peek: Molly   267

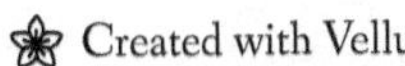 Created with Vellum

ALSO BY KAYT MILLER

Bedhead

Redhead

Deadhead

FarmBoy

Game Changer

One of a Kind

The Virginia Chronicles

Our of the Blue: The Flynns Book One

Mick'sology: The Flynns Book Two

Vested Interest: The Flynns Book Three

The Importance of Being Ernie: The Flynns Book Four

The Importance of Being Kennedy's: The Flynns Book Five

Quirky Girl: The Flynns Book Six

The Art of the Game

Lainie: The Palmer Sisters Book 1

Agatha: The Palmer Sisters Book 2

Sadie: The Palmer Sisters Book 3

Cortland: The Palmer Sisters Book 4

Keely: The Palmer Sisters Book 5

Violet: The Palmer Sisters Book 6

Molly: The Palmer Sisters Book 7

The Portrait Painter

Hopeful Romantic (Link coming soon.)

Thanks to Margie Dill (Link coming soon.)

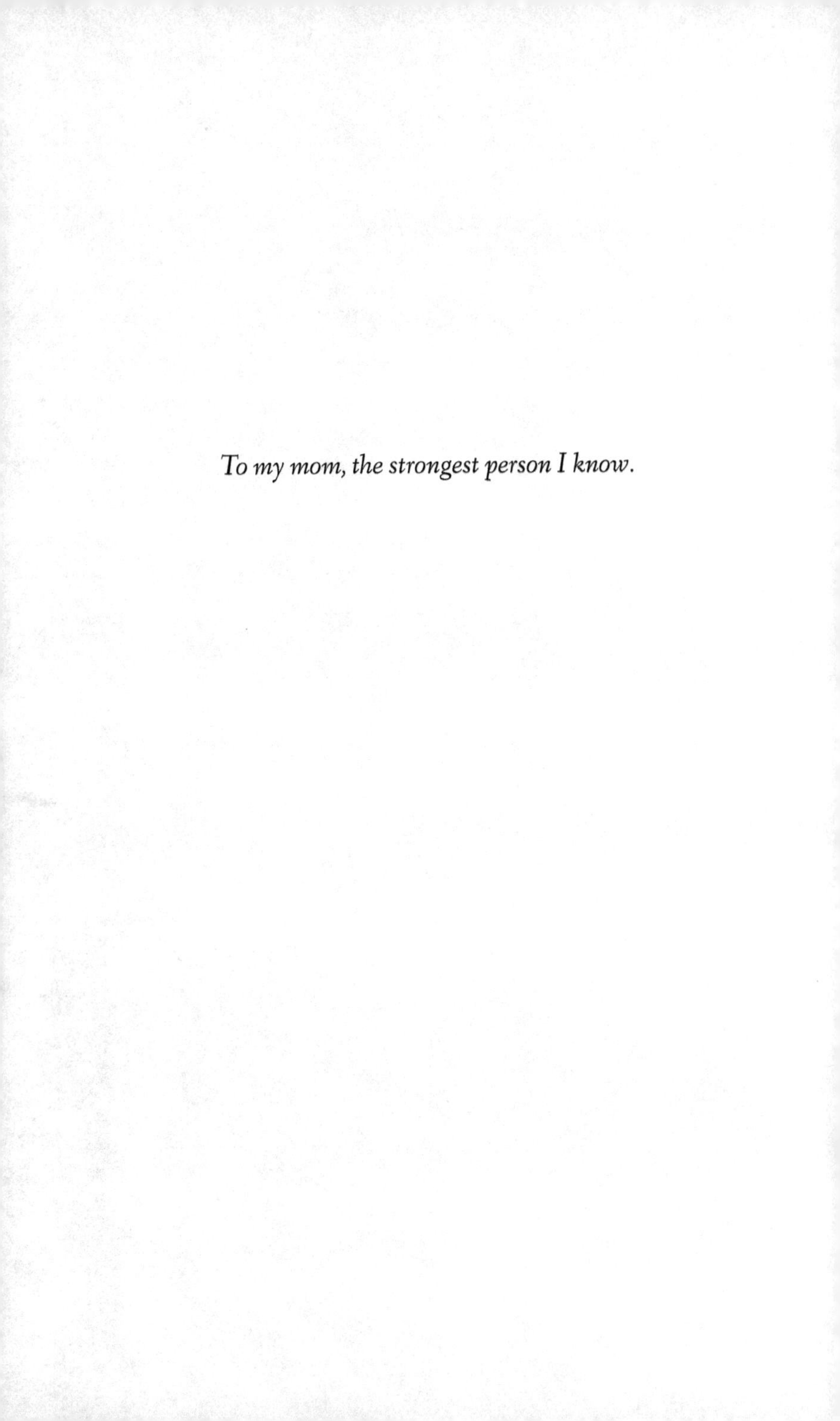

To my mom, the strongest person I know.

CONTENT WARNING

This book contains content that some readers may find disturbing including depictions of rape and sexual assault. Reader discretion is advised.

CHAPTER 1

VIOLET

"Hey, Violet."

I look up from my hiding spot in a shady corner of Keeton and Lainie's lower patio to see Nick Martelli approach.

Here we go.

Stepping closer, he points to the lounge chair next to me. "May I?"

"Of course." I know what's coming. I just didn't expect us to talk about it at my sister's rehearsal dinner. At least we're secluded back here; no one will be able to hear us.

"I've got news," Nick says as he sits on the side of the chair so he's facing me.

"News?" I'm not looking forward to this conversation at all. I've been dreading it, actually. We've had exactly two talks about Kyle Maines. Two excruciatingly uncomfortable and painful conversations. In the first one, back in May, Nick told me what he knew about Kyle, things that both surprised and frustrated me. First of all, he lives in Sedona. A city only about a hundred and fifty miles straight south of Page. Not a surprise, since I've seen him twice here in town. One of those times, the first time I'd seen him since *it* happened, he approached me at Murphy's Pub.

Kyle is what you'd call well-connected. His mom is Frances Abernathy, the Lieutenant Governor. Of Arizona. At the time *it* happened, she was the Pima County District Attorney. To be specific, she was the DA of Tucson. So, even if the Tucson police had done their job, nothing would have happened to Kyle anyway. She'd never have prosecuted her own son. It's no wonder the cops did what they did.

At our second talk, I gave Nick a copy of my original police report. What good it'll do him, I have no idea. I'm sure the Tucson PD have it too.

Nick sighs. "So, here's where I'm at on this, Violet."

A sigh isn't good. I lean forward, anticipating bad news.

"You know I've been working on this off duty, right?"

I nod. I knew he was doing his best to keep the promise he made to my twin, Keely. She didn't want me to have to deal with any of this again, and I don't either.

"And you know I've only been talking to people I can trust."

I nod again. He's been doing everything he can to keep things quiet. "I know. Thank you."

He arches his brow. "I'm not going to be able to keep doing it."

"What? You're done investigating?" I'm not sure how I feel about that. I mean, I hate Kyle Maines. I'd love to see him rot in jail, but the idea that this whole thing would go away now is appealing too. No. That's not right. He needs to be held accountable which means I need to be strong.

"No. I won't be able to keep it quiet."

Oh. "Oh? Why not?"

"You weren't the only one."

"Oh," I say softly. I knew that was probably the case. The guy knew what he was doing that night. It felt like it was all choreographed or something.

"In every city he's lived, there have been complaints filed, but..."

"No charges?"

Nick nods slowly. "No charges."

"Because of his mom?"

Nick nods, wincing. I can see why. The Arizona police have dropped the ball.

"How many others?"

"Keep in mind this is just speculation—educated speculation. My contact in Tucson says the cop in charge when you went to school in Tucson is gone. That's why they were able to dig into the archival records for other possible victims." Nick's jaw clenches. "We also found out that the cop from Tucson is now in Sedona."

I gasp. "Oh, my God. How is that possible? He moves wherever Kyle lives or something?"

"It seems that way, but we haven't looked into that yet. That's why I'm telling you this thing has to expand."

"So, you think that cop has been working to keep Kyle out of jail."

Nick nods. "Yeah, I think so. "

"Then there are probably more." It's not a question; of course there are. He was at the University of Southeast Arizona for four years and president of that fraternity for three of those. "Where else has he lived besides Sedona and Tucson?"

"He grew up in Scottsdale," Nick says. Scottsdale is a very wealthy city just outside of Phoenix. "His parents still have a home there. I've only been able to learn of one incident there when he was in high school."

Poor girl. I look up at Nick. "What about recently? In Sedona?"

"Nothing so far. But he's a predator and I'm guessing a serial rapist. He's not going to stop, especially since there's no one to stop him."

"Until now."

"Until now." Nick gives me a little smile. "There's no doubt in my mind that if he hasn't done it yet, he will. It's been his permanent residence for almost a year. It's only a matter of time."

I nod, hoping we can stop talking about Kyle soon. I'm starting to feel anxious. I do my best to keep Kyle from my thoughts. I guess that's not going to be possible now.

"Luckily, my friend in Tucson was able to do a little research on the sly." Reaching into the back pocket of his dress pants, Nick pulls out a folded piece of paper. "Your original police report."

I take it from him and quickly scan the report. "This isn't...."

"I know. It was doctored sometime after you left the station."

"Why?"

"Read it." Nick pauses. "Please."

I don't want to read it, but I will. Sighing, I start at the top. Everything related to my name, address, and my vital statistics are correct. But when I get down to the part where it summarizes the incident, it's different. Where mine goes into disgustingly great detail about what Kyle did to me, this one was much shorter, changed to:

__Synopsis__: The alleged victim in this case, Violet Leigh Palmer, age 19, reported she was sexually assaulted by

*possible suspect Kyle Joshua Maines at Omega Alpha Pi
fraternity located on the University of Southeast Arizona
campus.*

*__Narrative__: Miss Palmer alleged that she met Kyle
Maines at the party. She stated that he was concerned at
the level of her intoxication.*

I snort. "Concerned with the level of my intoxication?
That's a lie."

"Keep reading."

---

*She claims Kyle took her by the hand and led her upstairs
to a bedroom that she assumed was Kyle Maines's room.
There, he told her to lie down on the bed to rest, but
Maines claimed she didn't want to be alone, so Kyle
climbed into bed with her...*

Shaking my head, I look up at Nick. "I can't... that's not
what happened. This is nothing like my report."

"I know."

"Can't you just show them mine?"

"It's easy to recreate documents these days." He shrugs.

"So, just like the rape, it's my word against the Tucson
police?"

He nods but says, "If you were the only victim, I'd say yes,
but since we suspect there are others...."

"You can get their police reports?"

"We hope so. That's why we need to open this up. I can't

keep it a secret anymore. As a matter of fact, we may need to go public. As in, notifying the press."

I lay my head back onto my lounge chair. I knew this would happen. Looking over at him, I ask, "Do you think his mother knows?"

Nick arches his brow. "Yeah." He nods. "She's got to know."

"How could she let him...?" I mean, she's a woman. "Why would you stand by a man who raped multiple women, even if he *is* your son?"

"I have no idea, Violet." Nick reaches his hand out and touches the top of my wrist, patting my hand gently. "So." He clears his throat. "You need to prepare yourself."

I look up suddenly and my eyes meet Nick's. "Huh?" *What's he talking about?*

"I can't sit back and risk him hurting another woman, Violet. I need to make this an official investigation. I need to get the captain up to speed. As it is, he's not going to be happy that I've gone rogue on all this."

I stare at his face and blink like I've got something in my eye. I think I do. Tears. But I won't let those fall tonight. Not when we're all so happy about Lainie and Keeton.

Nick leans forward, whispering, "Shh. It's going to be okay, Violet. I promise you. I'll keep you safe."

How can he say that? It's going to get out. Everyone will know. I won't be able to keep this secret anymore.

"Violet." He pauses. "It's time you talked to your family."

I shake my head slowly, but I know he's right. It's time they all found out why I'm such a freak of nature. Why I'm the weird one in my family, why I turned inward almost six years ago and have been working all that time to bring myself out of it.

When it happened, I dropped out of college. I couldn't stay there. I literally packed my bags the day the police told me they didn't believe me, and never looked back. I lived with my dad for a year, working part-time jobs here and there. Since then, I've gone back to school. I've been making progress.

I hate this. It's going to hurt the people I love the most. I scan the crowd for my dad, and I spot him near the pool talking to Keeton's ex-wife, Deb. He's smiling, and I watch as he throws his head back, laughing at something she said. There's no one who deserves to smile and laugh more than my father. Finally, after all these years, he's happy, and this news, this drama, is going to kill him.

"Violet. It's time," Nick whispers.

I know. Turning back to Nick, I say, "Give me until after Keeton and Lainie get back from their honeymoon." No way am I telling them tonight or tomorrow, their wedding day. "Can you do that?"

"A week then?" he asks.

I nod. "A week."

CHAPTER 2

"Did he tell you?" Keely asks as she plops down on the lounge chair beside me.

"Yeah." I'm doing my best to act nonchalant about the entire conversation I had with Nick twenty minutes ago. It hasn't really sunk in, to be honest.

"You okay?"

I turn to my left and look at my twin. It's not often that my sister is this serious. It worries me. "I'm okay."

"When are you going to tell everyone?"

"After the honeymoon." I look out at the party, in full swing now, and sigh. My dad is still talking with Deb, but now Keeton and Lainie have joined their little circle. All four of them are beaming with happiness. "I don't want to ruin this."

I hear a scream, then a splash as Billy, one of Keeton's crew, does a cannonball into the pool, splashing everyone nearby. Everyone, including Agatha and Sadie, my other two sisters.

Keely snickers. "That's gonna piss off Sadie. That's a white dress she's wearing."

I look back over, and sure enough, Charlie Ashbury, Sadie's boyfriend, wraps his arms around her to hide her now transparent dress. "I think Charlie's the one who's mad."

Keely titters again. "He's so uptight." Turning to me, she asks, "So, where's the golden god?"

"Who?"

"Eric."

Okay. I don't know where to start with her question. "Eric?" I stare at her. "Eric Gustafson?"

"Uh, yeah. Where's that stud of yours?"

"Keely." I cough at her comment. "Mine? He's not mine."

Keely's feet quickly slide over the side of the chair until she's in the exact spot Nick was a while ago. "It's time for you to live, Vi."

"*I live!*" I say defensively. *What?* I do.

"Okay, how 'bout this. You need to *love*."

I scoff. "Just because you're all in love with Nick now doesn't mean it's for everyone."

"Honey," Keely says softly, "You deserve to be happy, and Eric Gustafson has the hots for you."

"He does not!" I say way too loudly, because there's no way one Mr. Gorgeous Eric Gustafson would even look at me twice. The guy is an eleven on the hot-o-meter—one that only goes to ten.

"He does. If he shows up—"

"He won't. Lainie said he's at the shop dealing with a last-minute repair or something. Some customer that's a pain in the you-know-what."

"Ass. The word is ass. You can cuss, you know. You're an adult."

"Shut it. I don't need to say those words to be an adult. I prefer not to. That's all. Feel free to cuss all you want."

"Fuckin'-a-right, sis." Keely laughs. She stops suddenly, looking me square in the eye. "Mark my words, Vi, that man has a thing for you."

"Keely, no," I whine. "He's too...."

"Hot? Sexy? Thor-like?" she says the last word in a husky voice.

I laugh. Yes. "No. He's a player. He could get any woman he wanted."

"And?"

"Why would he pick me?"

"Because you're gorgeous. And perfect."

I scoff.

"I have no idea why you can't see yourself like everyone else does. You look exactly like Mom."

"No."

"Yes. Look in a goddamn mirror, Violet. You're the prettiest one."

I look at her like she's insane. "I'm not."

"You are." She laughs, but it's not a happy one. "Just look at yourself. God, that pisses me off," she mutters. "You look *just* like her."

"I'm broken." It's my only defense. I know I look like our mom. A mom I miss every single day.

Keely slides off her seat and onto mine, forcing me to practically slide off the other side. "Vi," she whispers. "You're the least broken Palmer sister. You were raped, for fuck's sake. That fucker didn't *break* you. Hell, Vi, you're the strongest one of us."

I'm not the strongest. Not by a long shot. "I'm not ready."

"I call bullshit."

"Keely, that's not fair."

"I've watched you for six years. I've seen it all. I saw you the week after, when you wouldn't get out of your bed and when you dealt with the fucking Tucson police. I'd say you were broken then. Since then, I've seen you do everything you could to heal. I'm not just talking about therapy. I had a front row seat to your struggles when you moved back in with Dad, working all those shitty jobs while you tried to figure shit out. You went back to school, and now you're only a year away from your degree."

I nod. I did do all of that.

"You go out with us more and more." She looks up at me, then scans my body. "Your body be bangin', girl. Something we can all see tonight, since you're not wearing your typical huge T-shirt and sweats." She rolls her eyes. "I know you've been working out, eating better, not drinking as much, which sucks for me, but it's good too."

"I'm trying."

"I know. We all see it, but I'm the only one who knows how far you've come and the reason for it all. It's time you tell the four other people who love you most in this world what happened to you."

"I know." I say it so quietly I barely hear it myself.

~

I'm mingling. That's right, ladies and gents, I've left my hidey-hole in the back corner of the lower patio and I'm now walking amongst the guests at tonight's shindig. I pass by a small cluster of guys from Keeton's shop, better known as Gustafson Custom Motorcycles. They smile and wave, and I do the same. I'm proud of myself. A couple years ago, I'd never have been able to do that. Hell, I'd have stayed hidden a year ago.

Walking around the pool area, I stop to notice how pretty everything is. Lainie and Keeton didn't have to do much to make it look like this. The landscaping was already perfect. Lainie just added some pretty potted plants and new, colorful patio cush-ions and pillows. It's perfect. There are clusters of seating areas and small tables provided by the caterer. The same caterer, Beth of Class Act Catering, that Agatha works for now and then.

I make my way to the tables that Beth has set up. There are chafing dishes filled with yummy-smelling foods. One holds chimichangas—an Arizona staple—while another holds Sonoran hot dogs. The grill has been going nonstop producing grilled chicken, burgers, steaks, and pork chops. There are so many side dishes; there's no way we can eat them all. Then there's the dessert table. I helped Sadie with that. We baked pies, cupcakes, sweet breads, heck, everything you can think of for a picnic-themed party like this one.

Filling my plate with a variety of items, I move over to a small table near the pool where Sadie and Agatha sit with their men.

"Violet? You want a beer?" Ian, Agatha's fiancé, asks.

"I'll take a soda." I smile. "Diet, please. Thank you."

"No problem. Back in a second."

"Isn't my man the sweetest?" sighs Agatha dreamily.

"Nope, mine's the sweetest," Sadie coos as she reaches out to pinch Charlie's cheek.

"Well," Keely says as she sidles up to the table. "Mine's the hottest."

"Thanks, babe." Nick smirks. "I think you're pretty hot yourself."

"I know." Like Keely's heard it all before. *She has.*

We all laugh, though. Keely keeps us entertained, that's for sure.

"Now, we just need to find someone perfect for Violet."

"Done and done," Keely declares.

"Who?" Agatha leans over the table; her eyes look like they're popping out of her head.

My face gets hot, which means it's also turning a bright shade of red. I know they can all tell I'm embarrassed. "No one. She's full of it."

"Who?" It's Sadie's turn to ask.

"No one. Ignore her. She's drunk." I pause. "Or insane."

I guess that was funny, because they all laugh.

"Okay, it's just a theory." Keely glares at me. "Can I say that? Huh, Vi?"

"No."

"For fuck's sake. Who?" Sadie's getting testy. I think pregnancy does that sometimes.

Keely blurts out, "Eric."

The table goes silent. As in dead silent. Agatha and Sadie blink first at Keely, then turn their faces to me.

"Of course," hisses Agatha. "How did I miss that?"

"I know, right?" Keely says smugly. "You saw him with her at the pool party when Lainie moved in, right?"

Agatha jumps in with, "That's right. He never left Violet's side."

"No." I shake my head adamantly. "No."

Ignoring me completely, Sadie nods. "And the night we took the grill." She pauses. "He was so sweet to you. It's like you were the only one there." Sadie keeps right on blabbing. "He touched your shoulder. He waved *to you* as he left. He didn't even acknowledge the rest of us." Her words are coming out so rapidly she sounds out of breath. "Of course."

"No. You guys—"

"God, he's so fucking hot," Sadie giggles. "You two would be fucking gorgeous together. Imagine their kids."

"They'd be stunning." Agatha nods.

Sadie has gone wacko. Heck, they all are. It's like they're possessed with all this nonsense.

"He's taller than she is too."

Hello? I'm right here, Sadie. It's like they're all talking about me, not to me.

Agatha looks thoughtful as she says, "She'd have to have someone taller than she is."

"He seems sort of alpha," adds Sadie.

"Oh, my God, that's h-a-w-t. I love alpha men," Keely teases. "As long as I'm the boss." She winks at Nick.

"Uh-huh." Nick chuckles as he kisses Keely's cheek. "Whatever you say, beautiful."

"See?" Keely chortles.

Just when I thought we'd gotten past the whole Eric thing, Agatha starts it right back up. "So, Eric?"

"No."

"Yes." Man, Keely won't let it go.

Deciding that ignoring my sisters is the best way to deal with this, I bite into my chimichanga and moan.

"Beth's good, right?" Agatha asks proudly.

I nod. "Hm-mm. Good." The food is good and so is the change of subject. Finally.

"Well, speak of the devil."

I stop midchew at Keely's words. When I look up at her, I notice she's staring up toward the deck.

"Your boyfriend's here," she whispers for my ears only.

I feel the heat of embarrassment start at my chest again and slowly work its way up to my face. *Stupid pasty complexion.*

"He's looking down here," hisses Keely. "Act normal."

I cough and start to choke. *Act normal?* What the heck is that? There's nothing normal about me. Swallowing the bite of chimichanga, I wipe my mouth, place my plate and napkin onto the table, and turn slowly.

When I see him, I nearly choke again. My goodness, the man is beautiful. Even in his jeans and black Gustafson Custom Motorcycles T-shirt. Well, especially in that. The shirt is snug on him. The muscles in his arms are bulging out of the short sleeves, letting us all see the tattoos that he's accumulated throughout his adult life.

I'd like to run my finger over them, tracing each line and detail.

I quickly turn back to stare at the hands resting on my lap. What? No. I didn't mean to think those sexy thoughts. This is a new development. Honestly, I haven't looked at a guy, you know, in *that* way, for a long, long time.

"Oh, look who's here," Sadie sings. "And he's heading our way."

"He's looking right at you, Violet." I'm not looking up, so I'm not sure who said that.

Crap on a cracker. Why are my sisters doing this to me?

"Violet?" says a deep, raspy voice. My name has never sounded so good.

I look up just as he reaches my side. "Oh, hi, Eric." See? I can do it.

Placing his hand on the back of my patio chair, Eric bends slightly. Close enough for me to smell him. I get a hint of oil or grease from the shop, but it's not overwhelming. Behind that is a masculine scent that I just bet is all him, or maybe his soap. Either way, it's making my head spin. "We need to talk."

I nearly choke again, but since I'm no longer eating....

"Oh?" He wants to talk? My body is nearly vibrating. The hair on my arms is standing on end. He wants to talk *to me*.

"You need to catch me up on the rehearsal stuff that I missed."

Oh. Of course. I'm walking with him down the aisle. Of

course he needs to be brought up to speed before tomorrow. Ugh, why does that realization suck so much?

Eric looks around the party. When he spots the corner I just came out of, he nods in that direction. "Let's go over there."

"Oh, hey, Eric?" It's Keely. What the heck is she going to say? I'm going to have to kill her, I really am.

He turns to face her. "Yeah?"

"It's nice to see you too. We're all good over here." She points at my sisters and their partners. "Thanks for asking."

Eric chuckles. "Sorry." He smiles brightly. "Hey, everyone."

"Hi, Eric," say Sadie and Agatha simultaneously.

"Now run along and talk about walking down the aisle together." Keely snickers.

She thinks she's so dang funny. She's not.

Eric holds his arm out like he wants me to go first. He says quietly, "After you, Violet."

I walk quickly to a small patio table with four chairs next to my lounger and sit.

Eric doesn't sit. Instead, he holds on to the back of his chair. Looking down at me, he asks, "I'm going to grab a plate. Can I get you anything?"

I shake my head. "No, I just ate."

"It didn't look like you finished. There was still a lot of food on your plate."

He noticed my plate?

"How 'bout some of that cake?"

I love cake. I really do, but when you work in a bakery four days a week, well, cake isn't a priority anymore. "No, thank you."

"Something to drink?"

"Sure." I nod. I don't think the guy is going to relent unless I get something. "Iced tea?"

"Great." He smiles. "Back in a sec."

Not knowing what to do until then, I tap the table with my fingertips and look out at the party. The first person I see is Keely. She's looking right at me, smiling from ear to ear. I can read her lips as she says, "I told you so."

I mime right back to her, "It's not what you think."

She nods. "Yes, it is." Then she starts blowing kisses my way.

"Keely," I say aloud. She's such a dork. I shake my head and then laugh, because she's funny and she means well. But she's wrong about Eric, sadly.

"Here you go, beautiful."

I want to roll my eyes at his words, but I'd better not. I mean, I bet he says that to everyone.

Setting down a plate heaping with food, he sits next to me. "So, having fun?" he asks, biting into his chimichanga. With his mouth full, he adds, "Mm. Oh my God. This shit is amazing."

"It is." I giggle. "A friend of Agatha's did the catering."

"I wonder if she's single."

Oh. *Oh.* Well, I guess that's that. I look over at Keely again. Of course she's staring. I shake my head just barely. Enough for her to see, but hopefully not enough that Eric would notice. Holding in the sudden bit of sadness, I answer, "I, uh, I think she is."

Eric chuckles. "Good to know." Eating another forkful of food, he nods, then swallows. "So, tell me what I missed."

CHAPTER 3

ERIC

Why the hell did I just say that? *I wonder if she's single?* What the ever-loving fuck? I watched Violet's gorgeous face change from happy to sad in a millisecond. I mean, fuck, what asshole does that when they're sitting next to the most beautiful woman in the entire world? You don't bring up other women. Jesus, I'm a dumb fuck.

I do my best to change the subject, asking about the rehearsal they held earlier today. I missed it, thanks to the biggest whiny-ass customer we've ever had. I swear, if Keeton agrees to work on that guy's bike again, I'm quitting. The fuckwit stood over me while I tried to figure out what the hell he was complaining about. First he said it was "making a funny noise." Okay, heads up, people—bikes make noise. A lot of noise. Then he said it was "vibrating on the highway" so I tightened up the bolts that hold the seat on the bike. Bam, problem solved. But, oh no, that wasn't enough. Jesus. In the end, I basically tuned up the asshole's brand-new bike. It pisses me off, because it meant I missed the chance to spend time with Violet at the rehearsal and for most of this little party. Something I've been trying to do for months, ever since I met her here at Keeton's house back in June.

I was lost in my own thoughts and missed something. "I'm sorry?" I need to focus on this girl, not on work.

"Oh, uh, n-nothing," she stutters.

"No, sorry, I was thinking about work. What did you say?"

She stares at me, and I can practically see the wheels turning in her stunning head. "Um, I just asked if you were growing out your hair."

I quickly raise my hand to my head. It's true, I haven't gotten it cut for a while. Like months. It's crazy long now, past my shoulders. I tend to forget about my hair and shit. "Why? Should I?" Does she hate my hair?

"No." She titters. "I was just wondering."

"Does it look bad? I'll get it cut in the morning if you don't like it." Hell, I don't want to look like a crazy person walking next to her. I want her to like it.

She giggles again. "You look fine. It's just gotten so long. Almost as long as mine."

Shit. She hates it. "I'll cut it in the morning."

"No." She laughs. She straight-up laughs. Her head falls back, revealing more of that elegant neck, which makes my dick go from zero to sixty in a second. When her laugh subsides, she reaches out and touches my left forearm, making me shiver from the feel of her fingers on me. "It's fine. I like it."

Doing my best to ignore all the sensations caused by her touch, I ask, "You like it?" I run my right hand through my blond hair. "I was going to put it up tomorrow. For the wedding."

"In a bun?" she asks. I can't read her expression.

"No? Maybe? You don't like man buns?" Fuck. I need to cut this shit off.

"I like man buns."

"Yeah?" I smile at her. I can't help it.

"It doesn't matter what I think, but yeah, I like man buns."

It *does* matter. More than anything else has ever mattered before in my life. I want Violet Palmer to like me. Hell, more than like me. I want her to love me.

I smile at her and say softly, "It matters."

"So, you're house-sitting while they're on the honeymoon?"

Violet looks surprised. "No. Who said that?"

"Keeton. I thought he said you were staying here."

"I can't."

"You can't?"

"No."

Wow, she's not going to give up any info without a fight. "Why can't you?"

She looks at me while she nibbles on her lower lip. Leaning forward, she whispers, "I've got pets. I have to be home to take care of them."

First of all, why is she whispering? Lots of people have pets. "Why are you whispering?" I lean close, whispering in response.

Giggling again, she keeps her voice low. "I have *a lot* of pets."

"How many we talkin'?" Twenty? Thirty?

Violet looks around us like she's making sure no one is close enough to hear. "Ten. My family only knows about one of them."

I jerk back in my seat. I'm surprised. That's a lot of fucking pets. "Ten? What are they?"

Her brows furrow like my question is confusing. "Most of them are special needs animals from Page Second Chance Animal Shelter. I'm actually fostering four of them. The rest I've adopted."

This woman is precious. I knew she had a heart of gold, and this proves it. "Are they dogs? Cats?"

"Well," she says as she sips her tea, "I'm fostering one small dog named Charles Barkley."

I chuckle at the name. "Great name. Does he look like Charles Barkley?"

"Wait!" she stares at me, her eyes round with surprise. "He's a real person? I thought they just made it up to be funny. You know, Barkley? Like bark?"

I laugh again, loud. I pull my phone out of my back pocket and search for the pro basketball star. "Here." I turn the phone around and show her.

Taking the phone out of my hand, she touches the screen. Her eyes flicker back and forth as she reads. "Well, I'll be darned," she sighs. "I had no idea." Looking up at me, she smiles. It's beautiful. It's so perfect it makes my heart literally flip-flop in my chest. "They look nothing alike."

That's it, I lose it. I throw my head back as a laugh emerges from deep down in my chest. I can't help it. She makes me so damn happy. I laugh for a little longer until I finally get myself together. Looking over at her, I see she's giggling at me. It's cute. She's happy I laughed. Thank God.

"So, who are your other roommates?"

Violet scoots closer to the table. With her hands resting on the top, I can't help noticing her intertwined fingers. They're long, elegant fingers. Everything about her is elegant.

"Well, I've got two hamsters called Hammy and Sammy, and Carl, a parrot with only one wing."

"Only one wing?" I squeak. Yeah, I squeaked.

"Hit by a car. The person who hit him was kind enough to take him to the vet, who had to amputate the damaged wing."

I scoot my chair closer. Resting my elbows on the table, I ask, "What about your other pets?"

"I've got two cats."

"Names?" I'm enjoying this conversation more than I can explain.

"The male is Sherman. He's a big yellow tabby. My girl is Stella."

I smile and nod, encouraging her to keep going.

With a sigh, she says, "I've got a red-eared slider turtle I call Donatello, for obvious reasons."

"The *Ninja Turtles?*"

"Exactly." She nods. "Then there's my guinea pig, Binky."

"Binky?" I chuckle.

"He came with that name."

"So, two cats, a turtle, and a guinea pig? What else?"

"I have a fish. A beta. Her name is Beatrix. And last but not least, my dog, Max."

"Max. That's a solid name. What breed?"

"You name it, Max has it."

"A mutt?"

She looks affronted at the term. "No!" she snaps. "I prefer crossbreed. It's nicer."

"My apologies. I didn't mean to offend you *or* Max."

Violet nods, but she's no longer looking at me. Instead, her eyes are on the hands that are now resting on her lap.

"I'm sorry, Violet. I love animals. If I could have pets at my place, I'd have ten too." I'm not making that up. I love animals. I never had any as a kid.

"Really?" she asks, looking wary.

"Really." I pause, wondering if I should ask. What the hell. "Maybe I could meet them sometime?"

Nope. I shouldn't have asked. She's staring at me, her eyebrows so scrunched together it's got to hurt. "No?"

"No one knows I have that many." She pauses. "Well, Keely knows, because she hangs out at my house now and then. But, like I said, the rest only know about Max."

"Why don't they know? There's nothing wrong with having ten pets, Violet."

"Shh," she hisses. "No. My sisters would—"

"What? What would your sisters do?"

"Nothing." Pushing her chair out from the table, she stands. "I've got to get home. See you tomorrow."

"Sure. Yeah."

The skirt of her pretty dress swirls as she walks away at a fast clip. Shit, I can't leave it like this. Standing up quickly, I follow her into the lower level of Keeton's house. He's got a game room on this level. It's kick-ass. I look up as she approaches the staircase leading to the main level. "Violet. Wait."

She turns slowly, and I can't help scanning her from head to toe. She's tall. I'd guess she's five-nine or ten. I'm six-three, so standing next to a tall woman is sort of nice. Violet is long and lush, something I hadn't noticed before today. Probably because she's dressed up. The other times I've seen her, she's been wearing big shirts. Today I can see her body a little better, thanks to the pretty summer dress she's wearing. It's a pale yellow that makes her auburn hair stand out even more. Her hair is up, revealing her long neck. Tendrils fall here and there, making her look even more beautiful. Our eyes meet, and I want to keep looking at her blue-green eyes forever.

"Yes?" she asks, placing one hand on her hip.

"I'm sorry."

"Why?" Her stance softens, as does her expression.

"I shouldn't have invited myself over."

She takes one step toward me, then stops. "No, I'm sorry. I don't usually have people over."

"The pets?"

"Yes. No." She uses one hand to run down the side of her face. "Lots of reasons."

"Do you ever take Max and Charles Barkley out to the dog park?"

She nods. "Mostly during the week. Fewer dogs."

"Maybe I could meet you there someday."

"Sure. Maybe." She shrugs.

"Let me give you my number. You can text me sometime."

I stand silently, waiting for her to do something like get a phone out of a pocket or purse. I scan her body and see she doesn't have a purse. "Let me get your number. I'll text you so you have mine."

She stares at me for a good thirty seconds, then she says, "Five-two-three-nine-two-seven-four."

"Great. I'll send you a text so you have my number."

Violet nods. "Okay. See you tomorrow."

"I can't wait." I quickly add Violet's name to my contacts and cross my fingers I see her name appear on my phone someday very soon.

Ignoring my pathetic comment, Violet turns and walks up the stairs and away from me. I stand watching the stairs long after she's gone. I'm about to turn around when a voice startles me.

"Pace yourself."

"Huh?" I turn to face the shortest Palmer sister. "Hey, Keely."

"Pace yourself with Violet. It's a marathon. Not a sprint."

"Excuse me?"

"P-a-c-e yourself. You're going to have to work slowly with her. Give her time. Lots of time. If you don't, you'll lose her."

I blink down at the blonde twin. "I see."

"Do you?" She steps closer. "Because I can tell you're hot for my sister. I guess I should back up a little. If you want to just fuck her, you need to absolutely forget about that. That'll never happen. Ever. She's not a one-night-stand kind of woman."

"No, I—"

"But, if you feel the way I *think* you feel about her, then you'll need to be patient. She's been through some shit."

"What shit?"

Keely shakes her head. "Not my story to tell. I'm just saying, patience, grasshopper. You're going to need a lot of it." She starts to turn away but stops. Moving in closer to me, she whispers, "But, Eric?"

"Yeah?" I whisper right back. I don't know why.

"There's no one more worthy of your time. She's worth every single second that you try to woo her. If it takes you five years, you won't be sorry. Not one fucking day will you be sorry. She's the sweetest, kindest, and most gentle soul I've ever known. Well, except for our mom. You won't regret the baby steps you're going to need to take. Kid gloves. That's what you'll need." Keely stops talking, but I can tell she's got more to say. "You're going to hear some things in a couple of weeks. Those things don't define her. They happened but they didn't break her. Hands down, she's the strongest person I know. I'm in awe of her, and if you feel about her the way I think you do, you'll be in awe too."

I already am. "What are you talking about?"

"Patience, Thor. You're going to need it. Got it?"

Jesus, what the hell could she be talking about? "Got it."

CHAPTER 4

"Let's do this thing, bitches."

"Keely," I chastise. I'm a little shocked by Keely's statement, but I shouldn't be. Keely says stuff like that all the time. We're all used to it. It's just the setting. We're getting ready to step out of the bride's room at the church so we can line up to walk down the aisle at Lainie's wedding.

Lainie. She looks stunning. I don't think I've ever seen a more beautiful bride. She's wearing a glimmering ball gown that makes her look like a princess. All the layers of tulle on the skirt help to hide her baby bump. While everyone knows she's pregnant, Lainie wanted a dress that disguised it a little bit. I get it.

"Ladies," Lainie says, holding her hands out to us. We all move toward her, wrapping our arms around her. "I can't believe I get to marry the man of my dreams today. My best friend." She sniffles. "And I get to do it with my baby sisters, my future sister, and best friends by my side." She turns to look at Molly and Deb, smiling.

"We're happy to share this with you too, sweetie," Deb gushes. "I'm so happy for you both."

"Me too," says someone in the huddle. I think it was Aggie.

I merely nod. I'm getting a little emotional about this exchange and about this day. Heck, I've been nervous about it since Lainie told all of us the date of her wedding. That's also the day she asked me to be her maid of honor. Honestly, I thought Aggie would be her choice, but she asked me to meet for coffee one morning at the bakery and entered the shop holding a bouquet of pink and purple flowers. Handing them to me, she asked, "Will you be my maid of honor?"

I wanted to say yes. Of course I did, but for some reason I felt guilty. Of the four remaining sisters, I would have guessed I'd fall at the end of Lainie's list of choices. But when I saw movement from the corner of my eye and Sadie, Polly, Aggie, and Keely all stepped out from the back of the bakery, all three of my sisters smiling at me, encouraging me, I stood up and wrapped my arms around Lainie. "Yes. Of course. I'd be honored."

So here I am, lined up at the back of the church waiting for my turn to walk down the aisle. I'm nervous as heck. Not because I have to walk sixty feet to the front of the church. No, it's *who* I'm doing that with. Eric. Eric Gustafson, the groom's younger brother. Just the thought of him causes nervous chills to run through my body. No, I'm not scared of him, although the man is intimidating for sure. He's at least five inches taller than me, and that's saying something since I'm nearly five ten, the tallest of the Palmer sisters.

Not only is he tall, he's everything else too: broad, muscled, blond, and the most handsome man I've ever seen in person, or heck, even in movies. *The* most handsome. That's why he's intimidating. The fact that his voice is deep and just a teensy bit raspy is only a bonus. And when he says my name, I want to melt into a puddle of goo.

But I'm being ridiculous. I'm fantasizing. Something I'm exceptionally good at. For one thing, a man like Eric no doubt has a harem of women at his beck and call. For another, someone like him wouldn't be interested in someone like me. Sure, he's been sweet to me the two or three other times I've seen him. The first was at Keeton's house the day Lainie moved in. He showed up to help with the move and stayed for the BBQ and pool party afterwards. He introduced himself to me and laughed when I made an inappropriate "that's what she said" joke that surprised even me. After that, no matter where I was, in the house, near the pool, he was nearby. I suspect Lainie asked him to keep an eye on me or something. My sisters do that. *A lot.* They think I'm fragile.

I suppose they're right.

"Vi?"

I'm jerked back to reality by Sadie's voice.

"Yes?"

"Remember, Eric won't know what he's doing."

Right. Crud. Eric and I didn't actually talk about the wedding ceremony yesterday. *Pretend you're confident, Violet.* "Sure. No problem." Big problem, is more like it. I can barely speak when I'm around him. Less than usual, anyway. But this isn't about me; it's about Lainie.

As my turn to step through the doors gets closer, I see him. Eric. He's just moved into position at the entrance. My head is down, because I'm blushing like there's no tomorrow, and if we make eye contact, I may choke to death. Gosh, I'm so nervous.

I notice his shoes first. They're black and shiny—patent leather shiny. The bottom of his pant leg is a dark gray. I let my eyes follow up the leg; it takes forever to get to the bottom of the tuxedo jacket. The guy is all legs. Well, and muscles. (See above.) My eyes move up until I see his elbow jutting out at his side. I'm supposed to slide my hand through that arm and hang on to it as we walk. I'm supposed to touch him.

Last night, at the rehearsal, I did this with Ian, Agatha's fiancé. I had no problem placing my hand through the hole made by his arm. No problem at all. Heck, I didn't even think about it. But right now, I'm practically vibrating with nerves. Sucking in a deep breath, I glance up and see him looking right at me.

Bad move, Vi. Bad move.

Eric Gustafson has beautiful eyes. They're like a steel gray color. Sort of like Aggie's, only his are more metallic than hers, if that's even a thing. Not only are his eyes looking at me, the skin is crinkled at the corners. He's smiling.

As I step closer, I'm still looking at his face. I think it's the longest I've ever looked at him. He's bowing his head down like he's going to say something to me. I give him a small smile. *Pretend you're confident, Violet.*

"You're stunning, Violet." Those are the words that just came out of his mouth. They were a whisper, only loud enough for me to hear. I'm not sure if that's good or bad. I mean, if he didn't care what anyone thought about that, he'd have said it louder, right? Well, we *are* in a church, I guess, and this is about Lainie. Oh, crud. Why do I do this to myself?

With the smile still plastered on my face, I say, "Thank you. You are too."

A deep, rumbly laugh jumps out at me. I don't know why he's laughing. Is he laughing at me? At what I just said? What *did* I say? I blink a few times trying to recall words I said five seconds ago. *Oh.* I just told him he was stunning.

He's laughing *at* me. I'm sure of it. I feel heat flush over my face. Embarrassment. It's my constant companion. But right now, I hate it. The forced smile on my lips falls, and I swear, my eyes are burning. I'd like to turn and walk away—better yet, run away—but I can't. I'm the next one to walk down the aisle, then it's Lainie and my dad's turn.

This isn't about me.

I do my best to school my facial expression. Turning to face the front, I see that Agatha is almost halfway up the aisle, which means we need to start walking. I place my hand on Eric's elbow and nudge him forward. Focusing on the task at hand is just what I need to do. I'll just forget about making a total fool of myself for now.

As we slowly walk forward, I plaster a smile on my face like a normal person. I do my best not to look left or right at the guests and instead focus my eyes ahead, mostly at Keely. She's not looking at me, though. She's gazing at her boyfriend, Nick Martelli. I don't blame her; he's easy on the eyes, as they say. I don't think it'll be long before she gets engaged and married too. Lainie is the first to walk down the aisle. (Correction. She's divorced, but she and Lewis didn't have a "real" wedding, so this counts as the first time she'll walk down the aisle.) Anyhoo, the rest will follow quickly behind, leaving me the lone unmarried Palmer sister. It's okay. I want them to be happy. My family means everything to me. I want them to *all* get their happily-ever-afters.

"I'm sorry," he says softly.

I'm not sure if I should ignore him or look at him to see what he's talking about. I guess since I'll have to interact with him the rest of the day and into the night, I should probably get used to looking at him. I turn my head slightly and look at him from the corner of my eye.

He repeats, "I'm sorry. I didn't mean to laugh."

Oh. I shrug. "No worries."

"Yes. I worry."

We're almost to the front, and he wants to get into this now? "Don't."

I hear him release a breath, or perhaps it was a sigh. I can't tell.

"I wasn't laughing *at* you."

"Okay," I whisper. "Thank you."

"Shit." He says it under his breath.

I should probably say something, but we're at the front of the church already. I release his elbow and move to stand in the spot designated for the maid of honor. I turn to face the back of the church just as the wedding march begins. I peek over at Keeton so I can watch his reaction to Lainie in her dress. I'm glad I did, because it is sincerely the sweetest thing I've ever seen. I hear him gasp and watch him as he swipes his hand across his cheek. He's crying. And that's all I need to get my own waterworks going. I'm so darned happy for them. And just a tiny bit sad for myself. Just a tiny bit.

CHAPTER 5

Eric

I fucked up. Thirty seconds after seeing her, I fucked up. I watched her face change from a bright smiling one to a blushing, embarrassed one. That's one thing I never want to do to Violet Palmer. Ever. I laughed when she essentially called me stunning. It's a mistake we all make now and then, and one I found charming. That's what Violet has done to me—she's charmed me. Well, maybe charmed isn't the right word. She bewitched me the second I saw her at my brother's house back in June.

Since then, I've seen her a number of times from afar. Then, a couple weeks ago, I spoke to her briefly and touched her shoulder. The hair on my arm stood on end with just that touch. It happened the night we stole, or should I say, confiscated Sadie's BBQ grill. I brought my pickup and helped carry the huge motherfucker down three flights of stairs. I'd do it a million times over if it meant I got to talk to her. Touch her.

I'd thought my brother's reaction to Lainie Palmer was sort of insane. I mean, she walked into the shop and BAM, he was in love. One day. That's all it took for him to be in all the way with her. Don't get me wrong, I love Lainie. She's amazing, beautiful, and sweet. I couldn't ask for a better wife for my brother. She'll be an amazing mom too. I was just shocked, since Keeton Gustafson is the least romantic person I know.

But now I get it. The second I met Violet, I had what I suspect Keeton had. A *BAM* moment. I don't know why it happened with her and nobody else. There's just something about Violet. It's a combination of beauty and fragility. Her beauty... damn, she's incredible with her pale skin and long auburn hair. I don't know how long it is, because she always wears it up. I'd be sad about that, except when it's up, I get a glimpse of her neck. It's regal. Everything about her takes my breath away. She makes my heart beat double time. I swear to you, that has never happened to me before. I've never had that kind of reaction to a woman. Sure, I've been turned on by women, but never like this. I've never had a physiological reaction. Not until Violet.

As we walk down the aisle, I do my best to focus on my job —walking—but I can't. I need to fix this. So, as quietly as I can, I whisper, "I'm sorry."

She doesn't respond. Hell, she won't even look at me. So I try again. "I'm sorry. I didn't mean to laugh."

Still no eye contact. Violet shrugs. "No worries."

She's ignoring me. Sure, we're in the middle of walking down the damn aisle at my brother's wedding but still. I've got to keep trying. "Yes. I worry."

"Don't."

Don't? Don't what? Talk to her? I've been holding my breath, but I need to release it. Trying one more time before we make it to the front of the church, I lean closer to her. Close enough to smell her. Sweet. "I wasn't laughing at you."

"Okay. Thank you," she says so quietly I can barely hear her.

She still won't look at me. A sure sign she's just trying to get me to shut the hell up but it's not going to work. The sad thing is I know I screwed up. Can I fix this? It doesn't feel like I can. She shut down on me. So I mutter, "Shit," aloud.

I keep glancing across the aisle at her. When the music changes, I know that Lainie will soon be walking down the aisle with her father. I saw her at the back of the church when we were all lined up, and I know my brother is going to lose his shit when he sees her. He's been doing almost as much of the wedding planning as Lainie. Actually, he's the one who insisted they have a big church wedding and an even bigger reception, since she didn't get any of that for her first wedding. Hell, neither did Keeton. He and Deb just drove up to Vegas and got married.

This time, though, he wanted her to have everything she ever dreamed of, including the dress. *Especially* the dress. Keeton paid to have a limo take Lainie, her sisters, our sister, Molly, and Deb, Keeton's ex-wife, down to Flagstaff for a day of wedding dress shopping. He told her to buy whatever she wanted, that money was no object. The thing is, Lainie Palmer isn't like the women Keeton's used to. If he'd told any of his previous girlfriends, Deb excluded, that same thing, he'd be fucking broke. But I know for a fact, thanks to Molly's intel, that Lainie's dress was on sale and that she spent under fifteen hundred bucks for the thing. I peek down the aisle and smile. She looks like a million bucks.

Looking back over at Violet, I stare at her dress. It's pretty. Not as pretty as she is. The color is a deep purple shade that makes her milky skin almost glow. The top is tight, but not in a bad way. I think it's supposed to be like that. The other times I've seen her, except for yesterday, she's always wearing oversized shirts and baggy pants. Seeing her now in something that fits, it's a bit of a shock to see how small she is. Her collarbone is pronounced, and her bare arms are slim but toned.

I hear my big bro sniffle, bringing me back to reality. Seeing him all emotional like that, I can't help but get a little choked up, especially when he starts wiping tears from his eyes. I pat him on the back and say softly, "You're a lucky bastard, man."

"I know," he says with a shaky voice. "Fuck, man, I know."

Goddamn, I want that. He *is* a lucky bastard. I take the opportunity to look beyond my brother at Violet. She's watching Keet closely. When she sees him wipe away a tear, her brows furrow—with concern at first, but then a small smile appears.

I can't help wondering what Violet would look like in a wedding dress. I'm curious what style she'd choose for herself. Hell, she could wear a burlap sack and she'd still be gorgeous.

Turning back to the bride, I watch as she and Rob, her dad, approach Keeton. Lainie has tears in her eyes too. Swear to God, I've never seen two happier people in my life. I clear my throat, attempting to keep the emotions at bay. I can't let Violet see me like that—like a goddamn crybaby.

CHAPTER 6

*V*IOLET

The wedding ceremony was perfect. Emotional and perfect. I've never seen my sister happier in my life. And her new husband? He looks as proud as a peacock walking hand in hand with her to the dance floor for their first dance as Mr. and Mrs. Gustafson. Lainie took his name, no hyphen this time, which I think is sort of a sign. She used to be Lainie Palmer-Bottoms after she married the idiot Lewis years ago.

Sitting at the long table with the rest of the bridal party, I'm spellbound watching my sister and her new husband as they dance to "A Thousand Years" by Christina Perri. It's the perfect song for them. A tear slides down my cheek. No worries. It's a happy tear. I sip my water and wait nervously for their dance to end, because once it does, it's our turn—the bridal party will join them on the dance floor. Which means I'll be with Eric. He'll have his hand in mine. Dang it, I'm nervous.

As soon as the music ends, the DJ announces, "Let's give Mr. and Mrs. Gustafson a round of applause."

Most everyone claps while the rest hold their champagne glasses up in a toast.

"Bridal party!" he shouts into his mic, "come on down. It's your turn."

There's laughter beside me as Sadie stands up, holding her hand out for Deb. I guess they're going to dance together, which makes sense since they walked down the aisle together. Deb stood up on Keeton's side of the aisle, but she's really here for both of them.

"May I have this dance?" says a deep voice close to my ear. I shiver.

"Sure." I give him a small smile. I'm doing my best to keep my nerves in check.

I look up at the large hand he has extended. Placing mine in his, I can't help noticing how good it feels.

"I can't dance," he says softly. "Have mercy."

He makes me laugh. "Okay," I say with a giggle. The truth is, I have no idea what I'm doing either.

With my hand in his, he leads me to the dance floor not far from Lainie and Keeton.

Facing me, he smiles and says, "You ready for this? Better watch your toes."

I giggle again. "Noted." When his arm slides around my waist, I feel his palm on my upper back. He gently nudges me a little closer. With my right hand in his left and my left hand on his upper arm, an upper arm hard with muscle, I wait for the music to start. When Ed Sheeran's "Perfect" starts, I take in a deep breath. I love this song. It's one of my favorites.

"I love this song," Eric says softly as his eyes meet mine.

I look up. "Me too."

As we dance, I close my eyes so I can memorize what it feels like to be here in his arms. I feel warm and surprisingly protected. There's not one ounce of fear in me, something that has been a constant in my life for six years. Fear is that intangible emotion that never seems to go away. It's always lingering somewhere in the back of my mind. And not just fear of men. It's fear of doing anything that would draw attention to me, fear of trying new things, fear of meeting new people.

I'm brought out of my thoughts when I hear Eric sing just loud enough for me to hear. He's got a good voice. Sexy, like his speaking voice. But he knows the words. I look up at him, expecting to see some sort of silly smirk on his face, but that's not at all what I see. No, what I see is sincerity. I'd even say he looks earnest. I blink as he continues. Gah. Why can't I take my eyes off his face? His eyes are piercing mine. If I weren't me, I'd think he was singing those words to me. I swallow hard as he sings the final verse. Now I feel self-conscious. So, what do I do when I feel that way? I laugh. And blush. A lot.

The two of us are just standing on the dance floor as everyone else begins to file off. I'm not anxious to leave his arms, so I stay put as he asks, "What?" He smirks. "You don't like my singing?"

"No." My mouth opens and closes like a fish. "I mean, yes. You have a very nice voice."

"Oh, yeah?"

"Yeah."

Leaning down closer than he's ever been, he whispers, "I'm glad you like it. I'll serenade you anytime."

"Oh. All right." Giggling nervously, I pull away from him as the next song starts. A fast one. I look over and see Lainie and Keeton near their wedding cake. "I think I need cake."

"Cake, huh? I could eat some cake. Especially if it's Sadie's."

"You've had Sadie's cake before?"

"Cupcakes." He nods. "Lots."

Huh. I work part-time at my sister's bakery, and I've never seen him there. "I've never seen you there."

"I've seen you."

Oh.

I'm about to ask him when that was when I'm jostled from behind and into Eric's chest by someone who is really into the "YMCA."

He's able to stop my momentum by placing his hands on my upper arms.

"Sorry," I say, embarrassed again.

Placing my hand in his, he tugs me off the dance floor, saying, "Let's get that cake."

I'm not sure what to do. I know I should pull my hand out of his, but it feels so darned good. His hand dwarfs mine, but it's warm and slightly calloused. Instead of fighting it, I nod. "Let's."

CHAPTER 7

Eric

I need to play it cool with Violet. I want to be next to her all night, but I've got to let her do her thing at this reception. I can do that. I'll just stand back in the shadows so I can watch her. Yeah, I know, that's some creepy stalker shit. It can't be helped.

"So," says my sister as she sidles up to me with my beautiful niece, Maddy. I hold my hands out and wiggle my fingers in the universal sign for "gimme."

Maddy's little feet are kicking and jiggling about as I try to secure her using one hand on her diaper-covered bottom and my other on her back. I lower my head until we're eye to eye. Touching my nose to hers, I say, "Boop," in a high-pitched voice. It makes her giggle every time. A sound I'll never get tired of.

Peeking around Maddy to my sister, I ask, "How you doin', sis?"

Molly's had a tough year. A *very* tough year. She lost her husband in Afghanistan last January, a week before he was done with the Army Rangers and only weeks before this little sweetie was born. It's been fucking sad around the garage and Molly's place. My sister is strong, though. Unbelievably strong, and I know it's all due to Madalyn. She's stayed fierce for her daughter, because that's what Adam would have wanted. At least that's what my sister says whenever we give her props.

"Having fun?"

"Sure. Lainie and Keet." She sighs. "They're perfect for each other. I'm so happy for them."

I know she means it, even though her face says something else. She's sad and probably a little envious. I get it.

"So, I saw you talking to Sig earlier?" I nod toward the extra-large red-headed man standing in line for cake.

"You know him?"

"He came into the shop last week to apply for a job. Keet hired him yesterday. You were gone doing girly wedding shit."

She rolls her eyes at the last part of that sentence. Molly's not super girly, but she's no tomboy either. "I didn't think we needed anyone right now. What's he going to do?"

Molly is the office manager at Keeton's shop. Gustafson Custom Motorcycles is a thriving bike shop. We specialize in Keeton's custom designs, but we also do repairs and upgrades to existing bikes. "Mechanic."

"Oh? Like I said, I didn't think we needed anybody."

"He specializes in electronics. You know, the computer shit."

"Can't you do that?" asks my sister with a bit too much venom.

"He just got out of the army."

"Oh." She nods. "I get it."

I'm guessing she means Keeton hired him because he's a vet. I'm sure that's part of it. Keeton, along with the rest of us, does what he can to support our vets. "No, the dude knows every-thing about all the new computer technology. We need him if Keet wants to keep current. It has nothing to do with Adam."

There's a long pause before she says anything. "How long has he been out?"

"He just got out."

I'm looking down at my niece, pushing a blonde curl out of her pretty face when she asks, "So, Violet Palmer, huh?"

"What?" I say a little too loudly. She's changing the subject. Okay. I can work with that.

"I know you, baby brother. I saw the way you were looking at her. It's the same way Keet looks at Lainie."

I nod. I can't argue with her. "It was strange. That day I met her at Keeton's, it sort of hit me like a lightning bolt. Did *you* know...?" I hate to even say Adam's name again. It could ruin her night, literally.

"I knew Adam was the man for me the first day we met. Unfortunately, I was in middle school." She chortles. "Keeton brought him home from school one day—his new best friend."

"You knew it in middle school?"

"I did. I just had to wait six years for him to notice me."

"Oh, he noticed you long before that."

"What?" Molly's eyes are shiny, but the tears haven't fallen. Not yet.

"He used to get really pissed at us when we teased you. Told us to lay off."

She clears her throat, but I get a small smile. "He did?"

"Yeah. It was usually aimed at me, since I was the younger, brattier sibling, but he got on Keeton's case a few times."

"I had no idea."

"You remember how Keet used to drive by us in his old Chevy as we walked home from school? He'd barely acknowledge us. If he even lifted his fingers on the steering wheel in that asshole wave he used to do, it was notable."

Molly guffaws. "Yes. The asshole. He was too cool to give his younger siblings a ride home."

"Well, I mentioned that to Adam one day, and he punched Keeton over it."

"What?" Molly screeches.

"I swear." I hold up one palm. "He yelled at Keeton, saying stuff like he needed to protect his pretty little sister—not let you walk home."

I expect to hear Molly laugh, but that's not what I'm seeing when I look down. A tear is sliding down her cheek.

Shit. I've upset her. "Molls...."

"No." She holds up her hand. "Thank you for telling me that. I like to hear stories about him. No one wants to talk about him anymore. I miss him—" She releases a sob. "—so much."

"We all do, honey." I lean in with Maddy between us. Reaching the arm that's not holding up my niece, I wrap Molly up into a hug. "He was a good man, Molls. We didn't think he was good enough for you." I chuckle. "But we never thought anyone was good enough for you. It's a good thing you don't ever listen to us. We wouldn't have this little princess if you had."

Molly laughs through her tears. "She's my gift. My sunshine. I'm so lucky to have part of him in her."

I chuckle. "She's definitely got Adam in her. I can already tell she's going to be just as stubborn as that asshole."

Molly beams at her daughter, then laughs. "She's definitely her father's daughter."

"Here." I reach into my tux pocket and pull out the deep purple pocket square that matches Violet's dress and hand it to my sister.

"Thanks." She wipes her tears then blows her nose. Before I know it, she's stuffed the thing back into my pocket.

"Disgusting," I mumble. "Here." I hold Maddy out to her. "Take your kid. She's got a stinky gift for you in her pants."

I laugh as I walk away, and she shouts, "Asshole!"

It only makes me laugh harder.

CHAPTER 8

I can sense him nearby. No, not in a creepy, stalker kind of way. But, it's like I've got a sixth sense when it comes to Eric Gustafson or something. I look to my right and see him leaning against the wall, a beer bottle in his hand. When our eyes meet, he lifts the bottle and nods. He makes no move to approach me. It's strange. It's like he's watching out for me.

Wait....

No. She wouldn't.

"Lainie!" I say louder than I mean to. I spot her over near my dad, so I march over to her, stomping my sore feet as I go. Stupid high heels.

"What's up, sweetie?" Lainie chirps.

No, don't give in. Placing my hands on my hips in the way one does when they're trying to act all serious and irritated, I ask, "Did you ask Eric to watch out for me tonight?"

Lainie looks at me, then scans the room, looking for what, I'm not sure. "No. Why? What's he doing?" Lainie takes my hand in hers and pulls me around several tables and out into the hallway. "Why are you asking me that? What's going on?"

"Nothing." Why do I feel defensive? "I can't help noticing that Eric is keeping an eye on me. I assumed you put him up to it."

"Keeping an eye on you? No. Why would I do that?"

"I don't know." I lower my head. Gosh, I'm such a ninny.

"What's he doing exactly?"

"Nothing." I lift my head and smile. "Nothing." Fake it 'til you make it.

"Vi." Lainie steps closer to me. "What's he doing?"

"Nothing. Seriously. I just keep seeing him watching me. He's not doing anything." I'm getting flustered. My palms become moist with sweat.

Lainie moves some hair out of my eye and smiles at me. "I think he likes you."

"Oh, geesh," I groan. "Not you too. Did Keely put you up to that?"

"No." Lainie shakes her head. "Call it a hunch."

"Well, you're wrong. I bet Keeton put him up to it."

"Well, Keeton does know I worry about you, so maybe."

"Right." And that right there... I'm sick of it. I really am. I'm not an invalid. But, in her defense, I've acted like one for a long time. When she finds out the reason why right after her honeymoon, it's just going to get worse.

CHAPTER 9

VIOLET

About two weeks later...

I'm sitting on my dad's leather sofa playing with the slice of pizza on my plate. I scan the room and see my sisters and my dad chatting, laughing, and eating Lainie's doctored-up frozen pizza. Sure, we could order out, but doing it this way brings our mom into the mix. She always turned frozen pizza into a real treat. It was more economical too. Lainie is a pro at it now. I'm not too shabby either, but it's Lainie's thing, so I keep my mouth shut.

I hear Lainie telling my siblings all about her honeymoon. Keeton surprised her with a trip to Hawaii, someplace she's always wanted to visit. Lewis never took her anywhere. I think he went to Hawaii once, but he left her at home. My goodness, Lewis was the worst.

"Keely?" asks Sadie, loud enough for us all to hear. "Why couldn't I bring Charlie to this shindig?"

"Yeah," adds Agatha. "Ian is part of this family too."

Why do both of my sisters sound so hurt? I don't want anyone to be upset about this. Maybe we should have included them, but Keely suggested it be just us when I tell them about *it*. I agreed with her. I'd prefer it be just my immediate family right now.

"Stop your bitching. We need to be able to do shit together without the men." She turns to my dad. "You don't count."

"Gee, thanks, Kiki," Dad deadpans.

We all laugh. My dad has seemed extra happy lately. I'm glad, but I can't help wondering if it has something to do with Deb. They really hit it off. Gosh, I hope he finds happiness again.

"Anyway." Keely rolls her eyes. "Violet wants to talk to us. She wanted it to be blood only."

Like it was synchronized, every pair of eyes slowly turns to me.

"You pregnant?" asks Sadie. Then she laughs.

Why does that hurt? For whatever reason, it does. I know my face reflects it.

"God, Sadie. Don't be such a bitch." Keely moves toward me so she's sitting next to me on the couch.

"Sorry," Sadie says, grimacing as she lowers her head.

"Everybody sit your asses down. Let Violet say what she needs to say."

I can't decide if I'm glad Keely is taking over or not. I guess I am. If it were me, I'd go home tonight without ever mentioning the name Kyle Maines. The hair stands up on the back of my neck just thinking it.

"What is it, hon?" asks Lainie.

Setting the plate with the uneaten pizza slice down onto the coffee table, I place my now empty hands on my knees. I scan the room and see that they're all seated as Keely commanded. I want to laugh but can't. Not right now. Staring down at my hands, I begin with, "Six years ago...."

You could hear a pin drop in this room. I look up, then quickly back down at my hands that are now clutching my jeans. Keely's hand covers one of mine.

"You got this," she whispers.

Dragging in a deep breath, I begin again. "Six years ago, I was raped."

Gasps. I hear gasps come from each and every person in my family. The first person I see is my dad. God, I hope I never have to see that expression ever again. It's a mixture of shock, anger, and fear. I don't want anyone to say anything just yet, so I keep talking. "I was at a frat party at the University of Southeast Arizona." Keely squeezes my hand. "It was the first time I'd gone to a college party." I scoff. Figures. "My roommate talked me into going. She did my hair and makeup. I even dressed up."

I pause and try to swallow, but my mouth is suddenly as dry as a desert.

"Go on." Keely is doing her best to encourage me. I'm glad. I need it.

"I was nervous, so I drank a lot of beer. They were warm and gross." I half expected someone to laugh at that, but no one is laughing.

"A guy approached me. He was really good-looking." Reaching out, I pick up my glass of water and take a big gulp. "He asked me if I wanted something better than beer. Something cool. I said, 'sure.'"

"Oh, Violet." Lainie is the first to say something. "You should never take drinks from a stranger at a party."

I'm a little taken aback by Lainie's words. I mean, I know. *Now.*

"Jesus, Lainie. Like that's helpful. She was fucking nineteen. And stop blaming the woman here. That's not fucking fair."

"Sorry. I didn't mean...."

"It's okay." And it is. I've said the same thing to myself hundreds, maybe thousands of times. When Keely squeezes my hand, I keep going. "He was charming. Complimentary. I could tell he was important, because there were always other guys around him. They laughed at everything he said."

Keely adds, "He was the frat president."

"Wait," Sadie says with one hand up. "How do you know all of this, Keely?"

"I'll get to that," I answer for her. "Let me get through this, please."

Sadie says softly, "Sorry."

"He was president of the fraternity. I didn't know it at the time, though." Sitting back further onto the couch, I lean back. "He talked to me for a long time, always refreshing my drink when it ran low. We danced to a slow song." My mouth is dry, but I still try to swallow. "I was really drunk." I can't seem to emphasize that enough. "At some point, we ended up in one of the bedrooms. As soon as the door shut, he...."

I look up into their faces. I see sadness in my sisters' eyes, but when I look at my dad, my heart breaks. He's crying. And not just a little bit. "Daddy?"

He shakes his head. "Keep going, sweetheart."

I'm not going to get into graphic detail here, especially in front of my dad. "As soon as the door shut, he pushed me into the door and started kissing me. Honestly, I was flattered at first. I mean, he was good-looking, and he liked me." I scoff and roll my eyes. "Idiot."

"You weren't an idiot. You were a young college woman," Aggie says forcing a smile.

"I won't go into detail, but he-he pushed me onto the bed..." Rubbing my hands over my face, I finish with, "He raped me."

"So, that's why you quit school all of a sudden," my dad states. It's not a question.

I nod.

"You said you hated school. That you were flunking out. You needed more time at home." My dad sounds like he's sort of lost. "That was all a lie?"

"No. Not really. I *would* have flunked out. I had no plans to step foot on campus again or into a classroom." I mean, what if I saw him? He'd always be there—somewhere.

"I thought that was strange," says Lainie, like she's talking to herself. "You're the smartest one of us. School was easy for you. You were your class valedictorian."

Was there a question in there? "I was doing well before...."

Keely leans in and whispers, "Do you want me to tell them the rest, and about Nick?"

I nod. I do. I'm overwhelmed right now. A change in subject is just what I need.

"In answer to Sadie's earlier question, the reason I know is because Violet's roommate called me a week after it happened. Violet hadn't left her room and she was worried. So I drove down to Tucson."

"Why didn't you call us?" Sadie asks Keely.

"Because," Keely says, "my first concern was helping Violet, Sadie. It's not about you."

"That's unfair." Sadie sounds hurt.

"Get over it." Keely mutters. "Jesus."

I can't take this. "Please don't argue. Not over this. Please. Everything Keely did afterwards was because I asked her to do it."

"When I got there," Keely continues, "I could tell she hadn't been out of bed for a week. She told me what happened, and I talked her into going to the university clinic and then to the cops." Keely scoffs, "Like that did any good."

Dad asks, "What do you mean?"

Keely turns to face my father. "Because they told her, essentially, that she asked for it."

"What the fuck?!" My dad stands up fast, his face red with anger. "Who said that?" he spits out.

"Daddy?" I look up at him. "Let Keely finish. Please?"

"That's the reason you're all here." Keely sighs. "Nick has been looking into it."

"Nick knew before we did?" snaps Sadie. "Seriously?"

Keely growls, "What the fuck is your problem, Sadie? This isn't about you."

"I know. But she—we should have known before now." Sadie turns to me. "We love you. We could have helped."

That's what starts the tears and the blubbering. *My* tears and blubbering that I'd hoped to keep inside. "I know," I sob. "I couldn't." Covering my face with my hands, I wail. That's the only way to describe it. "For a long time, I thought it was my fault," I say between crying jags.

I feel arms around me and smell something like vanilla and cinnamon. It's Sadie. "No, baby. No. It wasn't your fault. Shh," she says softly, holding me tightly in her arms.

While Sadie hugs me, she says, "I'm sorry. I'm just upset I wasn't there to help. This has nothing to do with me or any of us. We all love you with our whole hearts, Vi. We all do."

I hear Lainie's sniffles. When I look over at her, I cry harder. Her body is literally shaking.

"I know. I'm sorry I didn't tell you all. I've been trying to work through it on my own."

The room is quiet except for the sniffling. There's not a dry eye in the house. Not even Keely's as she tries again. "I told Nick. When he did a search for Kyle Maines, I...." She looks at my sisters. "Do you remember a couple of months ago at Murphy's when that guy approached Violet?"

Sadie nods.

"We all thought he was hot—we teased Violet about him?"

More nodding.

"And Vi came back from the bathroom all flustered?"

"That was him?" Aggie squeaks. "That fucker is here? In Page?"

Keely nods slowly. "Sedona. But he sells insurance, so he's up here sometimes."

"That motherfucker!" shouts my dad as he jumps up from the sofa again. Pacing back and forth, he yells, "I'm going to fucking kill him."

"No, Dad," Keely says calmly as she approaches my angry father. "You're going to let Nick do his job."

"And what is that? What's he doing?"

"Well," Keely doesn't miss a beat, "with Violet's permission, he looked into Kyle Maines."

"And?" Dad snaps.

"He's done it before." I pause and swallow. "And probably since."

"Oh, no," Lainie says sadly.

"Why isn't he in jail? How has he gotten away with it?" Leave it to Aggie to ask that.

"Can everyone sit back down and let me fucking finish?" Keely sounds angry, but I can tell she just wants to get through this.

My dad is the last to sit as Keely continues, "Kyle Maines is the son of Francis Abernathy."

There's a pause before Aggie says, "Wait. Isn't that...?"

"The lieutenant governor of Arizona," my dad says. "Total bullshit. I'm still going to kill that motherfucker."

Ignoring that last outburst, Keely declares, "That's why

you're all here. Nick told Captain Morgan everything yesterday. There will be an official investigation. Shit is going to hit the fan. We wanted to prepare you for the backlash."

"There will be press," I add. Nick warned me about it yesterday when he called to tell me the captain was on board and, because of Frances Abernathy, they may have to bypass the state authorities and ask the FBI to work alongside them in something called a task force. I'm not sure what that is, but it sounds good.

"If the lieutenant governor is related to this guy, I would think the FBI would *have* to get involved," Aggie says matter-of-factly. She should know, since Ian is a former agent. "They won't be able trust the state cops to do anything related to Abernathy."

"True. But it's state, not federal," Keely replies.

I need to ask. "What if they find out he did it in other states like Nick suggested? The FBI would get involved for sure. Right?"

Keely and Agatha look at one another. "Not sure, Vi," replies Keely. "We'll find out."

"No matter what happens, Violet, we've got your back," Lainie says as she steps over to sit beside me.

"I know." I pat her knee. "I know."

CHAPTER 10

Eric

I'm working late on a vintage Harley when I hear the click-clack of ladies' shoes. They're moving at a fast clip so, naturally, my head pops up to see Lainie Gustafson race past me and into the back half of the garage. The half that Keeton uses to build his custom designs. Keet's working late too; just the two of us tonight.

I've known Lainie long enough to know she'd never just race past me without saying hello unless... unless something is wrong. *Is something going on with the baby?*

I hate being a sneaky shit, but I can't help it. I'm worried. Setting my tools down quiet-like, I stand and move toward the large opening between our two spaces. Sure enough, I hear Lainie, and I can tell she's crying. *What the hell?*

Leaning in closer, I can hear her sniffling and hiccupping as she talks. "Sh-she was ra-raped."

Who was raped?

"Who, baby?" asks my bro. He's real gentle with her. Something I'd never seen before he met Lainie.

"Vi-Violet."

"Violet? Raped?" my brother asks, concern in his voice. "When? Who?"

"What!" I shout. I can't stay out of this conversation now. I need to know what the hell's going on. I stomp around the corner and stop when I'm inches from the two of them. "What? Tell me."

"This is none of your business, little bro." Keeton looks pissed.

"I heard Violet's name."

"And?" Keet asks with an arched brow.

"She's my business," I growl. So now he knows. It's out there. Now, he'd sure as shit better not keep something about Violet from me.

Keeton is a smug asshole sometimes. "She know?"

Ignoring my brother, I turn to Lainie. "What happened? Is she okay? Where is she?"

"Oh, hon," she sniffles. "She's okay. It happened a long time ago. When she was a freshman at the University of Southeast Arizona. We didn't know. We just heard about it tonight."

Why didn't they know until tonight? Why now? Wait a second. I step back until I bump into Keeton's workbench. "Keely."

"What about Keely?" asks Lainie.

I focus on her. "She told me."

"She told you?" Now Lainie seems angry.

"No. Not about that. The night of the rehearsal party. She told me I'd learn something about Violet soon, but she wasn't specific."

I remember exactly what she said: *You're going to hear some things in a couple of weeks. Those things don't define her....*

Now I get it. She was raped, but it didn't break her. I can see now why Violet is so timid. Maybe it's not timid though; what if it's fear? What if *I* scare her?

"Shit," I mutter, running my fingers through my wild hair.

"She's okay, Eric," Lainie says, approaching me. "She'll be okay. It's just the guy has done it to others, and they're finally investigating."

"What? Why finally?"

"Nick. Nick found out about it and started digging. He, the rapist, is Lieutenant Governor Abernathy's son."

"What's the motherfucker's name?" I growl again.

"Oh, geesh. You and my dad." Lainie's face is flushed from crying, but at least she's no longer shedding tears. I can't take the crying. "Let law enforcement handle it. Besides, what good would you be to Violet in prison?"

Ignoring Lainie's warning, I snap, "What's his name?" I want to know.

With a sigh, Lainie stares at me. Finally, she says, "Kyle Maines."

"Maines?" Keeton asks intently.

"He sells—"

"Insurance." Keeton chokes out. "He's my fucking insurance agent."

"No," Lainie says softly.

"Yes," he snaps. "But not for long." Keeton stomps around his wife, through the open doorway, and into the showroom that leads to his office.

Turning to Lainie, I place my hand on her shoulder. "Is she okay?"

"I think she's okay. It's going to get bad once they make the investigation public."

"Can't they keep her name out of it?" I mean, she's the victim.

"I hope so." She places her hand over the one I've got on her shoulder. "She's going to need us."

If only I could be one of "us." I knew it was going to take time to show her how much I care about her, but now? Now it's going to be nearly impossible.

"Don't," Lainie says suddenly. "Don't give up on her. I think you'd be good for her. She deserves to have a good man by her side."

"A good man?" She thinks I'm a good man? I feel my chest puff out just a little bit. Damn it, I *am* a good man. Squeezing her shoulder once, I pull mine out from under hers. If Keet saw me touching her, he'd probably belt me. I'd like to laugh about that, but I can't. Not right now.

"If you're anything like your brother...."

"I am," I say proudly. My bro is a straight shooter. A no-bull-shit kind of man. One who is loyal to a fault. He's been looking out for Molls and me forever, since our parents died. I look up to him, count on him.

Now that Lainie has given me the green light, I'm unsure about my next step. Looking down, I do the only thing I can think of. I ask, "What should I do?"

I can tell she's thinking. She's nodding, and her pretty eyes are squinting up at me like she's devising a plan. "Okay." Lainie places her right hand over her round stomach. My niece or nephew is cookin' in there. "Baby steps. But I think you should just *be there.*"

"Be there?" What the hell does that even mean?

"Be around. Stop into the bakery when she's there. Hang out with us when we all get together. We'll let you know when the Palmers are doing stuff."

"So, a stalker?"

Lainie laughs for the first time since she's walked into the shop tonight. "No. Not a stalker. You just need to start showing up to things. Be present."

"I told her I could meet her at the dog park."

"Dog park? Why?"

"To meet her dogs."

"Dogs? Plural? As in, more than one?"

Oh, shit. I think she mentioned that only Keely knew about the rest of her pet menagerie. "Uh...."

"She's got Max. Is there another one?"

"One more, I think." Damn it. I already fucked up the secret. She's counting on me to keep my damn mouth shut.

"Hmm, interesting." Lainie nods. "I had no idea. I'm glad she's got dogs. She has always loved animals." She pauses. "I guess I can figure out why I didn't know about the other one. She never brings them with her, and she doesn't like visitors."

"I don't know." I need to keep my damn mouth shut about her secret.

"See? You already know something about her that I don't. That's a good sign."

"You think?" I run my fingers through my hair. Damn, I need a cut. But Violet likes it, so it stays. Maybe a trim?

"Yes. I think." Stepping away from me she starts to walk through to the other side of the garage. Turning back, she says softly, "Be good to her. She's special."

"I know."

CHAPTER 11

Violet

"Come on, Max," I say, tugging on his leash. He found an interesting patch of grass that has taken his complete attention. He's not a huge dog but big enough to be able to stop my momentum. As I urge Max on, Charles Barkley tugs my other arm. I guess he's anxious to get to the dog park. "Me too, buddy. Me too."

"Are they giving you a tough time?" asks a deep, raspy voice coming from somewhere behind me.

I know who it is without even looking. I feel the smile slide across my face without even giving it a second thought as I turn to see a shirtless, sweaty, and gorgeous Eric Gustafson. "Oh, hi," I squeak.

Eric squats down in front of the good dog. I look back at Max as he finally decides to join the fun. "Which one is this?" Eric rubs Charles behind the ears, earning him a very wiggly tail. Lucky dog.

"That's Charles Barkley." Max chooses that moment to squeeze between my legs, causing me to wobble off balance.

Eric stands quickly to grasp my upper arm. "Thanks," I say with a nervous laugh. "And that rascal," I point down, "is Max."

Eric bends at the waist to pet Max. Charles, getting jealous, moves over and attempts to shove Max out of the way.

"Be nice, CB," I chastise.

I listen as Eric talks to both of my sweet boys. "Are you a good boy?" he asks Max. "And how 'bout you, CB? You a good boy too?"

My dogs are eating up the love like it's kibble. "I think they like you."

Pushing himself up to his full height, he puts a big palm on each side of his narrow hips, causing his loose running shorts to pull down just a little bit. Just enough for me to see he's got those lines that start at his waist and move down at an angle like an arrow pointing to his, uh, his—

Thankfully, my thoughts are interrupted when Eric says coolly, "What's not to like?"

"Oh, uh...." Crap, what do I say to that?

Then Eric chuckles. He also reaches out to touch my upper arm. "Just kidding. Animals seem to like me." He shrugs.

I have no scientific evidence to back up this claim, but I'm positive animals can tell the difference between good and evil. We all give off vibes, good ones and bad ones, that I'm sure they can sense. I've known Max for several years, and in that time, he's never been wrong about a person or another animal. He saves his growly remarks for when they're absolutely necessary.

"So, you guys going to the dog park?"

I release a gust of air between my lips making propeller sound. "Trying, but Max keeps finding interesting things to sniff."

"What if I take Max and you take CB?"

"Oh, no, you don't have to do that."

"I want to. Remember, I can't have pets at my place. This lets me live vicariously through you."

"Oh." I nod. "If you don't mind."

"Not at all. Hang on." I watch as Eric pulls something from the back waistband of his shorts. A shirt. I stare as he slides it over his head, then I gape as his muscled arms pull though each of the sleeves. I want to cry as the tee slides down over his stomach and feel a sense of loss at the disappearance of his pretty abdomen. I'm distracted by his hand as it reaches toward mine. When his fingers curl around the handle of the leash, I help slide it off.

"Shall we?" Eric says, pointing to the park.

CHAPTER 12

I don't remember the last time I had such a good time with a girl. We spent over an hour at the dog park trying to corral her hilarious sidekicks. After that, we walked on the trail until we came across an ice-cream stand. She let me buy her a frozen yogurt and two bottles of water for the dogs. I got myself a hot fudge sundae, my favorite. We made our way to a shady spot near a small pond for a little rest. I held the leashes as Violet sat first. I moved next to her but not so close as to make her nervous. I slid down until I was on my back lying in the shady grass, my sundae long gone. CB decided to plop his sloppy, wet head, thanks to the water, onto my stomach as Max crawled onto my legs. It was hot as hell, but I wasn't about to push them away. I patted CB's head and looked up at Violet, who was watching the entire scene with hawkish eyes.

My heart beat so hard in my chest, I was sure she could hear it. I felt the burn of tears in my eyes, but I cleared my throat to keep myself from becoming emotional. Because, well, never in my life have I felt so sure of anything. I've never felt so happy, so alive. Sitting there with Violet and two of her beloved animal friends, I know this is all I'll ever need. If I could bottle up this moment, I would. Better still, I'd spend more days like this with Violet. *Just* like this.

God, I hope she gives me a chance. She's perfect.

Because, in my experience, women are high maintenance. Not only that, they're usually fake and overly obsessed with their appearance. The few times I've made the effort and taken a woman to dinner, they've barely eaten. It drives me crazy. I mean, I paid for the damn steak, eat the damn steak.

Violet isn't like that. I bet if I bought her a steak, *she'd* eat it. She's elegant, sure, like I've said before, but it's not a guise. No, she's naturally that way. Soft-spoken unless she's trying to get CB or Max to listen, and very shy with me. It sounds ridiculous, but I'm a little jealous of the dogs.

I'm not sure how long we sit like that, but as I pet CB's back, I sneak a peek at her again. She's beautiful today in a girly baseball cap sitting low on her head. Her high ponytail that finally shows me how long her auburn hair is, is poking out the back hole of the cap. I'd say it's down the middle of her back if I was able to pull that hair tie out. And I'd like to. I'd love to see it fanned out on our bed. The one we share every night. *Hey, if I'm fantasizing, I might as well plan every night with her while I'm at it.* Her face is clear of any makeup; she doesn't need it. I can see the freckles that dot her face perfectly. Her lips are a shiny berry color, no doubt their actual color.

When she catches me looking at her, I smile.

"You look pretty today." What am I saying? Pretty isn't a grand enough word, but if I tell her she's fucking gorgeous, she may run away. But even in a simple flowered top that flows around her and tan shorts, she's gorgeous. It could be because it's my first glimpse of bare leg. Long bare leg. I'd say, like me, she gets most of her height out of her legs. Her gams are curvy too. Her thighs are thick and perfect. I'd love to kiss my way up those legs.

After we finish our ice cream, Violet starts to get up. I've spent the last thirty minutes going back and forth in my head about how I should do this with her. Should I tell her how I feel? What if I told her that I knew about the soon-to-be-dead Kyle Maines? While the words of two of her sisters roll around in my head, I can't help thinking that being patient sucks. Not only that, it feels wrong. I mean, if she has no idea how I feel, she could misinterpret my intentions. No, staying quiet is only doing Violet and me a disservice.

Before she has a chance to get up, I hold out my hand. "Violet?"

She stops her momentum and looks at me. "Yeah?"

I sit up, which displaces CB from my chest. He chuffs at the imposition while Max stays firmly planted on top of my legs. Holding my hand out in front of her I ask, "Hold my hand?"

She's tentative, but she does it, holding her palm out like I'm trying to shake her hand rather than just hold it. Giving her hand a gentle squeeze, I keep hold as I say, "I've had fun today."

"Me too." Damn, her voice is soft.

I push up further, and poor Max is forced to move off my legs. I turn until I'm completely facing her, never letting go of her hand. Clearing my throat, I begin. "I need to say some things, and I hope you'll let me get it all out before you run away."

"Run away?" She shakes her head hard enough that her shiny ponytail swings from side to side. "I won't run away."

"You might."

"I won't."

"Promise?"

She's silent for a few seconds. "Promise."

Placing my other hand over hers, I look into her eyes. "You know how Lainie and Keeton knew?"

She nods. I don't have to explain it. Thank fuck.

"That day I met you at Keeton's. Remember that day?"

Violet's head barely moves up and down.

"That day, I understood what Keeton must have felt when he first saw Lainie. Except, for me, it was you."

Violet's face turns fuchsia. I've never seen anything like it. One minute she's pale as cream, and the next her face is flushed hot pink. I feel her start to tug her hand out of mine, but I hang on tight. Not too tight; I don't want to scare her.

"Violet, you promised."

"You don't know what you're talking about," she chokes out. "You don't feel that way about me."

"Please don't tell me how I feel, baby."

I think I startled her with that endearment, because her eyes bulge as her head jerks back. "Baby?"

"What? You don't like that expression?"

"No." She blinks. "I don't know." She tries again to tug her hand free, and I let it go because her face suddenly reads angry. "Who put you up to this? Keely?"

"What? No!" What the hell is she talking about? "Well, she did tell me to 'be patient' and 'give you lots of time.'" I use air quotes, by the way. I may have also used a fake snarky voice. Because now that I think about it, it pisses me off. "Lainie essentially said the same thing last night."

"Keely and Lainie know about this? Before me?" Violet pushes up to her knees, then she's on her feet so fast I blink. Reaching for the dog leashes, she starts to tug them away from me.

I jump up onto my feet and move closer. "You promised me you'd let me finish. Are you a person who goes back on her word?" Ha! I've got her.

"No, but it sounds to me like you should be talking to my sisters. Perhaps you should meet up with Agatha and Sadie," she snaps. Muttering under her breath, I hear her say, "I'm so sick of people thinking I'm that pathetic."

"No one thinks of you like that."

She stops suddenly. "How the heck do you know? You don't know me, Eric Gustafson. You just want...." She growls. "I have no idea what you want, but I'm not a-a floozy."

I want to laugh, but if I've learned one thing the last couple of times I was with Violet, it's that I should only laugh at things that are funny—to both of us. "I know you're not a floozy. I know about Kyle."

"What!" she screeches. "Who told you?"

"I overheard."

"Crap. Crap, crap, crap," Violet chants as she moves back and forth in front of me. "I just told them yesterday."

"I heard your name and tried to listen."

"What?" She stops in front of me. "Why?"

"Because. Lainie was crying. She said your name. You're my girl. I had to know if you were okay."

"She was crying?" Violet blinks. "Still?"

That's what she took from that? "Yes. She was upset. I was concerned about you. I had to know."

With a leash in each hand, she rubs her face. "This is too much for me right now, Eric." Turning away, she begins to make her way to the walking trail. Before she gets there, though, she turns back to me. "Thank you for spending the day with us, Eric."

And then she's gone. And I know in my heart I fucked up. Now all I need to do is figure out how to fix it. I've got to fix this.

CHAPTER 13

VIOLET

I don't know what to think about what just happened with Eric. I'm confused. It feels like my brain is whirling around with a lot of mixed-up thoughts and feelings. On one hand, I'd like to strangle my sisters. How could they talk to Eric *about* me without talking *to* me first? On the other hand, they could just be playing matchmaker for their pathetic sister. Okay, I know we only have two hands. But for this, I need more than two. Way more. So, the other, more far-fetched hand is the one where Eric actually likes me. You know? *Likes me* likes me.

There's just no way.

Guys like Eric Gustafson don't go after girls like me. They just don't. The one time a hot guy hit on me, it was to do *it* to me.

God, I can still hear them laughing....

"No!" I say aloud. It brings Max's attention away from the car window and back to me but for only a split second. "I won't think about *him* or *them*, Max. Right, buddy?" I reach out and scratch him behind his left ear. "You'll protect me, won't you, boy."

Max nods. I swear it. The dog is amazing.

Doing my best to change the thoughts running rampant in my head, I clear my throat and ask, "So, did you boys like Eric?" First of all, why am I asking them? It's like asking a kid if they like ice cream. Duh! Of course they liked Eric. And Eric liked them. I blow out a sigh, making that raspberry sound. "I'm a mess, guys." A complete and utter mess.

Pulling up to my little rental, I notice a car at the curb. A shiny black BMW that I've gotten to know well these past couple of months. Pulling into my driveway and beneath the carport that's attached to my house, I hesitate, mumbling, "CB, you're about to meet your aunty."

I slide out of the car, and Max follows me, making a beeline to Lainie. I pull open the back door, and CB hesitates. It's quite a drop for the small dog from the back seat of my old RAV-4. Reaching in, I pick him up around his belly and set him down so he can join his brother.

"There *are* two dogs," Lainie states. "I heard you had two."

Flipping Eric. Can't keep a damn secret.

"CB," I point to the little one, "is a foster dog."

"You foster dogs?"

"Among other things," I say only loud enough for me to hear.

I know I should be mad at her for surprising me with a visit, since I'm not the kind of person you just drop in on, but I can't do it. Her heart is always in the right place. "What's up, Lainie?"

"It's Sunday."

I'm well aware. It's my day off from everything. The bakery is closed, and I've got no classes. It's the one day a week where I don't have to do anything if I don't want to.

"Keeton and I are having a BBQ tonight. We'd like you to come."

This is odd. Why is she doing this in person? "You could have sent a text." I mean, it's how we usually arrange get-togethers.

"I also wanted to see you, alone."

Uh-oh. This is getting serious. "Oh?"

"Are you going to invite me in? I've never been inside your little bungalow. I'd love to see what you've done to it."

Sure, it's probably strange that only one of my sisters has been to my home, but it's my sanctuary. I've been renting this house for over three years from my high school best friend, Jess. It belonged to her grandmother, left to Jess in her will. When Jessica landed her dream job in New York, she offered to rent me this place for practically nothing. I pay the taxes, all utilities, and I make sure to keep up with repairs. She knows about the pets and she's fine with them. The few times she's been back, she's stayed with me. She'll want it back someday, but until then, it's mine.

Looking down at the dogs then back up at my sister, I nod.

"I've got more pets." What else is there to say? She probably knows already, thanks to the blabbermouth that is Eric Gustafson.

"How many more pets?"

"Several."

"Okay," she responds hesitantly. "Are there snakes?"

I snort, then laugh. "No, geesh. Snakes give me the willies."

"Me too." She pauses. "Spiders?"

"Not as pets." I want to laugh at the visible shiver that

comes out of Lainie. None of us are spider fans, especially spiders indigenous to northern Arizona.

Unlocking my front door, I push it open and let the dogs run inside first, then Lainie. I hear squawks and other cute noises coming from inside the house. When I step up, Lainie has stopped in her tracks. Her eyes are on the sofa where my two felines, Sherman and Stella, are napping together.

"Cats?"

"Yep."

"From the squawking, I'd say there's a bird in here somewhere."

"Parrot." I walk past her, pointing in the direction of my small kitchen. "Come on, the kitchen is a pet-free zone." Most of the time.

It's a snug fit in the kitchen thanks to the full-size appliances. I've got a small round table and two chairs there and about two linear feet of counter space in which to work, so the table is useful. "Would you like some green tea? Sugar-free lemonade?"

"Water? Please?" Lainie asks, her eyes taking in my eat-in kitchen.

"Sure." I open up one of my upper cabinets and take out two glasses. Adding ice to both, I fill hers with bottled water from my fridge and get lemonade for myself. Placing the glass in front of her, I offer her something to eat.

"I've got some pretzels." I open the fridge again and peer inside. "I could make you a salad." I turn to her. "I've probably got the stuff to make you a sandwich."

"No." Lainie chuckles. "I'm fine. Sit." She points to the other chair. "Let's talk. I don't have much time."

Ugh, why does that sound so ominous?

"After that, I'd like to meet the rest of your pets and see your home. It's really adorable."

I nod. "Thanks." I've done a lot to the little place. It's not like Jess or her grandmother left it in disrepair, it's just that the entire thing was beige. I've painted all the rooms bright, happy colors, and decorated with equally colorful accessories. It helps disguise all of my thrift store furniture. "So?"

"So." She smiles. "I was worried about you after last night."

"I'm okay. Are you?" I recall Eric telling me Lainie had been crying over my news.

"I was upset. Yes. I wish you'd told me...."

I take a drink of lemonade and wish it wasn't the sugar-free kind. I could use real sugar for this conversation. "It never felt right. I knew it'd become this thing." I wave my hand around, demonstrating what, I'm not sure.

"We all love you so much." I can hear Lainie's voice start to quiver. She's going to cry.

"I love you too." And I do. I love them with all my heart.

"With everyone all freaked last night, I didn't get to ask you..."

I sit completely still, waiting.

"Have you been to therapy?"

"Yes." Multiple times. But since I'm no longer on my dad's insurance, I've had to resort to self-help books.

Lainie laughs nervously. "Wow, you're not giving up much, are you?"

"Look." I reach my hand out and take Lainie's in mine. "It's been nearly six years since it happened. In that time, I've been to therapy, read every book there is out there ever written about or by sexual assault survivors. I've called sexual assault hotlines when I've needed it. I journal, and this past year, I've worked hard to get physically healthy. Something many of the books recommend."

"Wow." Lainie wipes her cheek. "You're so strong."

"I am. Now."

"Are you prepared for everything that will probably happen when Nick and the police do whatever it is they're planning to do?"

"Yes." No. But I'm going to keep up the front that I am prepared.

"I love you, Vi."

"I love you too." I squeeze her hand that's still in mine. "I know you're all worried, but I'm ready to deal with this head-on."

"I can't believe he's Keeton's insurance agent," Lainie says absently.

"What?!" I screech, standing up so fast my chair falls back. "He's what?!" Oh, my... "He's Keeton's agent?"

"Oh, shit, sorry. I should have led with that. I told Keeton about it and he recognized his name. Keeton's going to fire him tomorrow. I think he wants to murder him first, but I think I've talked him out of that."

"Maybe he should talk to Nick before he fires him."

"Oh, right." Lainie looks upward like she's thinking. "Maybe Keeton could help?"

"Maybe. But they might not want to make Kyle suspicious."

"Right," she says distractedly. "Right."

After I show Lainie around my place, introducing her to all of my pets, of which Binky the guinea pig is her favorite, she reminds me to be at their place by six for the BBQ. I wish I hadn't agreed to go. I'm not in the mood to be around a lot of people today and I know everyone will be there. *Everyone.*

CHAPTER 14

*V*IOLET

It was a mistake. I shouldn't have come. They're doing exactly what I thought they'd do, only times a billion. I'm pretty sure every single person here has patted my back sympathetically, offered to bring me food and drinks, and every now and then, they all look over at me with puppy dog eyes. Heck, even Nick and the other guys have been hovering. I've been here forty-five minutes, and it's been forty-five minutes too long. *I've had it.*

Just as Agatha starts to approach me holding a plate of cookies and a sad face, I stand up from my spot in the corner and move closer to the pool until I'm pretty much front and center. At the top of my lungs, I shout, "Enough!"

That gets everyone's attention.

"Enough with all of the coddling and sympathetic looks and creepy touching and patting my back. You're making me uncomfortable." I clear my throat. "If you don't all go back to normal, I'm going to leave, and it'll be years before I attend another family function. You got it?"

"But," starts either Aggie or Sadie.

"No 'buts.' I mean it. It's why I kept it to myself. I don't want you to treat me like I'm some stupid porcelain doll. I'm fine. Now get over it."

I see a few nods and awkward expressions that make me growl in frustration. "I mean it!" I do. I'm about two seconds from marching out of here and never returning. Taking my spot back in the corner, I decide to give them one more chance. I scan the crowd and spot Eric first. He's been avoiding me like the plague. It was only a few hours ago that I ran away from him at the park. I guess he took the hint, unfortunately. My eyes move left and land on my dad. Again. He's been sitting alone in a chair beneath a large umbrella since I got here. He's holding a bottle of beer, but his head is down, resting in his palms as he leans over, elbows on his knees. Of all the people here, my dad is the only one who hasn't approached me. Come to think of it, after his outburst last night, he stormed out of the house, and I haven't talked to him since.

I'm such a selfish wench. This is what my dad does when he's dealing with things. He plays the avoidance game just as well as I do, maybe better. Heck, I probably learned it from him. Standing, I slowly make my way over to him.

"Daddy?"

He won't look at me. God, I'm the world's worst daughter.

"Do you want to talk?"

"No." His voice is hoarse, but he begins to nod. "Yes." When he peeks up at me, he isn't smiling. "Why didn't you tell me, Vi?"

I've hurt him. "Dad...."

"I could have helped you. I would have helped you. Hell, I'd have loved to kill that fucker."

"Then you'd be in jail."

"So?" he spits before taking a drink of his beer. "Worth it, Vi. You're worth it. I'd die for you girls. You know that."

Crap. That's all it takes for the stupid waterworks to start. One tear slides out of the corner of my eye, followed by a bunch more.

"Daddy," I whisper. "I know. It was just something I had to work through on my own."

"I knew you were seeing a therapist. I just figured it was girl stuff."

I hadn't thought of that. I'd used his insurance, so of course he'd see the bills.

"If I'd known, I could have kept you on my insurance, baby doll. It wouldn't have cost me much at all."

"Dad, the therapist helped me. I was okay stopping then. I'm doing really well now." The truth is, the therapist wasn't that helpful. He was nice enough, but at that point, I didn't trust him even though he was old enough to be my dad. I just didn't feel like I could tell him everything. Maybe I should have found a woman. Too late now, I guess. I probably didn't do myself any favors trying to figure things out on my own, for the most part.

Dad sets the empty beer bottle on the ground next to his chair, then covers his face with his hands again. When he sniffles, I officially lose it.

"Daddy?" I squeak. "Please." I move closer and put my arms around him. "Please."

When his strong arms wrap me up, I can barely breathe, but I keep that to myself. He needs this as much as I do.

"You're my hero, Dad," I say in his ear. "I knew you'd protect me. I just didn't want to upset you. I couldn't stand the thought of you doing something drastic. I need you here with me."

"Vi," he chokes out.

That's all he says for several minutes. He releases me slowly, wiping his eyes as he does. "Violet, from now on, I need you to come to me whenever you need me. Either that or I'm going to come live with you and all those damn pets."

"Hey," I shout. "How did you know about my animals?"

My dad looks nervous. He moves from side to side looking around then back to me.

What is going on?

"So," He pauses "you remember about a month ago... Jess had your air conditioner replaced?"

I nod. The work was done while I was at school.

"Well, I supervised the job. Jess asked me to make sure they did everything right. I know how you are about your privacy, Vi. I swear, I didn't snoop. I just went in while they worked and made sure they did it right."

My mouth drops open. I'm surprised that Jess would ask my dad to help. Wait. No, I'm not. Jess adores my dad. Heck, not to mention the fact she's got a thing for "hot old guys." Her words, not mine. My dad fits that bill, I guess. Heck, she called him a silver fox the last time she was home. Couple that with the fact that Jess has always worried about me. So, I guess I'm not that surprised.

"For the record, your little dog is a pain in the ass."

I blink.

"He's cute, though."

"Dad." It's all I can say.

"What? You think your doorknob just fixed itself?"

I blink more. My dad is a finish carpenter. That means he works with a builder and does all of the nice woodwork inside houses and buildings. Actually, he's done everything related to construction. He's super handy. I know he'd like to build furniture instead, but there's no room at his house to set up a woodworking shop. At least that's the excuse he's used for the past twenty or so years.

"My doorknob?"

"I fixed it while the guys installed the a/c unit." Dad's face looks sheepish. "Did you not notice it doesn't stick anymore?"

"No." Yes, I did. "I figured it was a seasonal thing." Then, I laugh. "You're a sneaky devil."

I feel his arms again. "A sneaky devil who loves you with all his heart." He kisses my cheek. "I promise you, though, I never snooped. We did what we meant to do and got out of there."

"Oh, Dad." I know he does. "I know. I know you're not a snooper. Thank you."

"Correction. I had to search high and low for the dog treats. That little dog is a pain in the ass."

"So you said." Stepping back, I look up at him. "From now on, let me know when you're planning to fix things behind my back. I'll clean the place up and make you lunch. Deal?"

"Deal."

"Oh, that reminds me." I reach out and place my hand on my dad's arm. "I've got a loose board in the spare bedroom floor." More than one, actually. I know my dad and letting him in now and then to fix things will make him happy. He's been there for all of us because he loves us and wants to help us and I can let him. Especially now, after all of this...

"Oh, yeah? So, you're going to give me a Dad to-do list now?"

"Possibly." I smile up at him. "I'd love to have a couple of those Adirondack chairs for my back patio." I hesitate. "Oh, and there may be more than one loose board—in other rooms too."

"I hadn't noticed but, like I said, I did what I went to do and got out of there. I didn't want to impose on your space."

"I know, Dad. You're only looking out for me." I nod in the general direction of my sisters. "For all of us." Squeezing his arm, I'm about to walk away, but I have to say, "And for the record, the little white dog is called Charles Barkley and he's not a pain the butt."

"No?"

"Nope." I shake my head. "He's just misunderstood."

My dad laughs. A deep, rumbling laugh that makes my heart swell with warmth. We are so lucky to have him. So damn lucky.

"Hey," my dad says before I can walk away. He leans down like he wants to kiss my cheek. Instead he whispers. "That Eric character hasn't taken his eyes off you tonight."

"Oh?" I noticed, actually.

"Do I need to kick his ass?"

His question surprises me so much I laugh. "No, Dad."

"You sure?" He winks.

"I'm sure." As he turns, I decide on a little payback. "What about you and Deb?" I ask with an arched brow. "You two were thick as thieves at the wedding."

Dad smiles. "I like her."

Oh my God!

"She's amazing, Dad. She owns her own shop. She builds classic cars." It's right up his alley. He loves cars and motorcycles. Heck, ever since Keeton and Lainie gave him that vintage bike, that's all he drives. He's become a motorhead.

"I know." He winks again.

"Yay," I say, clapping my hands. "Invite her up. We'll have a family dinner."

"We'll see." He reaches out and squeezes my shoulder. "We'll see."

OMG. My dad likes a girl!

CHAPTER 15

ERIC

I've been keeping my distance. After the outing at the dog park and my confession earlier today, I decided the next time I saw her I'd keep my distance—let her come to me. So far, not a great plan. She's been here at Keet and Lainie's party over an hour and she's barely looked my way. I know because my eyes have been on her nonstop. She's talked to nearly everyone *but* me. Hell, she talked to the cop, Nick Martelli, and Agatha's man, Ian, for a good fifteen minutes—probably about her case, but still. I was a little jealous.

Then I watched in stunned silence as she yelled at all of us to knock off the hovering, and I did my best to keep the big smile from my lips. If she saw it, she'd misinterpret my expression. I smiled because I'm so damn proud of her. I don't know Violet well, but I'd bet my new bike that she's never had an outburst like that in her life. I can make that wager confidently due to the reaction of her sisters, two of whom were standing next to me. I'm pretty sure both Sadie and Aggie gasped when Violet first shouted, "Enough!" I guess they're with me. Who knew Violet had lady-balls beneath that pretty summer dress?

Afterward, I watched her with her dad. I tried not to stare, but I couldn't help it. I've gotten to know Rob a bit since he and Lainie got together. Rob helps Keeton out at the shop now and then, and I've never seen him so withdrawn. He's been sitting off by himself all afternoon. I know because I came here after the dog park for a swim. He's been in that exact spot since then. I kept wondering when Lainie or Keeton were going to talk to him, but they haven't done a thing. I guess the man needed space.

When the food was ready, we all took turns filling our plates. Keeton grilled chicken and some kind of fish this time. I'm not usually into fish, but I took a piece and, man, am I glad I did. "Fucking delicious, brother."

Keeton nods, then winks. "Lainie's recipe."

"She a good cook too?" Damn, my brother hit the jackpot with that one.

"Amazing cook." He smirks. "And she's all mine."

"Not for long. When's baby Gustafson due again?" I damn well know the baby is due in February, but I love the look on my bro's face when he talks about his future kid.

"February." He beams. "I can't wait, Eric. I can't wait to be a dad."

"You'll be great at it, man." I slap him on the back. "You practically raised me and Molls."

I watch Keeton take a big swallow. "Thanks, little brother."

"I'm not blowing smoke up your ass. You're going to have a sweet little family soon." I tap my chin. "What do you give a newborn for a gift? How 'bout a kid-sized drum set?" I hold my finger up. "We could start a band as soon as he or she is old enough." I've started to laugh now. "Can we practice in your garage?"

"Shut it, little bro. No drum kits. Payback's a bitch," Keeton snickers. "I'll give you and Vi's kid somethin' worse."

I stand frozen. Dumbstruck.

Me and Vi's kid?

I feel a smile unfurl, and I can't keep it in. "Me and Vi." It's not a question.

"If you meant what you said the other night. I—"

"I did. One hundred percent. I just have to get her onboard."

"Patience."

"I know. Jesus," I grumble. "Patience." I've heard it too many times now. I *am* patient. "For something as important as this is, I'll be as patient as a saint."

Keeton nods toward the house. "She's huggin' people. I think she's taking off."

"What?" I turn to see Violet hugging Keely. "I didn't get to talk to her."

"Then go, man."

Right. "Back in a bit."

"Or not," Keeton mumbles. "I want some alone time with my woman."

"Right. Later." As I turn to head in Violet's direction, she's gone. I pick up the pace and jog right past her dad.

"Patience," Rob says as I pass.

"I know," I grunt. I'm starting to fucking hate that word.

"Violet!" I shout as she approaches her little SUV.

Reaching for her door, she turns her head. Without a word, she releases the door and turns fully to face me. "I wondered if you were going to speak to me again." Her pretty auburn brow is arched. She's what? Testing me?

"I wanted to give you space."

Violet crosses her arms over her chest, which does the opposite of what she probably intends. It pushes her pretty tits up and out instead of hiding them. I suddenly realize I'm staring at them when she says, "You succeeded."

"Look." I run my fingers through my unruly hair. I never combed it after my swim, so I imagine it's all over the place. I'm stopped midsentence when Violet opens her car door. "You're leaving? You aren't gonna let me speak?" God, this girl won't give me a goddamn chance. "Seriously?" I'm a bit put off. More than a bit.

When she holds her hand out toward me, I see something dangling from her fingers. A hair tie? "Oh." I feel my cheeks heat. I'm a dick. "Thanks."

"You're welcome. Now." She sighs and crosses her arms over her chest again. I wish she wouldn't do that. It's so fucking distracting.

"Uh...." I quickly pull all my hair back and tie it into a mess of a bun. I blow some air between my lips. "I'm not sure what to do or say."

Violet's brows furrow. "About what?"

"You." I pause. "Me. Us."

"Us?" Those pretty red brows are now pressed together in the middle of her forehead.

"Us. Yes. I'd like to, uh, court you."

Bam, the furrow is gone, replaced by a look of utter surprise. "Court me?" She starts to giggle, placing her long fingers over her mouth to hold it in. It's not working. The giggle gets louder, until I'd call it more of a full-blown laugh. "C-court m-me?"

Damn, she needs to get control. This is sort of pissing me off. Not sort of—*it is*. I've practically served my balls on a platter for this girl, and she laughs at me? Well, fuck this. I turn and stomp away toward my car. At least I hope it's where I parked my car. That was hours ago.

"Wait! Eric?"

I turn my head to look back at her, but I keep walking, right into the fucking mailbox. The box part hits me right in the gut, and the foo-foo metal scroll shit below that hits me right in the dick. I bend fast, hitting my head on the top of the box. I'm on my ass in the road curled into a ball before I know it. I fall to my side in the fetal position using my hands to cover *my precious*.

"Eric?" Violet says sounding panicked. "Are you okay?"

"No," I grunt. I'm able to get the one word out, but it's pained and raspy sounding. That's all I can muster, since my main job right now is protecting the family jewels. Getting wracked in the nuts hurts so fucking bad.

"Eric?" Violet is on her knees next to me. "I'm sorry. I didn't mean to make you mad."

Now is not the time to talk. No, now is the time for me to do whatever I can to get my nuts to come back out from inside my body where they went to hide. *Fuck, it hurts.*

I force out, "It's okay." And it is. I don't want her to feel badly because I can't walk and talk at the same time.

"I wasn't laughing at you. It was just a funny concept. Courting." She's talking quickly beside me, her hand on my upper arm. "Like in the olden days."

I'm able to turn my head now without wincing. Looking up at her, I see her eyebrows are scrunched up again. "If that's what I need to do," I say, forcing air in and out of my lungs. "I'll court the hell out of you."

My eyes never leave her face, so I watch her expression morph from concern to worry to something calmer. Her eyes meet mine. "What does *courting* entail, exactly?"

Feeling like I'm not going to puke anymore, I push myself up until I'm seated. I bring my legs up and rest my arms on my knees. Releasing a breath to get myself together, I shrug. "I know we need to go slow."

"We do?" Her pretty lashes are fluttering, but she's not doing it to act flirty. She really wants to know.

"We do." I nod. "I'd like to spend time with you. That could be taking the dogs for a walk, watching a movie, having a meal." I shrug. "I'm just throwing some stuff out there." I'm really starting to feel like I have no idea what I'm talking about anymore.

"I like the sound of all those things."

"I want the other stuff too, eventually." I look up. When our eyes meet, I blurt, "I want to kiss you so bad." I squeeze my eyes shut and run a palm through my now constrained hair. "But you're not—" Before I can finish, I smell her sweet scent and then I feel her lips on mine. *She's* kissing *me*. She's fucking kissing me. What do I do now?

I open my eyes just as she pulls away, but she doesn't go far. Reaching my hand out, I gently place it on the back of her neck.

"Kiss me again. Please?" I ask softly.

She moves closer. My heart feels like it might explode. The anticipation of our lips touching again is making me sweat. When her mouth touches my lips, I open mine slightly. Enough for my lips to surround her plump lower lip. I suck for just a second, then I rotate my head to the left so I can deepen the kiss. Still no tongue. I don't want to freak her out. When I feel her little tongue touch my mouth, I want to devour her. But I can't.

Patience.

Fuck, I hate that word.

"Yo! Get a room!" shouts someone behind Violet. She quickly pulls away, her face pink with what? Embarrassment? Lust? God, I hope it's lust.

Pulling my eyes from her, I see the culprit. Keely.

"You didn't waste any time did you, Vi?" Keely snickers. "What'd you do? Push him down?"

Keely is full-on cackling as her man, Nick, rolls his eyes.

"Sorry about her." He nods toward Keely.

I half expect Violet to bolt, but when I look back at her, she's smiling.

"You're not upset with your sister?"

Violet shakes her head. "It's the first time in a long, long time that I felt like I was normal." She clears her throat. "As it relates to boys."

Boys?

"Well, men," she quickly amends. "I know you're all man, Eric." Then she laughs. Loudly.

"Right." I push myself to standing. Reaching my hand out, I wait for her to take it so I can help her up. When she does, I gently pull her into me. "We do nothing you're not ready for. You control everything. I will never be upset if you need to slow things down. I'm here for the long haul. You get me, babe?"

She nods. I can tell she's still not sure.

"I know you're uncertain."

"No, I—"

"It's written all over that gorgeous face, and it's okay. Little steps. I'm just happy you're giving me a shot..." I point to both of us, back and forth. "At this."

"I'll try," she says softly. "But, if you decide it's not what you want, you have to tell me. Don't lie to me."

"Never."

"Never." She repeats it like she's memorizing the word.

CHAPTER 16

Shit... meet fan.

That's my thought as I look around at the sea of people swarming around inside the Page Police Department. There are people walking in and out of a large conference room. If I crane my neck, I can see some people standing in front of a large whiteboard filled with notes. There are images taped to the board, but I'm not close enough to see what that's all about. The only thing I can make out is "Kyle Maines" jotted in large script at the top of the board.

I should probably be terrified, but I feel okay thanks to the fact that Aggie is sitting next to me in the waiting area. Ian, her beau and former FBI agent, is in the chair next to her. I contemplated bringing a lawyer with me, one Cortland Ashbury, but criminal law isn't his forté. His words. No, he's mostly into business and finance stuff, but he's the only lawyer I know, thanks to Sadie's relationship with Charlie Ashbury.

We're all pretty quiet as the police do their thing. I'm doing my best to eavesdrop on what they're saying, but they're either too quiet or I'm going deaf. I'm certain Agatha is doing the same. She's good at this crime and detective stuff. When I hear the words "task force," I turn to look at her.

"They just said 'task force,'" I whisper.

"Ian called a friend of his with the Bureau," she says, leaning close to my ear. "This isn't federal, but he thought someone from the Agency should be in on the initial discussions. If they get a few more agents involved, they'll call that a task force. You know, so they can work with these guys on the investigations." She shrugs.

Ian picks up the thread. "The FBI have more resources at their fingertips if this gets too big for Page PD. For today, Agent Banks is here to advise and give feedback."

"Sure. Of course." I let my eyes roam again, listening for more, but I don't get the chance.

I hear my name and look to my right and see Nick Martelli standing at the opening of another room. He's giving me a small smile. "You ready?"

I shake my head but stand up anyway. Agatha follows, as does Ian. We walk toward Nick, who steps aside for us to walk into a small office. Well, maybe I should call it a conference room, since, instead of a desk, there's a small round table with six chairs.

"Sit anywhere, guys."

I sit in the chair the furthest from and facing the doorway. I can watch who comes and goes this way. Agatha takes her place on my left just like in the waiting area; Ian sits beside her.

"There's water there." Nick points to a small pitcher of ice water and six glasses. "But if you want coffee or soda...?"

"I'm good with water."

"Me too," adds Agatha.

I reach out and pour several glasses and hand them over to

Aggie and Ian. I'm so dang nervous, my hand is shaking, so it's no surprise I splatter water on the table.

Minutes later, Captain Morgan enters the room, followed by a guy in a dark suit.

He must be the FBI agent. What was his name? Barnes? No matter; the first thing I notice is that he's handsome in a tall, lanky, clean-cut kind of way.

The FBI agent sits down on my right. Reaching out his hand to shake he says, "Agent Ryan Banks." Before I can reply he leans close and sniffs. "You smell like cookies."

I'm about to explain that I left work to come here when Agatha jumps in. "She works in our sister's bakery." Agatha raises her hand to him. "Agatha Palmer."

"Nice to meet you both."

Once the other men are seated, Nick asks, "We'd like to ask you some questions. Are you up to it, Violet?"

"Sure." Honestly? It depends on the questions.

Seated directly in front of me is Nick, with Captain Morgan on his right. Next to me is Agent Banks. His cologne is somewhat strong, but it's not making me queasy or anything. I do my best to avoid looking at him until I have to. He makes me nervous. I mean, I know everyone in this room. Captain Morgan is a friend of my dad's, so the agent is the odd man out.

Nick begins. "Violet, as you know, we have two copies of your police report from your alleged assault on October 30 nearly six years ago. Correct?"

Alleged?

I nod.

"The officer who completed your report signed here." He points to the line at the bottom. "Do you remember his name?"

"Sergeant Smalley, I believe." My voice sounds hoarse, like I've just smoked a pack of cigarettes. I cough into my fist to clear my throat. Then, just to do something with my hands, I sip some water.

Gosh, I'm nervous.

"Can you read the signature on this report? The one we received from the Tucson PD?"

I lean over to read the signature. "It looks the same." I lean down further. "No, it looks like Smith."

"Do you remember an officer by that name?"

I shake my head.

"Vi, would you mind speaking? We're recording this," adds Captain Morgan.

I nod and respond to the captain. "Um, yes." Looking back at Nick, I address his question. "No, I don't remember that name. Maybe Keely would remember."

To the rest of the table, Nick adds, "For the record, Keely Palmer does not recollect the name." Nick turns to me. "We interviewed her this weekend."

"Oh." She didn't tell me. "Okay."

"Tell us about that night."

That question didn't come from Nick. It came from a rather deep voice at my right.

"That night?" I croak. I turn to Nick. "I have to talk about that night?" I look left, then right, looking for someone to tell me it's okay if I keep it to myself. I do my best to swallow down the bile that suddenly rises into my throat. "Nick?"

"Yes," the FBI guy says loudly. His head is turned to Nick. "If she's your centerpiece, we all need to know what happened. All of it."

Centerpiece? What does that even mean? I feel a warm hand wrap around the one I've got clutching the dress I decided to wear to this stupid meeting. It's Agatha. I know she's trying to help, but it's not working.

"I've..." I swallow down again. "I've never told anyone all of it."

"Why don't we let her tell Amy behind closed doors? We can record it," suggests Nick. He looks at me. "Amy's our only female officer currently, Violet."

"Jesus," gripes Agent Banks. "You want to do this right or not?"

"Yes, of course...," Nick states hesitantly.

"She'll have to tell a jury. She might as well get used to this." He looks down at me. "You want them to catch this guy, right? You're not just here to look pretty, yeah?"

"Knock it off, Banks," grumbles Ian. "Cut her some slack."

"Why, because she's your girl's sister?" Banks scoffs. "You know how this works. It's going to be harder than fuck to get this guy, thanks to his connections." He looks around the table. "Which reminds me." He glares at everyone, including me. "If any of this gets out before you're ready, your investigation will go *poof*," he says softly as he makes a jazz hands kind of gesture, "disappear, thanks to mommy dearest."

"What crawled up your ass, Banks? You don't have to be a dick here," Ian grumbles.

"I'm doing this shit on my own time, man. You said yourself you didn't want the Bureau tuned into this yet. I'm doing this out of the goodness of my heart. So either you take my advice and get this girl"—he points his thumb at me—"to talk, or...."

They're talking about me like I'm not here. "I'll...." I swallow again. I'm certain I'm going to lose the coffee I drank this morning. "I'll do it."

"Vi—" Agatha starts, but I shake her off.

Fine. Okay. I can do this. I take another drink from the glass of water in front of me. "I'll start at the beginning."

"That'd be swell," says the jerk, Banks.

So, I start at the beginning. I tell them I was a freshman at the University of Southeast Arizona. That it was my first semester and I was studying Environmental Engineering.

"What's that?" asks the captain.

"Glorified garbage collector," grumbles Agent Banks.

What the heck is his problem?

"No." I glare at him, then look back at Captain Morgan. "It's about developing sustainable systems to protect, clean up, recycle, and reuse the world's natural resources." I want to give the FBI agent another dirty look, but that'd be overkill.

"Continue, please, Violet." See? Captain Morgan is nice.

I tell them I was studious and that I didn't go out much, well, at all. That got a scoff from Agent Jerk-face, but I ignore him. "My roommate talked me into going to the party. She did my makeup—"

Agent Banks asks, "What were you wearing?"

That's it! I'm not going to sit here and listen to the same crap Tucson PD dished out. "Are you going to let me tell you this or not?" I glare at Banks. "What I wore had nothing to do with the fact that Kyle Maines raped me. I was a v-virgin, okay? I didn't just give it away. That part of me, I was saving for...." I clear my throat. "Virgin or not, Kyle did this. It wasn't my fault. We both know rape isn't about a woman's clothes. It's about control."

"Knock it off, Banks. If you're going to be an asshole, you can leave." Ian says loudly. "Let her talk."

"Fine," Banks says, a little remorseful, but I don't believe it for a second.

"Shoot. Where was I?" I glare at Agent Banks again.

"You were getting ready for the party," I hear Nick say.

"Right." I explain again how I hadn't gone to any parties and that my roommate talked me into attending a fraternity party because she liked someone who lived at the fraternity house. "He was in one of her classes."

Captain Morgan asks, pen poised, "What was his name?"

"I don't remember. I'm sorry; I believe you have my roommate's information. She'd remember."

The captain nods.

"So, we got ready." I turn to Agent Banks and tell him I wore skinny jeans and a flowy top and some short boots. "I also wore a sweater since it was the end of October and could be chilly at night."

Nick nods, jotting down more notes.

"We got there at about nine at night. By then, the party was in full swing. The place was packed with people. Stacy, my roommate, took off as soon as she spotted her, uh, love interest, leaving me alone." No matter. I didn't mind. It just meant that I could stand off in the corner and people watch. It was my favorite pastime. It also meant that I didn't have to talk to people unless I wanted to. "I saw a couple of people from my classes next to the keg. Someone handed me a beer—"

"Who handed you the beer?" Agent Banks again.

"Whoever was pouring at that time. I don't know."

"You should never accept a drink from a stranger."

What the heck is this guy's deal?

"Come on, Banks," Nick interrupts. "Lay off."

Ignoring his help, I repeat some of the words Keely used the other night, I attempt to defend myself. "So I deserved to be raped because I took a beer from the guy pouring the beer? Is that really what you're implying, Agent Banks? You think I deserved to get raped because of my outfit and because I was nineteen at my first college party? Wow." I shake my head. "I take it you never went to any parties when you were in college. Did you ever take a drink from a stranger?"

I don't think he likes my questions, because he snaps, "This isn't about me."

I snap back, "No. It's about me and the other girls that

predator probably raped. So, let me finish my gosh-dang story so you can do what you need to do to catch this jerk-off."

"Gosh-dang? Jerk-off?" Banks scoffs. Leaning forward over the table he growls, "The guy raped you. *Allegedly*." He pauses. "And the most you can say is gosh-dang and he's a jerk-off? Really?"

"Fine!" Standing up from my seat. I put my hands on my hips. Turning to face him, I yell, "He's a fucking asshole who needs his dick removed. Is that better, Agent Ass-face?"

"Much." He leans back in his seat. "Continue."

The room is completely silent. I'm panting in my spot. I'm so angry, I feel like crying. Hell, I'm dying to cry right now. Crying is cathartic. But that has to wait. "If you'll shut the hell, uh, I mean, *heck* up, I'll tell the story. But one more interruption from you, Agent Banks," I say snidely, "and I'm out of here."

"Noted," he says smugly.

God, what a jerk-off.

"Where was I?" I squeak. This is too much.

"You were getting a beer," Agatha says softly next to me. She sniffles beside me.

Turning to look at her, I whisper, "You don't have to stay. I can do this alone."

"No." She clears her throat. "No way. Keep going." Leaning closer, she returns the favor. "Let me know if *you* want to leave. I'll get you out of here."

"No. I'm okay. Thanks, Aggs."

I continue, telling them that I had several beers, all warm and gross. I glare at Agent Banks. It feels good to glare at him. I can focus all of my vitriol on him. "I'd had several beers. I'd danced with the two girls I knew from my class and drank one or two more beers. That's when he approached."

"He?"

"Kyle."

"Violet?" Nick stops me.

I wait for his question.

"Had you met him before? In class? Seen him on campus? Anything?"

I told him no, because it was the truth. He wasn't in any of my classes, nor did he hang out with anyone I knew at the time.

With that answered, I talk about how he approached me, making me feel like I was the prettiest girl at the party. I didn't tell the people in this room about the guys behind him who kept laughing—the laughter that still haunts me. At the time, I assumed they were just having a great time and liked to laugh. In hindsight, I know they were laughing at me and at the way I fell for all of his lines. All of them. "He took my beer away and got me a cold cocktail." I look over at Agent Banks with an arched brow. I was waiting for him to say something, but he kept his pie hole shut.

"So he got you several drinks. What else?" Nick asks.

"He pulled me onto the dance floor. It was a slow song. He whispered things in my ear."

"Can you remember any of the things he said?"

I'm not sure which one of the men asked the question, but I nod. I wish I didn't have to repeat the things he said. I guess it's time. "He told me I was beautiful." I half expect Agent Banks or someone else to laugh, but no one does. "He said I was special." I snort at that one myself. I was ridiculous to believe such bullcrap. Aggie squeezes my hand again. I know it's her way of telling me I *am* special, but it's not working. Not today.

"What happened after that?" Ian asks.

"He...." I blink. I feel beads of sweat start to gather at my hairline. My dress is suddenly too tight and sticking to my body. I feel nauseous.

Damn it, Violet. You can do this.

"He took me by the hand and pulled me along with him. I remember going up a set of stairs."

"Did he ask you to come with him?" Nick's question.

I suppose it's a good question. Maybe if I'd just agreed to go with him, maybe this whole thing would have been my fault. Heck, maybe it was anyway.

I shake my head. "No. I don't remember him asking."

"That doesn't mean he didn't."

I glare at Agent Banks. "I thought we agreed you'd keep your pie hole shut for the rest of this."

I hear chuckling and see it's coming from Ian.

"So I did, Miss Palmer. So I did." Banks nods.

I look over at Nick then back at Banks. Honestly, I'm not sure where all of my strength is coming from, but I'm drawing from somewhere because I say, "This is hard enough as it is. Just let me get it out. Then you can ask questions. Yeah?"

"Yeah." Nick nods. "We won't interrupt again." He looks at Banks. "Will we?"

"Nope."

I tell them what happened. How Kyle Maines took my hand and led me up a set of stairs into a bedroom. That I didn't know whose bedroom it was. That as soon as the door was shut, Kyle pushed me hard against the door and started kissing me and biting me on the mouth, cheek, and neck.

I explain that I remember feeling the pain of the bites, but I didn't realize what he was doing at the time. It wasn't until the next morning that I'd seen them all. Everywhere. *Everywhere.*

"He tore open my top with both of his hands and I just stood there, shocked." I shake my head. "I still can't believe I didn't run right then, but it was happening so fast. Maybe a minute or two after he had me in there, he put both of his hands on the cups of my bra and yanked them down hard. I had bruises on my shoulders from it."

This is getting easier. I think it helps that I'm not looking at anyone. I'm staring at that spot right between Nick and Captain Morgan. There's a light switch near the door that seems to fascinate me.

"He slid his hand into my hair and yanked it hard until I followed him to the bed. He pushed me down and moved on top of me. He was heavy. I remember feeling like I was suffocating." I swallow hard. After taking a drink of water, I continue. "I started to fight back then. I could feel his, his, um, penis hard against my leg. When I hit him with my fist, he quickly placed a hand around my neck."

I pause for another drink of water. "I remember his words like it just happened. He said he'd kill me if I fought back. That n-no one would miss...." I breathe in and out. "That no one would miss the ugly fat chick."

Agatha gasps next to me. But if I'm going to finish this, I need to ignore her.

"He said I sh-should be lucky he chose me. That no one else wanted me."

A hot tear escapes, and I do nothing to stop it. I've literally never repeated those words aloud—ever. I've only ever said them in my head.

"I froze for a second or a minute, I don't know. Enough time for him to have my pants and, um, underwear down around my knees. He grabbed me by the waist and made me roll over." Clearing my throat, I made myself go on. "He wrapped his arm around me and pulled me up. He was talking the whole time about how he had to do it from behind because I was so," I blink the tears out of my eyes, "I was so f-fucking ugly. He didn't want to see my face."

Agatha is full-on crying now. I'm pretty sure Nick looks like he's about to lose it too. I feel terrible about it, but they asked. Right?

"I heard a wrapper. I guess I figured it was a condom wrapper. He did something else, but I don't know what it was because the next thing I knew I felt him inside me and pain." I sniffle some more. I'm trying hard not to lose it entirely.

"A *lot* of pain. I yelled, but he pushed my head down onto the bed, telling me to 'shut my fat mouth.' He did it to me for what seemed like a long time, but it could have been minutes, seconds. I don't know. When he was done, he pulled out and said something about blood and fucking virgins."

I lay my head back and sigh. Almost done. "He told me to get dressed and 'get the fuck out of his room.'"

I've said the f-word more in the last hour than I have in my life, but they were his words. Not mine.

With that done, I stand. "May I be excused a moment?"

"Sure." Nick clears his throat. "Of course. Let's take fifteen."

Only fifteen minutes when I need hours. Whatever.

"I'm going with you," Agatha says.

I look at her. She's upset. I know she is, but I have to tell her, "I need a moment alone, if that's okay."

"Oh." She blinks. "Of course. Yes. Absolutely."

"I just...."

"Go." She waves toward the door. "Go."

As I'm about to cross over the threshold, I hear, "I didn't mean to upset you."

Agent Banks.

"Okay?"

"If this thing opens up, you're going to be asked worse than what I dished out. You need to prepare yourself. You should prepare everyone you care about. This is only the beginning. The easiest part just happened right there." He uses his thumb to direct my eye back to the round table.

I stare at him. He's handsome if you like jerk-faces. I know he's right. I thought I was prepared for everything that's probably going to happen, but I think this proves that I'm not.

"You did well, though, Violet." He releases my arm. "Just remember why you're doing it."

I nod. *Why am I doing it?*

Agent Banks must read my mind, because he adds, "You're doing it for those he hurt before and after you. You're the brave one. Remember that."

I nod and walk away from the suddenly nice Agent Jerkface.

After our short break, everyone returns to their spots at the table. Nick begins by asking me if it's all right for him to recount the story about our experience with the Tucson police. "Keely gave an official recounting this weekend. Mind if I read it?"

"No." I shake my head. "A lot of that is a blur."

Nick turns to Agent Banks. "Here's Keely's recounting of their experience with Tucson P.D." He starts to read:

We went to the police and they did nothing. Worse than nothing. They told her she waited too long, that it was her word against his and no one would believe her. The officer we spoke to had the gall to tell her it was her fault for going to the party in the first place.

It was obvious that cop wasn't going to do anything, so we asked for the captain or superior officer, whatever he was called, but that was worse than useless. They wouldn't even let us talk to him. They said he wasn't interested and that it was a pointless exercise.

Then we were escorted out by a different cop, a younger one. When we got to the front door of the station, he stopped us. He put his hand on Violet's arm to stop her from leaving so he could mock her. He told her she should be lucky someone paid that kind of attention to her.

"Despicable," spits out Agatha.

"Puts a black mark on cops everywhere," mutters Captain Morgan.

"Dirty fucking cops," Agent Banks says, looking disgusted. Turning to Nick, he asks. "Who was in charge of the department at that time?"

"He's no longer there. Chief Brent Carter."

"Where is he now?" Ian asks.

"He's in Sedona."

"Of course he is," Banks says, rolling his eyes. "This," he points to the table, "is a fucking conspiracy. Mark my words. Carter is the dirtiest motherfucker in this shit, thanks to mommy dearest. I bet if you looked into his recommendations, Abernathy has played a key role in his advancement, at least since that fucker left Tucson."

Nick nods. "I looked into it and you're right. Everything you just said is right."

"We need to nail that asshole as well." Agent Banks appears to be more engaged in this conversation. "Okay, let's back up a bit to the point when your sister showed up. What happened at that point?"

I tell them about my roommate's attempt to get me to unlock my door and her subsequent call to my twin. "Keely drove down and practically broke down my door." I want to laugh, recalling Keely yelling profanities at my bedroom door, but now's not the time.

"You went to the hospital first?"

"We went to the university clinic."

"So," the captain asks, "you went to the clinic first before the police?"

I nod.

The captain asks, concern in his voice, "Why didn't you call the police right away, Vi, honey?"

"I was terrified. He said he'd kill me, and honestly, I don't remember the order of things after Keely swooped in there."

Luckily, Nick answers that for me. Clearing his throat, he says, "Yeah. Keely stated that several of the bite marks were still very red and swollen. He had broken the skin. She was concerned about infection and her overall physical well-being. She thought it would be less intimidating for Violet to start there."

I nod. It makes sense.

"Did they do a rape kit?" asked Nick.

"Yes." I remember that part vividly. I'd still hurt down there. "But it'd been five or six days."

"Did they take photos?" asked Banks. "From Keely's statement, the marks were still visible."

I shrug. "I remember they prescribed antibiotics for the bites. I don't know if there were pictures."

"Did they, the clinic, call the police?"

"The clinic people? No. Well, I don't know."

"They're mandatory reporters." Banks looks at me; his eyes have softened. "People who work in clinics, educators, they're all mandatory reporters. They should have notified the police. Did you happen to tell them who raped you?"

Nick answers for me. "Keely said you mentioned his first name. She thought you knew his last name at the time and she recalls you mentioning the fraternity."

"Oh. I don't remember any of that."

Banks speaks. "You're going to want to subpoena her

records from the university. Something isn't sitting right with me about all of that."

"Do you think the university was protecting him?"

Banks shrugs. "His mother was the DA of Pima County. Also, an alum of the University of Southeast Arizona and a big donor."

"There's a building with that name," I say absently.

"Like I *just* said, a big donor." Agent Banks is back to his old grumpy self. He turns to Captain Morgan. "You're going to need to subpoena employee records at the time of the assault to find out who was working there. If they covered up other rapes, those employees would know about it."

Oh. Right. Wow.

"It also means," Banks continues like he owns the place, "if the university is somehow involved in a cover-up, you may want to get the FBI involved, *officially*."

"Why?" I ask. It's probably not my place, but I don't under-stand how this works.

Agatha whispers, "More resources."

I nod, thinking about that for a second. "Oh, right." Either she or Ian mentioned that.

Clearing his throat, Banks adds, "Either way, you're going to hit a shit-ton of roadblocks due to the fact your Lieutenant Governor is involved."

"You think she's involved?" asks Captain Morgan.

Agent Banks deadpans, "Up to her fucking neck."

Moving on, Nick turns to me, asking, "Did the officers at Tucson PD who took your statement take any photos?"

"Not that I recall."

Nick looks at Banks. "There weren't any photos with her statement."

Ian jumps in, asking, "You said he bit your cheek, neck, chest, and...?"

I guess I didn't say any of the other spots. "My back, my..." I pause. "My butt, shoulder, and upper arm."

Agent Banks looks at me blankly. "They took no pictures?"

I shake my head. "Not that I recall."

Captain Morgan looks at me softly. "Sweetheart, a female officer would have been with you and taken the pictures. You would have been, erm, naked. I'd think you'd remember that, don't you?"

"Yes."

"Goddamn dirty cops," spits out Agent Banks. "I fucking hate dirty cops."

Me too.

"Violet? One last thing." I turn to look at Nick. "Keely mentioned that you've seen Kyle since the attack. As recently as March of this year?"

I nod. "I've seen him twice."

"What!?" says a shocked Agatha. "You've seen him since we saw him at Murphy's Pub?"

I turn to her. "He hasn't approached me since then."

"Jesus," mumbles Agent Banks. "The balls. He approached you?"

I'm not sure if he's talking about my or Kyle Maines's balls, but I'll assume he's referring to Kyle. I look at Agent Banks. "I was there with my sisters. He approached the table and said something like 'Hey girls' to the rest of my sisters. Then he looked at me and it was then that I realized who he was."

My rapist.

"What did he say to you?" asks Ian.

"I can't remember all that well. I was shocked. I think he said it was nice to see me and that it'd been a long time."

"Jesus," mutters Agent Banks again.

"Keely mentioned that he complimented you, saying something along the lines of you looking nice or pretty."

I roll my eyes. Leave it to Keely to remember that. "Maybe. I don't remember. I remember getting up and walking to the ladies' room to gather myself."

"He followed you." Agatha isn't asking. "I remember that much." She turns to Ian. "That was the day I got fired from H&S."

"Ah." Ian nods but says nothing else.

"He followed you?" Captain Morgan asks.

"He was waiting for me outside the restroom."

"What happened?" Agatha asks, her voice cracking. "Did he hurt you?"

I assume she means physically, but I can't be sure. "He...." I swallow. "He told me I'd improved with age."

"That fucker," growls Aggie. "That motherfucking fucker."

I can't help it. I giggle nervously at that. Agatha doesn't cuss like my twin Keely or even Sadie, so it sounds funny coming from her.

"Did he say anything else?" interrupts Agent Banks.

"Just that he hoped to see me again soon."

"Jesus," mutters Banks again. "You need to watch your back, Violet."

"You've seen him two other times?" asks Nick, ignoring Banks for now.

"I saw him at a convenience store in June, I think. We didn't speak, but he saw me. I know because he winked at me." God, it gave me a shiver down my spine. I vowed never to go to that store again, even though it's close to my house. "And one other time—he didn't see me, though. I was in the bank. He walked by the window."

"He didn't see you?"

"No, I don't think so. He was with an older woman. He was talking to her."

"When was this?"

"A couple of weeks ago. Before Lainie's wedding." I remember because I was running wedding errands that day.

I watch as Nick does something on his phone. "Was this the woman he was talking to?" Nick turns the phone around; on it is a professional photo of a woman in her midfifties, I'd guess. Her hair is golden blonde and cut in a severe bob style. Almost as severe as the expression on her face. It's hard to forget that face. She looks like a bird of prey. "Yes. That was her."

Nick looks at Agent Banks. "Kyle's mother."

"Oh, right." I nod.

Why was his mother in town too?

CHAPTER 17

ERIC

I'm awoken from an after-work doze when my phone chimes. Picking it up, I stare down at the number. *Violet.*

Violet: Can you come over?
Me: You okay?
Violet*:* No.

Shit.

Me: Yes. Be right there.
Me: Text me your address.
Violet: 9102 Heron Dr.

She's never written before. Hell, she's had my number for a couple of weeks and this is the first contact. Usually, once a chick has my number, they text nonstop. Leave it to my girl to use it sparingly. The one person I'd love to hear from all day long.

Me: Be there in 10.
Violet: Hurry.

I choose not to change out of my work clothes. Shit, I need to shower, but this sounds serious. Honestly, she's scaring me. I wish I got more information from her. I'd like to know what I'm walking into. I jump onto my bike and race to her place. I speed so I'm there in less than ten minutes. When I pull up to her curb, she's sitting on her front step with Max and CB on their leashes beside her. The second I stop, the dogs take a keen interest in me, plus Violet is up on her feet, racing toward me, her canine buddies in tow. I round the bike just as she throws her body into mine, her arms wrapping around my neck.

"Baby, what's wrong? You okay? Did someone hurt you?"

"Sc-scorpion."

"Scorpion?"

"In m-my kitchen," she sniffles in my ear, obviously upset.

"Okay. Okay. Let's go take a look."

She jerks back from me, growling, "I'm not stepping foot in there!"

"Okay. Fine, beautiful. You stay here. I'll take care of it." I start to walk toward her house. "Was there just the one?"

"What?!" she screeches. "Do they move in packs or something?"

"Not that I know of. Where was the little bastard?"

She visibly shivers. "K-kitchen. On the floor. By the sink."

I'm going to assume it was alive, but if it's out in daylight, it may be dead. They're typically night crawlers. The question is, why didn't her cats get it? Cats love to play with and eat those nasty things.

I reach her front door and turn the knob. Stepping inside, I look down at one huge-ass yellow cat sound asleep by the door. Walking in the rest of the way, I look up and see through to the kitchen from the entrance. Since I'm wearing biker boots, I'm not too worried about the scorpion, but I still keep an eye out. Confession? I'm scared shitless of them too, but I'm not about to let Violet know that. I can't have her thinking I'm some pussy who can't kill spiders and shit for her. It's job one in Keeton's house. Or maybe job two.

In the kitchen, I look over toward the sink, then down to the floor. I see it. It's dead. Most of the body is gone, which tells me that Garfield lookalike by the door had a tasty snack. I feel something rub up against my legs and look down at a much smaller version of the cat near the front door. Bending down, I scratch it between its ears. "Did you eat it, little guy?"

He or she meows and moves along, sniffing the bug as it goes.

Pulling a paper towel from her dispenser, I pick up the carcass and toss it in the nearby wastebasket. "Bam. Saved my girl in less than five minutes."

"Eric?" her soft voice sounds from the front of the house.

"Got it. All clear."

"Really?" she asks hesitantly. "You sure?"

"I'm sure. The remains are in the garbage."

"Oh, yuck," she says loudly. "What if it crawls back out?"

I quickly pull out the bag that's only half-full and tie it off. "Where's your garbage can, beautiful?"

"In the carport," she says, stepping into the kitchen tentatively. "You sure?"

"Positive." I step around her with the bag as far as I can get it from her. "Back in a second."

When I make my way back into the kitchen, Violet is still standing near the small table, biting her lip. "I'm sorry I bothered you with that. It was stupid, but my dad's phone went to voicemail, and my sisters are more terrified of bugs than I am," she says as she rolls her pretty blue-green eyes.

"I'm glad you did. It made me feel manly and important."

A smile spreads across her lips, opening them just enough to show me her straight teeth. "You are manly and important." She giggles. "Thank you, Eric." Now she's getting shy.

"As a matter of fact, you should call me first, baby girl. I want to be your go-to guy in emergencies."

Ignoring my request, she asks, "Have you eaten?"

I shake my head.

"Because I was going to make myself some dinner. There's enough for two. Would you like to join me?"

"I'd love to." It's my turn to show my toothy grin. "Can I help?"

"No, there's no room for two cooks in here. Why don't you relax? Turn on the television. I've got Netflix if you want to watch a movie; otherwise, I've only got basic channels."

"A movie sounds good." I turn to step out into the living room. "Any suggestions?"

"I don't care for horror movies. Well...." She stops. "Nothing bloody."

"Got it. I'll find us a comedy."

"Okay."

This night is getting better and better. Not only is Violet cooking for me, I'm staying for a movie. This is, hands down, the best night of my life. So far.

CHAPTER 18

VIOLET

The truth is, I was just going to make myself a little salad for dinner, but since I've got company... a shiver sweeps over my body.

I've got company.

I don't remember the last time I had someone over. Sure, there's Jess. But it's been months since her last visit. Keely pops over now and then, mostly to steal clothes, makeup, accessories, and shoes. Shockingly, we wear the same size shoe. She's got big feet for her height. I like to tease her about it since it's one of the only things I can tease her about. She's pretty close to perfect. Correction—she's almost perfect. She can be a tad rude at times. Oh, and she cusses like a sailor. Other than that, she's pretty perfect.

So, back to dinner. Since I can't feed the six-foot-three behemoth sitting in my living room only a salad, I pull out the ingredients to make my mom's lasagna. I'm replacing the ground beef and Italian sausage with Italian flavored ground turkey. It's just as good and fewer calories. I also use those lasagna noodles you don't have to boil first. They're amazing. I cook up the meat, then build the lasagna.

"Damn, it smells good in there," Eric says from my living room, loud enough for me to hear. "You sure you don't need any help? I'm a great taste-tester."

I laugh because he's funny and endearing and hot. Not only that, Eric Gustafson *Is. In. My Living. Room.*

OMG! I can't believe he's here.

"No, thanks." I chuckle as I slide the pan into the oven and set the timer. "What kind of salad dressing do you like? I've got lite Ranch, fat-free Italian, and lite French."

His head pops around the corner, startling me. I slap my hand over my chest and jump back. "Eric." I pant. "You startled me." Catching my breath, I can't help noticing how he had to bend down to walk through the archway into my kitchen. Man, he's tall. And muscular.

Ugh. Stop it, Violet!

"Sorry. Can I have all three?" he asks shyly. "I like to layer them."

"Sure." Gross, but sure.

"You gonna introduce me to your other pets? I'm pretty sure the cats love me." He points down to his feet where both Sherman and Stella are rubbing themselves on his legs.

"Huh," I say in disbelief. "They hate people."

"Told you, doll. Animals love me." He bends down, picking up the big guy, Sherman, bringing him up to his face. When they're inches apart, I brace myself for the claw that I'm sure will sweep out and get Eric's face.

"Be careful—" I'm stunned silent when Sherman nuzzles his face, then he licks Eric's nose. "Well, that's just bullcrap, Sherman." I've got my hands on my hips now. I'm not happy. "You never let me snuggle with you, let alone get a kiss."

"*I'll* give you a kiss," Eric says, setting Sherman down.

"Oh. Well..." I turn to open the fridge. "Maybe later."

"I'll look forward to it." His voice is deep and extra husky.

The truth is, I'm looking forward to it too. I'm just not ready. Not yet.

Choosing to change the subject, I pull the dressings out of the fridge and set them on my little table. I've already got two placemats, two plates, glasses, and silverware out. Our salads are sitting on top of the plate.

"You work fast," Eric says, staring down at the table. "The salad looks delicious, and I'm not much of a vegetable fan."

"Oh. I'm sorry." I reach for the bowl. "Let me...."

Eric's hand stops me before I can grab the bowl and take it away. He's touching the top of my arm as he says softly, "No, Violet. It looks great. I mean it."

"Oh. Right." I step back, now embarrassed. "Do you want to meet the rest of the crew?"

Good save, Violet. Good save.

"Sure. I can't wait to meet Carl."

My head jerks to look at him. "You remember his name?"

"Of course," Eric says, looking a little affronted. "You can't forget the name of a one-winged parrot. That guy sounds like the bomb."

God, I want to cry. Like really cry. I'm always afraid people will make fun of my little animal family. It's one reason I keep them a secret. That, and I don't want to hear people tell me it's too many, that I don't have room for them, or that it's not good for me.

I lead Eric into the spare bedroom. I push the door open and step aside so he can pass. I sniff the air, quickly making sure the animal smell isn't overwhelming. I clean their cages daily, so I know they aren't terrible, but this many critters in one room can stink.

Eric passes by me into the room. I see him nearly stumble over one of the loose floor planks my dad's supposed to fix soon. "Watch your step. There are some loose boards."

"I see that." He smiles back at me. "Want me to fix 'em?"

"My dad's going to do it."

I mean, Eric could do it, but now that I've asked Dad, I need to let him do it.

"No problem. I get it," he says, approaching Carl's cage. "Hey there, fella," he says softly. "You're a brave little guy, aren't you?" Eric looks over at me. "Can I touch him?"

"Sure. Open up the cage. He'll either bite you or...."

I watch as Carl jumps onto Eric's finger. "You really are some kind of pet whisperer. It took me months to get him to do that."

"You just warmed him up for me." Eric winks. I watch as he whispers things to Carl. I can't hear him from my spot near the door, but dang, I'd love to know what they're talking about.

Eric places Carl back into his cage.

"This is Beatrix." I point the small fish bowl on my desk.

He leans down close to the bowl. "She's pretty. I like how colorful she is."

Bea, the Beta fish, is mostly blue, but she's also got purple, turquoise, and black on her.

Pointing to Binky's habitat he says, "Binky, the guinea pig, I presume?"

"Yep."

"He's big. I imagined something this size." Eric holds up his thumb and first finger about three inches apart.

"No, that'd be a mouse or a hamster." She points to another plastic habitat. "Meet Hammy and Sammy. Those are hamsters."

He nods, then moves along to Donatello's house. "You've got a cool setup for the turtle."

"I do." There are rocks, a few plants, a small log, and water, of course.

Standing up to his full height, Eric turns to face me. "I like your little family, Violet. They're cool."

I blink a few times to keep the misty feeling I'm getting behind my eyes at bay. Doing my best not to choke up, I nod. "Thanks." Sure, it sounds raspy and emotional, but it can't be helped.

He steps closer. "Now, about that kiss we discussed earlier...."

I try to say something, but nothing comes out of my mouth. I look like a dang fish out of water.

"Will you kiss me, Violet?"

If he'd asked me that three days ago, after that terrible morning at the police station, I'd have said no. I mean, the idea of anyone even touching me after I'd described my assault in sordid detail.... But here's the weird thing about all of that. I've never felt better. Not in six years, at least. I've thought about it a lot since the day at the police station, and I think maybe it's because I finally, *finally* told my story. All of it. Heck, I never even told my therapist about most of it—not about his words or about him making me roll over to my stomach, or the pain. So while I've been cautious about my own emotional responses to the police meeting, I can see how cathartic it was. It also has me thinking about going back to therapy. Therapy helped a little at the time to let me know my feelings were valid and that I'd need time to heal. So now that I feel like I can talk about all of it, therapy could help even more. While I'm no longer on Dad's insurance, I know I could go to the counseling office at my college. It's a resource I haven't taken advantage of yet, but I think it's time. I'll call them on Monday.

As for Eric... I trust him. I'm not sure why, exactly. Maybe it's because he's honest with me. And patient. I'm positive he won't kiss me unless I give him the signal that it's okay.

"Yes."

This time, *I* step closer to him. Placing my palm over his pec, I move up onto my bare toes. I lean in and press my lips to his. Eric holds perfectly still; his lips don't even move. Not until mine do, at least. When they do, I feel a warm hand on the middle of my back and another one touching my cheek. Eric's kisses are soft and exploratory. He kisses the corner of my mouth, then my nose, cheek, and left eyelid. He moves to the right eyelid and over to my ear. There he suckles my lobe in his mouth, and I moan.

Wow, earlobes are an erogenous zone?

His lips move across my cheek and back to my mouth too soon. I'd like him to do that to my ear again, but I'm distracted from that when his tongue touches my lips. I open for him like I did on our first kiss. Eric pulls away slowly, and I chase him a little bit. Dang. It ended too soon.

"Something's beeping," Eric says, so close to me I feel his breath on my cheek.

"Huh?" I'm literally in a fog.

"Something's beeping," he repeats.

I hear it then. My kitchen timer. "Oh, shoot." I step away from him and race to the kitchen. Pulling open the oven door, I remove the aluminum foil from the top of my lasagna and close the door again.

"Damn, it smells so good. What'd you make?"

"Lasagna."

Eric's hand slaps his own chest. "Be still, my heart."

I'd laugh except I've never seen him more serious.

"My absolute favorite meal." He holds his palm up. "Swear to Harley Davidson."

That makes me laugh. Eric's a funny guy. It seems every

time we're together, he has me in stitches. When I calm myself, I start to prepare the garlic bread. "So, is that the kind of motorcycle you have? The one out front?"

"It is." He's closer now, watching me work. "I traded in my old one last month. This is my dream bike."

"What is it?"

"It's called a Dyna."

"Dyna? That's a funny name."

"Before that, I had an XL Forty-Eight."

"You have a truck too, right? We used it when we, uh, retrieved Sadie's BBQ."

"Yeah, plus I've still got my first car."

I'm done preparing the garlic bread, so I slide it into the oven. "What's that?"

"A Chevy Caprice."

I blink a few times. "I'm not sure I know that one."

"Before I got it, it was a police car. So, you know what that means, don't ya?"

I don't, but I'll give it a guess. "It's big?"

"Well, yeah. But the real reason it's kick-ass," he winks at me, "is it's got a 6.0-liter V-8 engine, 301 horsepower with 265 pounds of torque." Eric nods proudly.

"So...." I'm not sure what to say. "That's good?"

Eric looks affronted. "Good? Woman!" he says loudly. "That's one hundred percent awesome."

"Oh. Okay." I smile at him because I'm not sure what else to say. I go with, "My first car was a Chevy too."

"Yeah?"

"A Cavalier. It was eleven years old when I got it. But it was a solid little car."

"Sounds awesome." Eric is patronizing me. I can tell. But I don't think he means it in a mean-spirited way.

"Obviously not as awesome as yours. Maybe we could take

it out for a spin sometime. You could show me what all of that engine stuff means."

"Yeah?" Eric's beaming now. "Really?"

I smile back. "Really."

He nods for a second or two, but then he stops. "I don't remember the last time I've had such a good time with a girl, Violet."

"Yeah?"

"You're even better than I imagined. Cooler. Sweeter. Prettier, if that's even possible."

"Thanks." What else can I say?

"You're so easy to talk to. And I mean that like it sounds. We're talking. It's not just me talking about cars and bikes or you just talking about girl shit. We're conversing."

I know what he means. "We are." I nod. Peeking into the oven, I see the bread is toasted and the lasagna is bubbling. Perfect. "Ready to eat?"

"Hell, yeah."

"Have a seat. What would you like to drink? I've got diet soda, lemonade, water, and I think I've got one lonely beer." It's been there a while, but beer doesn't go bad, does it?

"I'll take the beer, if it's okay."

Bending, I extend my arm to the way back of my fridge, pulling out the lone beer for him and a diet soda for me. Handing him the can, I reach into my cupboard for a glass. He shakes me off. "The can's fine, honey."

Honey. That sounds nice.

I set hot pads on the table and bring the entire pan of lasagna to the table. Placing the bread in a small basket, I set it next to the casserole.

"Dig in," I say with a nod. I watch as Eric does exactly what he said he'd do; he layers his salad dressing. First, he moves some of the lettuce aside, pouring Ranch dressing in its place.

Covering that up with greens, he adds a layer of Italian. Hiding that, he ends with the French. Then, he mixes it all around. It's the most interesting way to eat a salad I've ever seen. I'm tempted to try it, but I only get two tablespoons of dressing thanks to my healthy eating program; because of that, I'd like to focus on Ranch.

I prepare my salad and watch as he takes his first bite. With his eyes squeezed shut, he moans. "Oh, my God," he says with his mouth full." Shaking his head, he swallows. "Sorry. Bad manners."

"I'm glad you like it."

His salad is gone in two minutes tops. I've been so mesmerized by the speed and fervor at which he's eating, I haven't taken a bite yet. I grab his empty bowl and set it in the sink. Cutting the lasagna, I place a large rectangular slice on his plate. My eyes never leave him as he uses his fork to cut away a piece about two inches by two. Lifting it to his mouth, he finally looks at me. "What?"

I giggle. "Nothing. It's fun watching you eat. Go ahead." I nod to the food. "I hope you like it."

"I'm sure I will." Placing the cheesy casserole into his mouth, he squeezes his eyes shut again. He chews slowly but stops to moan. His eyes slide open, but only partway. They're sort of hooded and sultry-looking. He continues to chew, swallowing finally. "Marry me."

"What!?" I squeak, then laugh.

"Marry me." Eric isn't laughing.

"Why?"

"This is the best lasagna I've ever eaten."

I shake my head. "Better than Giovanni's?" Giovanni's is one of our local restaurants. Their food is to die for, and nobody makes better lasagna than them. Nobody.

"Way better."

"No way. I didn't even use beef," I say defensively. Why am I defensive? "It's ground turkey, for heaven's sake. I didn't even make my own sauce this time. It's from a jar."

He shrugs. "I'm not blowing smoke up your pretty ass, Violet. It's the best I've ever eaten." He lifts another bite to his mouth. "You normally make your own sauce?" His left brow arches. "I bet that's fucking amazing."

I shrug. "It's pretty good. I use fresh tomatoes."

His slice is gone in minutes. Heck, I still haven't eaten my salad. I've just been watching him.

"May I have another helping?"

"Of course." I smile. No, I grin. "I'm happy you like it." Heck, happy doesn't cut it. I'm downright giddy.

CHAPTER 19

Our conversation has waned somewhat, so I ask, "You go to college?"

Violet nods. "I do."

I wait for her to expand on that, but she doesn't. "Where?"

"Where do I go?" she sips her drink. "Northern Arizona."

"You drive to Flagstaff?"

"A couple of days a week, yes. I also take online classes. That helps."

"What's your major?"

"Ah, well." She sets her fork down. "It's still Environmental Engineering but...." She hesitates.

"What?"

She shrugs. "I guess I'm not excited about it anymore."

"Why is that?"

Violet shrugs again. "Honestly," she chuckles, "it's a bit boring. Important work, but it's boring to me." She looks past me out the small window at my back. "Funny you bring this up, but

I've been thinking, recently, that I need to do something more..."
She must be thinking of the word or something because she's
quiet for several seconds. "...personal."

"More personal?"

"Yeah."

"Like?"

"Well, I don't know, but something related to social work or
possibly counseling." She shrugs again, picking her fork back up.
"School guidance counselor sounds kind of interesting too."

"All of those would be rewarding." I hesitate before I say
this. Maybe I shouldn't. Hell. "Do you think that could be
related to the, er, the assault?"

She nods once. "Definitely." She answers fast, which tells
me my question was okay. At least I hope it was.

She adds, "Since this has all gotten dredged back up, I've
been thinking I need to do more to help other people who've
experienced trauma or who just need someone to talk to. I have
a unique perspective on the matter."

"You do." I stop shoving food into my mouth long enough to
really look at her. She looks different than the last time I saw
her. Prettier. Her eyes are brighter, and I can't help noticing a
few more real smiles than last time. "You okay?" I ask softly.

Violet's head moves up and down. Affirmation. "I had a
meeting with the police a few days ago."

I wait for her to continue.

"They asked me to tell them what happened, and I did. I
told them *everything*. It was the first time I ever told the whole
story, and ever since I've felt..." Violet looks up then down at
me. "...lighter."

"Like a weight's off your shoulders?"

"Exactly." Violet takes a bite of lasagna. "Mm, this is really
good." She giggles. "If I do say so myself."

"You can say so yourself. *I* would."

As soon as we're both finished with dinner, we move into her small living room. The only furniture in the room is a long couch covered in orange and yellow flowers, circa 1970, a small rocking chair and the old trunk they're facing, on which sits, I'd say, a thirty-two-inch television. Picking up the remote, Violet asks. "What did you want to watch?"

I'd queued up one of my favorite movies, perfect for a date. "The Princess Bride."

"No way," she says breathlessly. "That's one of my favorite movies."

"Mine too." I smile at her. "One of them. I've got eclectic movie taste."

"Me too."

I watch as Violet presses a few buttons on the remote and the movie begins.

"Do you need another drink?" she asks, getting ready to stand.

"Nope." I take her hand in mine and give it a squeeze. "Not right now. Sit, honey. Let's just watch for a while. Maybe we could go get ice cream at intermission." I release her hand as she takes a seat next to me. Where she belongs.

"Intermission?" She giggles. "Sounds good."

"I'll take you on my bike."

Violet's eyes get as round as saucers. "I've never been on a motorcycle."

"*What?!*" I fake scream. "Not even on Rob's?"

Keeton and Lainie gave my dad, Rob, a vintage motorcycle the day Lainie moved in with Keeton. That's also the day I met Violet. "Nope."

"Well, I'll drive extra safe, then." I smirk. Once she's seated next to me, I scoot a little closer to her so I can place my arm behind her. "This okay?"

Violet nods shyly, never taking her eyes off the television. It's okay, her hand is still in mine. I'll take that.

CHAPTER 20

VIOLET

Riding on the back of Eric's motorcycle tonight was exhilarating. I've always been scared to ride. My dad has offered, but I always turned him down. I can't tell you why I said yes to Eric. Oh, well, that's not true; it's because I got to sit right up against him. I had my arms wrapped so tightly around his hard stomach; my nose was close enough to smell him.

I stop thinking for a second. *I didn't mind touching him.* Heck, I've spent some serious time thinking about Eric touching *me*. Ever since the wedding and the dance. It bothered me then, that I could enjoy how close he was, but more than that—he gave me chills. Sexy chills. That's a part of me I thought died six years ago. I've literally felt numb down there. Until now.

My stomach flips. Guilt hits me like a tsunami. Just like I did the days after the wedding, I asked myself: *Should I want him touching me? Is it wrong?*

CB is sound asleep next to me, so as I slide out from beneath the covers, I do my best not to wake him. If I do, he'll want me to take him outside, and I'm not up to that this late. I crawl out of bed and head into my living room. A couple of days after the wedding, I stopped at the public library in search of something to help me with my new questions. To ease my mind about these new feelings. The self-help section of Page Public Library has never let me down, and that visit was no exception. I found a book about exactly this issue: a book about desire, passion, and pleasure *after* sexual assault. Patting Max's head as I pass him on his spot next to my bed, I slide back beneath my covers. CB stirs but doesn't wake up. Opening it up at the spot I've got bookmarked, I say, "I hope this tells me it's okay to feel things for you, Eric."

I must have only read for a short time, because I'm awoken by whimpering next to me.

"CB," I croak. "Not now." I guess he needs to go out. Peering at the clock, I do my own whining when I see it's only 3:00 A.M. Rolling out of bed, I reach over and pick up the whiny pooch. "I really need to fence in my yard, CB. Then you could run around and do your business whenever you want to."

Since that's not going to happen tonight, I set him down and call Max to come along. Might as well kill two birds, as they say. With both leashes in hand, I bend to attach my guys to their leads, unlock the front door, and step outside. "Hurry," I urge. "I want to get back to sleep."

I stand in my yard and let the guys do their thing. If they do, I'll pick it up tomorrow. Barely able to keep my eyes open, I do my best to encourage their progress. That is until Max begins to growl. That wakes me right up. Max doesn't growl unless he's got a reason. One time, he growled at a creepy guy who was hovering around the playground adjacent to the dog park. It was loud enough that it drew the attention of some of the parents who were sitting back on benches socializing. It also had the guy turning on his heels quickly and jogging away down the path. Max has a sixth sense about stuff like that. And about squirrels. According to Max, squirrels belong in the same category with creepy pedophile types.

I look down at Max, who is now pulling at his leash, struggling to move in the direction of the neighbor's bushes. Bushes that sit next to my bedroom window. I tug back.

"Come on, Max." I do my best to calm him down, hoping it's just a jackrabbit or other wildlife making him agitated, but it doesn't work. Max's growl turns from a deep rumble to a full-on tooth-baring snarl. "Max. Knock it off." He's scaring me. I tug on him, but he's strong for a midsize dog.

"Come on, guys, I'm tired," I say urgently. I'm also freaked the heck out. "Let's go." I tug harder, and Max comes with me. "Probably just a bobcat or something." Yes, I'm totally talking to myself. It happens, especially when I'm nervous.

Once I get the boys back inside, I hit the deadbolt, the lock on the knob, and the chain. I do the same thing at the back door since I usually only flip the deadbolt. Walking through the living room on my way to my bedroom, I can't help noticing Max is now pacing back and forth in my small living room. "Come on, boy. Bedtime." I feel my eyes burn with the need to cry. I cry when I'm scared. I can't help it. "You've scared me enough for one night. Let's go!" I say loudly. It must work, because Max finally follows me back to my bedroom. Before I get into bed, I make sure my windows are locked and pull my blinds down as well. "It was just a squirrel," I say to no one in particular. That's followed by a deep breath and, "Just a squirrel."

Sometimes I really hate living alone. Sometimes I wish I had someone here to calm me down in situations like this. I certainly don't need someone fighting my battles for me, but a little help for night squirrels and scorpions now and then would be okay. More than okay.

CHAPTER 21

ERIC

It's been four days since I saved Violet from the dastardly scorpion. In that time, she's remained completely silent. Each day since I've checked my phone repeatedly hoping for a call or a text, but no. Nada. Nothing. I finally give up and send one to her.

Me: Hey beautiful. How's your day going?
Violet: Good.

That's it. That's all I get. She doesn't even ask me about my day. Well, that's okay. She's just shy. So, the next day, I ask her a question. One that forces her to reply with more than one word.

Me: Let's play 20 questions. I'll start.

Again, no response from her, so I assume she's going to play along.

Me: What are your top five favorite songs?

This ought to be good. I know she loves "Perfect" by Ed Sheeran. She said so at the wedding.

She doesn't reply. I wait for two-plus hours before I attempt to text her again.

Me: Hello? Did you see my texts?

Two minutes later...

Violet: Yes.
Me: I'm not giving up. 5 favorite songs, please?
Violet: Fine.
Violet: In no particular order. "Perfect" by Ed Sheeran, "Allison" by Elvis Costello, "Dear Future Husband" by Meghan Trainor, "Just Waiting on a Friend" by the Rolling Stones, and "Baker Street" by Gerry Rafferty. Your turn.

I'm blown away by her list. Sure, I expected people like Meghan Trainor, I guess, but never the Stones, Elvis Costello, or fucking Gerry Rafferty. Classics. I love classic rock.

Me: In no particular order. "Perfect" by Ed Sheeran...

Because it was our first dance. But I leave that part off.

Me: "A Day in the Life" by the Beatles, "The Immigrant Song" by Led Zeppelin, "Sympathy for the Devil" by the Stones, and "Holiday" by Green Day.

Violet: Good choices. Growing up, my dad always
listened to classic rock.

Me: Mine too. Do you want to ask me a question or
should I do the asking?

Violet: You, but I'm about to walk into class so I'll
answer when I get the chance.

I give her the thumbs-up emoji and wait to ask my next
question. It'll give me time to think of something good—a question that will get her to talk.

I must have waited too long. I got busy with a rebuild and
lost track of time. By the time I get home, shower, and eat a
shitty frozen pizza, it's eight. I dig my phone out of the back
pocket of my work jeans in time to see her one and only unso-
licited text message that starts off with the little eye-roll emoji.

Violet: I guess I'll ask the question. If you could be any
fictional character, book or movie, who would it be
and why?

I laugh the second I read her question. It's creative and
funny. God, I love this girl.

What? That surprises you? Why would it? What's not to
love?

Me: First off, sorry I didn't text. Got busy with a bike at
work. Okay, let me think. I'll write back in a bit.

It takes me a good thirty minutes to think of something.

Me: You know I've got to choose a superhero, right? I
mean, I killed a scorpion for you.

She sends me the eye-roll emoji again. I laugh.

Me: People say I look like Thor…

I wait for the eye roll again but get nothing.

Me: He's mythological, noble, honorable, hot, and of course, humble.
Violet: LOL. Humble? You're humble?
Me: Of course. Now, you. Who would you be?
Violet: Hermione Granger, because she's confident, trustworthy, loyal, and a better wizard than the guys.

I know I've heard that name before. I quickly do an internet search and see she's one of the main characters from the *Harry Potter* series by J.K. Rowling.

Me: I've only seen snippets from the movies. I'll have to take your word for it.
Violet: …
Violet: Seriously?
Me: Yes. Sorry ☹
Violet: We need to change that. The books are better, but the movies will do. When should we begin your tutelage?

Hellz yeah.

Me: Tonight?
Violet: Sure. My place?
Me: Be there in a jiffy.

I get to her place in less than twenty minutes. I'd already showered and put on clean sweats. All I had to do was swap those out
for clean jeans and my boots. I grabbed my wallet and leather
jacket on my way out the door and jog down the steps of my
apartment building. On the road, I pass by a convenience store
close to Violet's house. Deciding not to show up empty-handed,
I pull into the shop and grab a tallboy of Bud for me, a bottle of
lemonade for Violet, a bag of plain chips, and a package of
cheese puffs. Who knows if she likes either of those? Now I sort
of wish I'd asked her to list off her five favorite snacks. As I
approach the counter, I look down at the rows and rows of
candy. Without much thought, I grab an assortment, including
licorice, candy bars, and gum.

"Havin' a snack attack, man?" a guy next to me says, chuckling. He's dressed like a preppy, about my age, but with slighter
build.

I shrug. "Gonna watch a movie."

"With your girl?" he asks with a smirk. It's a weird fucking
question for a weird fucking dude.

I shrug again but choose not to answer.

The clerk tosses everything into a bag, and I'm out the door
lickety-split. Stowing the bag in my saddle bag, I'm off again. In
minutes I'm knocking at my girl's door, anxious to get this date
started. The second she opens the door; I feel my heart start to
pound in an unnatural rhythm. Pushing the door open, she
deadpans, "Thor."

It surprises me and makes me laugh. "Hermione."

Except I must pronounce it wrong, because she giggles and
says, "It's Her–my–oh–nee."

Stepping past her into her home, I shrug. "Hermione. That's
what I said." I lean in and kiss her cheek softly. "Hi, Violet." She

blushes, and it makes my blood burn hot. "I'm glad you invited me over."

"Me too," she replies shyly.

Holding up the plastic bag, I say, "I brought movie treats."

"Yay!" She claps. "I haven't eaten anything today, I—"

"What?" I interrupt her. "You haven't eaten?" Setting the bag down, I turn to face her. "Let me run out and get you something."

"No. Junk food is good."

No, it's not. So I lie. "I haven't eaten dinner yet either. Let's order a pizza from Giovanni's." I wriggle my eyebrows up and down. "They deliver." She hesitates, so I add, "My treat, since I'll probably eat most of it."

"Okay," she agrees. "But I'm a little picky about my pizza toppings."

I nod. "No problem. We'll get whatever you want. I'll eat anything." I pat my stomach. "Stomach like a steel trap."

CHAPTER 22

VIOLET

"You don't like it?" Shoot. Nobody likes my pizza toppings, and I can tell by his face that he's not a fan either.

"No." He smiles right after he takes a bite of my white chicken pizza. "It's good." He rubs his flat stomach. "Mm. Love it."

Laughing, I shut the lid of the pizza box and stand. "Let me make you something else."

Eric reaches out placing his hand on my arm. "No. I'm good. Let's get comfy and watch the movie. If I get hungry, I'll eat some cheesy puffs."

"Fine." I take the box into the kitchen and set it on the counter. "Can I get you anything else while I'm up?"

"A kiss," he says from behind me. It startles me right out of my flip-flops.

"Eric," I pant. You can't do that." I'm serious. He can't. "I'm jumpy on a normal day." I'm not sure why. I could probably find some sort of psychological reason, but I'll just attribute it to being Keely's sister. She's made it her life's work to scare the crap out of me whenever she can. Example: Hiding behind our childhood bedroom door and jumping out at me or leaving a fake spider on my plate when my back was turned. Heck, she did that a couple of months ago at my dad's, and I nearly peed myself. The brat. Oh, and don't get me started on horror movies. Keely has a field day pulling horror movie pranks on all of us.

"Shit," he mutters to himself. "I'm sorry, babe."

"It's okay. You're like a ninja. I didn't hear you at all."

"A ninja, huh? Not Thor?"

I laugh, because he looks a little saddened by the notion. "Nope, not Thor. He's the god of thunder. He's noisy."

"True." He gives me a warm smile. "I'm sorry. I'll make sure you know I'm heading your way next time."

"Good." I reach out and take his hand. "Let's watch Hermione in action."

"Cool. I want to get a look at the superhero you aspire to be." I lift her hand to my mouth and kiss the top of her fingers. "Something tells me you're more interesting than that Herman chick."

I laugh again. "Her–my–oh–nee. Not Herman."

"Right. Got it."

Watching movies with Eric is turning out to be my favorite thing to do. Not once during the movie did I feel like he wasn't enjoying it. He asked questions about the story and characters and after it was over, he asked when we could watch the second film. Not only that, he told me he could see what I saw in Hermione (yes, he said her name correctly this time), but that I was much prettier. Ha! If he saw a picture of the actress, Emma Watson, today, I'm sure he'd say something else. But I'll take the compliment. I'll take it and wrap myself up in it like a warm blanket.

My favorite part about watching a movie with Eric is his ability to cuddle. We sat so close to each other our thighs were touching. His arm was behind me most of the time, his fingers playing with strands of my hair. A couple times during the movie, he leaned over for a kiss. Nothing dramatic, just light kisses first on the corner of my mouth, once on my lips, and several kisses on the hand he held some of the time.

Gah! Just thinking about it all makes me swoon. Could this be real? Could a man like Eric Gustafson really like me? I can't believe it's possible now that he knows about Kyle. He may not mind my damaged self right now, but long-term? Highly doubtful. Especially when things really get crazy. The minute the police make their move with Kyle, everything in my life is going to change. And not in a good way.

I feel my shoulders slump. *That's right, Vi. The minute my rape is front-page news, this thing with Eric will be over. He won't be able to take it.*

What man would?

CHAPTER 23

VIOLET

I'm calling a family meeting to order. Strange. I've never done that before. It's usually one of the others who orders us to appear. It's sort of nice being the boss for a change. So, yeah, I've summoned my sisters to Keely's apartment—with wine, of course. I haven't hung out with my family in a while, so they haven't been brought up to speed about the day I spoke to the police with Aggie in the room. Honestly, I assumed she'd tell my family everything, because that's what my sisters do: they blab to each other. I'm convinced there's no possible way that Agatha didn't rush over to Lainie's house afterward to tell her. It's okay, I don't mind. If I'm being honest, I'd hoped she'd do the dirty work for me.

But maybe not. The minute we left the conference room that day, Aggie pulled me aside and led me into the women's restroom. Once inside, she grabbed some tissue and wiped her eyes, saying, "No words, honey. I've got no words for what you went through."

She kept sniffling as she spoke. I was tempted to give her a hug but thought better of it. Instead, all I said was, "It's okay."

"I need time to process all of that back there." She pointed at the bathroom door. "After that, Ian and I are going to do whatever we can to help the police bring that fucker down."

"All right. Thank you, Aggie." I believed her.

Aggie nodded and left the bathroom.

Stepping up to Keely's door, I raise my hand to knock, but the door's yanked open before I get the chance. "'Bout time you got here," Keely says with a grin.

I look down at my Fitbit watch and then back at Keels. "I'm early."

"Yeah, yeah. Get in here. The gang's all here. Sadie ordered pizza."

"Oh?"

"She even ordered a small one with your gross toppings."

"Ah, that's so sweet." I mean it. "Thanks, Sadie." I say as I enter Keely's small living room. I'm surprised Keely still has her apartment. I half expected her to move in with Nick by now. But Keely is as stubborn as a mule, and she wants to wait until they're more serious. Ha! I don't think she could get more serious, but I see her point. She's probably smart to wait.

I scan her small space and notice one person is conspicuously absent. Dad. I didn't want him here for this. There's no way I could recount it in front of him, and I doubt he'd be able to hear it. Sitting on Keel's love seat next to Agatha, I look over at her and arch my brow. "You called everyone, right?"

"Yes, I did."

"Thanks for doing that." While I asked for the meeting, Keely took care of contacting everyone. When my eyes meet Aggie's, she reaches out for my hand and leans closer. She's got something to say. "What?" She knows something. Not surprising. Ian probably knows things since he's former FBI. If that's the case, he'd surely tell Agatha.

"Not much. I know they reached out to the clinic you went to at the university. I think it was a dead end."

"How so?"

Agatha shrugs. "You'll have to ask Nick, but Ian said he didn't think there were any records."

"No records? Like from the day Keely and I went there?"

"That's what Ian said."

Wow. I blink a few times, attempting to get a grip on that information. "That's serious." I seem to recall Agent Banks saying the FBI would get involved if the university covered things up. Or is that what he said?

Agatha states, "It is," but doesn't elaborate.

Before I can find out more, Keely claps her hands like the kindergarten teacher she is and says, "Let's get started. The pizza will be here in twenty." She turns to me. "Are you ready, Violet?"

I nod. I *am* ready. There was such a sense of relief after speaking to the police, it can only make me feel doubly so telling the people I love most in this world.

"*As much of it as you're able,*" says Sadie in a soft voice. I'm used to bossy Sadie. This is weird.

I look over at Agatha. "I'm surprised you didn't tell them."

She slowly shakes her head; there's no smile on her lips. "I want them to hear it from you. It wasn't my place to tell your story."

Right. "Fine." Sitting back on the little sofa, I begin. I repeat the parts they know about Keely coming to help me, about our visit to the college medical clinic, and then about the rape.

The rape. I can't believe I can say that word now. For years I've referred to the rape as "it" or the "assault"; at least that's what I said in my head. Now I can say the word *rape*. Honestly,

I'm surprised how much more empowered I feel than I did even a month ago.

During the bad parts, the parts in that bedroom six years ago, there isn't a dry eye in the house. Even Aggie's crying again. I don't try to comfort them. I know it was a tough story to hear, but they asked me to tell it. When I'm done, I explain to them what I think is going to happen with the investigation, at least as much as I can say.

When the doorbell rings, no one moves to get it. I start to stand, but Keely beats me to it. Before she goes, though, she turns to me. Her eyes are angry and red from tears. I've never seen her so angry. "If I ever see that fucker again, I. Will. Kill. Him."

"Get in line. Right after I do," Sadie says with a sniffle.

"Yeah?" Keely says sharply, "I mean it. I. Will. Fucking. End. Him."

"Keely. Who would that help?" I know my twin; she means what she's saying. "I asked Dad the same thing. How would that help me if you were in prison?"

"I think I'd look great in orange. Plus, I'd be fine in prison. Chicks dig me."

I roll my eyes but laugh too. "Idiot," I mutter as she moves to open the door to our pizza order. With the delivery kid right there, Keely yells back, "I'm serious. He's a dead man."

The poor pizza guy looks like he wants to swallow his tongue. Keely notices and says sweetly, "Not you, hon. You're cool as long as you didn't screw up our order."

"Keely!" I shout, then laugh. "Stop it." I jump up and move to the door quickly. Smiling at the delivery kid, I say, "She's just drunk. Ignore her."

"I'm not drunk," Keely snaps as I hand the guy the five dollars I've got crammed into my pocket.

"Thanks, ma'am," he says with a shaky voice.

"Ma'am?" Keely squeaks. "She's barely twenty-six."

"Yes, ma'am. I'm sorry, ma'am," he says nervously to Keely, which makes everyone laugh.

I push the door shut and take one of the pizzas out of Keely's hands. "Let's eat."

Everyone chews in silence. It's deafening, if that makes any sense. Not much has been said since I finished telling them about the rape. It's just a matter of time, though. My sibs can't keep their mouths shut for long.

Lainie clears her throat. I'm not surprised she's the one to start. She's our matriarch, in a sense. She's the oldest, and when Mom died, she did her best to fill in the gaps. They were huge gaps, though. Gaps too big for anyone to fill.

"I'm blown away by you, Violet."

Okay, I didn't expect that. "What do you mean?"

"I've known you your whole life, and I don't think you've ever been this strong. I see determination in your eyes. You're smiling. A lot. Maybe it's because Eric is wooing you or maybe it's because—"

"What? Eric's wooing her?" asks Sadie. "Since when?" She scoffs. "Nobody tells me anything."

"This isn't about you, biatch," snaps Keely.

"Fuck you, Keely. Stop saying that," Sadie growls. "Violet and I are close. Hell, she works in the shop three days a week... oh." Sadie goes silent. Turning to me, she smiles. "My bad. Eric's suddenly started coming to the bakery three days a week. If I didn't have pregnancy brain, I would have seen that for myself." She turns to Keely and points at her. "But you're still being a bitch."

"Whatevs." Keely shrugs as she takes a huge bite of her meatlovers pizza.

"Anyway." Lainie sighs, exasperated. "You're strong, Violet, and that's not all due to Eric."

I nod, because I know she's right. "I feel stronger." And not necessarily because of Eric. But having him as my friend has been nice. "Not just physically."

"You look great too." Agatha pats my knee. "What's your workout?"

"Kickboxing is my favorite, but I swim at the YMCA too."

"I'd like to try kickboxing," Lainie says, patting her round belly. "Maybe after the baby comes?"

"Sure. I can take a guest with me. You can try it out."

"I'd love to punch some shit," grumbles Keely.

Sadie laughs. "Definitely. You need an outlet for that rage of yours." She looks at me. "You'd better take her with you next time. She can go all fists of fury on the bag. Poor Nick." Sadie giggles.

"Screw you, Sadie." Keely is glaring at Sadie. "Nick loves me just as I am."

I decide to end this. "He does. You all have men who love you just as you are. Now, can we eat instead of arguing? I'm tired of it."

When I don't hear anyone agree, or disagree, for that matter, I look up and see every eye in the room staring at me.

"What?"

Lainie smiles. "I'm so proud of you." Tears start to slide out of her eyes in a torrent. I've never seen anything like it.

I look over, and Sadie's doing the same thing.

"Fucking pregnancy hormones." That came from Lainie. She never cusses.

"No shit, right?" Sadie adds.

"We're proud of you, Violet. You just told us to shut the fuck up." Keely nods. "Love it."

I nod, setting my slice of pizza back down onto my plate. Changing the subject, I announce, "So. Dad and Deb, huh?"

Like it was planned, three of my sisters spit something out of their mouths. Keely and Aggie whine, while Sadie nearly chokes on pizza.

"What?" screeches Keely.

"No way," Aggie says conspiratorially.

"Serious?" asks Sadie.

"Yep." Lainie nods, smiling from ear to ear. "It's true."

"*Hooooly* shit." Keely looks sincerely shocked. "At the wedding?"

Lainie nods.

"It's about damn time," Sadie says with a smile. "He deserves..."

"Everything." I'm the one who says it, but all four of my sisters nod.

"Absolutely." Whoever said it spoke for all of us.

When Lainie and Sadie start bawling again, I merely smile. Pregnancy hormones sound sort of terrible.

CHAPTER 24

Eric

It's feast or famine with Violet and me. We're currently at the famine level—again. I haven't seen her for five days. It's not her fault; she's busy with school and work. Besides, the shop has been crazy busy lately, ever since my bro was on the cover of another magazine. It's happened before. He gets a write-up and they take a bunch of photos of him with his bikes and orders start flying in.

The new guy we hired, Sig Engel, turned out to be the best thing we've ever done. He's a talented motherfucker. He knows all the computer shit with the new bikes, like he's a robot, but he's even better with the custom side of things. He's creative as hell. I have a feeling he'll be working with Keet on his side of the garage full-time soon. That means we need to hire some new blood to work on my side.

What I do isn't glamorous, but I enjoy it and I'm good it. I'm in charge of the side of the business that fixes bikes and rebuilds or upgrades factory motorcycles. We work primarily on Harleys and Indians, but we can figure out all the other brands too. I love the work. I enjoy solving the mysteries customers bring into the shop every day. For the most part, I get a kick out of the customers too. Of course, there are always assholes, like the guy who *had* to have his bike fixed the night of Keeton and Lainie's rehearsal party. Those assholes are everywhere, but usually I'm jovial enough to handle it.

As for Violet, like I said, she's busy with school and working at the bakery. We haven't talked much, even though I've popped in to get a cupcake now then. Okay, I pop in whenever she's at work. I swear I've gained five pounds already.

There have been text messages and even some real conversations over the phone, but she's had to study for midterm exams and such. I've been meaning to ask her if she's thought any more about changing her major. Hell, I've been meaning to ask her about lots of things, but our talks have usually been less than ten minutes.

I miss her.

I miss her like crazy. Just thinking about it makes my chest feel tight; like I can't breathe. I'm not an idiot; I know what it means. I know I'm not having a heart attack. I'm pretty sure I'm in love with her. I've never felt this way before, so I'm a little cautious about making that proclamation.

Checking the clock on my phone, I see I'm right on time. I'm at the park, next to the fenced-in doggy area, waiting for Violet to show up. No, we didn't arrange this. I decided to get in a run to burn off the calories from my new cupcake diet and to hopefully see Violet too. A bonus.

I bend at the waist to stretch out my hamstrings before they tighten up too much. When I push up to full height, I see them. CB and Max are pulling their leads so hard, Violet has to jog to keep up. She's smiling and laughing at the dogs. She hasn't seen me yet, so I get to observe her without her knowing.

When she sees me, I raise my arm and wave.

"Eric?" she squeaks as CB and Max race over to me, jumping up onto my legs. "Down, guys." Violet tugs on their leashes.

I squat down so I can scratch CB's head, which gives Max a chance to lick my face. The dog sure can slobber.

"Ooh, ick, Max," Violet says, laughing. "You're going to need a shower, Eric."

"I'm sweaty from my run. A shower was needed before I got the kisses." I lean closer to her. "What about you? Do I get a kiss from you?"

"No." She laughs again. "Yes." Leaning closer still, she barely touches her lips to mine.

"Hi," I whisper.

"Hi," she whispers back.

"I hoped you'd be here."

"You were waiting?"

"I was."

"Oh." Violet smiles shyly. "I'm glad."

Picking up CB, I take one step closer. In a low voice, I admit, "I've missed you like crazy, baby."

Violet's pretty face turns to a bright shade of pink. "Me too."

That's all I need. I can die happy now. *She missed me, too.* Giving her my best smile as I pet CB, I point to the dog park. "Shall we?"

"Yep. Let's wear them out so they'll sleep tonight."

"They're not sleeping?"

"CB sleeps like the dead. Max has been up making growly noises for days and days. I finally had to kick him out of my room so I could sleep. I put his bed right outside my door, but still. I feel bad. He's always slept next to me, and I can still hear him growling through the door."

"That's not normal? The growling?"

"No. Ever since that night I took them out to do their business in the middle of the night, he's been like that."

Okay, this is bullshit. "Violet?" I stop walking and turn to face her.

"Yes?"

"Are you scared?"

"No. Of course not," she says too quickly as she begins to walk to the park again.

Reaching out, I touch her upper arm. "Violet. Don't lie to me."

Releasing a deep breath, Violet shrugs. "A little. But, it's probably just someone's cat in my yard. Max is very territorial."

"What if I stayed with you for a couple of nights?"

"No." She blushes again. Shaking her head, she repeats, "No."

"I could sleep on the couch." I bend to release CB from his leash as Violet does the same to Max. We watch them run off together.

"No. That's okay. We're fine. He's just getting senile."

"Please?" I hate the idea that she's scared at night. Violet looks up at me. Her eyes are searching mine like she's trying to read me. I do the same back at her. "Please, Vi."

"I'm sure it's just a cat. Or a squirrel."

Squirrels sleep at night. But I'm not going to say that to her. "I'm sure it is too. Just let me stay. I'll keep Max with me so you and Charles Barkley can sleep."

"Sure. Okay." She shrugs. "Fine."

"Great. After this, I'll run home and pack a bag. What do you want for dinner?"

"No. Eric—"

"I'll pick up some groceries so you can cook for me. It's payment for being your big, strong, bodyguard."

She rolls her pretty eyes at me, and it makes me laugh.

"We could grill," I say, envisioning a thick steak with a giant baked potato and all the fixin's.

"I don't have a grill."

"I've got one. I'll throw it in the back of my truck." Then I can just leave it at her place. That'll give me one more excuse to visit. God, I'm a genius.

She glares at me. "You're not going to let me say no, are you?"

"No." I smirk. It's smug, but oh well.

"Fine." She sighs stubbornly. "You bring the grill; I'll get the food."

"No. I'll get the food."

"You're so stubborn," she says, gritting her teeth a little.

"How 'bout this. I'll get the meat and bring the grill. You do the other stuff."

"Fine." She practically stomps her foot. It's adorable.

It's fun to rile her up. "Great. It's a date." I lean down and kiss the top of her head. "Maybe we could watch the second movie."

"*Harry Potter?*"

"Yeah."

That makes her smile. "I'd like that."

I stand up taller, puff out my chest a little more. I'm fucking proud as a peacock that I get to see her tonight. Not only that, I get to sleep over. Granted, it's not in her bed, but I'll take it. Baby steps. Just like Keely said.

The next time I volunteer to sleep on a sofa, I need to make sure it wasn't made in 1971. This thing is hard as a fucking rock, and I'm pretty sure there's a spring sticking into my thigh. I roll over to get a look at Max in his dog bed. He's sound asleep. Hell, he's even snoring.

"I'm so glad you can sleep, Max," I grumble. Lord knows, I can't. I reach my hand out, feeling around for my phone. I'd guess it's around two in the morning, but I need to see for sure. When I make contact with my smartphone, I bring it to my face and touch the screen. 3:12 A.M. "Shit."

"Eric?" says a sleepy voice from somewhere in the room. I hold my phone out to illuminate the vision that is Violet Palmer.

"Sorry. Did I wake you?"

"No." She hesitates. "Maybe. Do you want to switch spots? That couch isn't the most comfortable."

No shit.

"I'm fine, honey. Go back to bed. You need to rest."

"Has Max made any noises?"

"Not yet. He's been sound asleep all night."

"Hmm."

I'm still holding up my phone. Her hands move to her hips when she makes that little noise. I can't help noticing she's wearing a sweet pair of pajamas. I also can't help taking a long look at those same sweet pj's. The shirt buttons all the way up to her pretty neck. Her shirt comes with a matching pair of shorts. *Short* shorts. It gives me an eyeful of long leg, which makes my dick stiffen. Since I'm only wearing athletic shorts—no shirt—I pull up the single blanket I've got on my legs to cover the evidence. I don't want to scare her.

"What if..." She sighs. Sounding tentative, Violet continues, "Come sleep with me. I've got a big bed."

"No. Violet."

"Yes. I, er, I trust you."

I stare at her for a good minute. I can't be sure, but I think about what she just said—she trusts me. I believe, in my heart, that statement was profound. "I'd never do anything..."

"I know." She starts to turn. "So, come on. You need your beauty sleep, Thor."

I'm up and reaching for my pillow in a split second. I reach down and pick up Max and his dog bed and carry him with me.

Once we're in her room, I watch her slide beneath the covers. Placing Max down next to her, I walk around the bed. "I can sleep on top of the covers—"

"Just get in bed, Eric. Let's not make this more awkward than it already is."

"I need to warn you."

Violet lifts her head. Looking up at me, she seems to be waiting for my warning.

"I'm a snuggler. I like spooning." Truth? I've never been a spooner in my life. Violet makes me want to be a better spooner.

"Spooning?"

"I'm the big spoon, by the way."

"Okay," she replies. "Noted."

Sweet. I get to spoon my girl. Hell, I never *wanted* to spoon anyone before her. Sliding beneath the covers, I move toward the center of the bed, displacing a grouchy CB. He gets up and moves to the end of the bed on Violet's side, all the while making funny snuffling noises. "Sorry, buddy." *Not sorry*. With her back to me, I ask, "Scoot back so you're closer."

Without a word, Violet scoots back. "A little more."

She scoots close enough for me to touch her hip. "Is this okay?"

"Yeah."

I move closer until I'm against her back. I slide my arm around her middle and place my palm on her stomach. "Is this okay?"

"Yes." Her voice is shaky.

"Violet? Are you sure?"

"Yes. Go to sleep, Eric. Stop worrying. I promise to tell you if it's too much. Deal?"

"Deal."

I let my head fall onto my pillow. I pull her into me so we're as close as we can be. The soft skin of her thighs is touching my hairy legs. Damn, it feels perfect. I lie in silence listening to her breathing. When it becomes a steady, rhythmic sound, I close my eyes and fall fast asleep.

CHAPTER 25

*V*IOLET

Whimpering wakes me up. I rarely need an alarm clock, thanks to the bladders of my two canine friends. Not only them, I guess. Stella and Sherman like to sit on me when they think it's feeding time. I blink a few times, trying to figure out what's different about today. When I feel a warm palm slide over my hip, I remember.

Eric.

Eric Gustafson is in my bed. *My* bed.

I feel myself stiffen at his touch. I'm not scared, by any means, but I'm well aware that my pajama shorts have slid down my hip, leaving that part of me bare, and his palm is on that bare hip. Skin to skin. I should move. I need to take the boys out to do their business. That's what I should do, but I don't want to. I like it which surprises me, honestly. I like how his palm feels touching my skin. I like it a heck of a lot, and if I move, his hand could go away. It would go away when I want more of it instead. Maybe if I moved backward....

I scoot back trying not to wake him up. As I move closer, I feel his palm slide over my belly. My bare belly. Eric makes a sleepy noise as he readjusts himself. In the process, he's moved closer to me. I feel his arm tighten around me and his mouth touch my neck. In the best deep, scratchy morning bedroom voice ever, he asks, "You awake, beautiful?"

God, his voice. Hearing it right up against my ear is doing things to me. Things I should probably try to avoid. But, dang it! I don't want to. So, in my own, not nearly as attractive, morning voice, I say merely, "Yeah." Not only that, I do two things simultaneously. I place my hand on the one he's got on my stomach, and I arch my neck so he knows I like him there.

"Vi," he whispers.

His voice makes me feel things all over my body. His breath touches my neck in such a way that I can't seem to lie still.

"Touch me, Eric." Okay, where did that come from?

"Where?" He kisses my neck. "Where do you want me to touch you, angel?"

Since my hand is already on top of his, I use mine to push his upward. Beneath my pajama top. Up, up, up, until his hand is covering my breast.

His hand sits absolutely still as he asks, "Violet? Are you sure?"

"Yes. Touch me." I'm sounding a little whiny. Where is that coming from?

His palm slides back and forth over my breast, and I find myself arching my back, pressing my chest further into his palm. It also means my butt is right up against him. I can feel him. He's—he's excited.

"Is this okay?" He sounds breathless as he pinches and plucks my left nipple.

"Yes," I moan. I want more. I want both of his hands on me. I push up to sitting, my back to him. I reach for his other hand as he sits up and moves so close, I feel his chest against my upper back. Taking his right hand, I bring it around me and push it up to cover my right breast.

"Jesus, Violet. Are you sure?"

I lay my head back onto his shoulder. "Yes. Eric. God, it feels good. Your hands...."

I feel his body against my back. He's as close as he can get. His lips touch my neck. His breathing seems labored. He's kissing and sucking there while doing amazing things to my breasts; kneading, pinching, pulling, and rubbing the hard tips.

"Eric." I'm sounding a little desperate.

"Baby. You feel so good. So beautiful."

I arch into his palms again, but it's not enough. "I need...."

"I've got you." His right hand slides down, away from my breast. The move makes me whimper in loss. As it moves to the elastic of my shorts, it stops. "I'm going to put my hand on you, Violet."

I nod.

"I need to hear your words, angel."

"Yes. Please."

Without another word, Eric's thick fingers move beneath the band of my shorts and into the front of my panties. When he touches me, I nearly jump off the bed.

"You're so wet, honey. Is this okay? Are you okay? Tell me."

"I'm okay." His big fingers move back and forth between my legs, then settle at the front. When they circle my clitoris, I practically meow. "Yes. Keep doing that."

His fingers are magic. His left hand is moving back and forth between my breasts while his right is playing me like a harp.

"Eric," I pant. "Almost."

His fingers move quicker, pressing just a little harder. It's the change I need. A wave of release hits me. I feel it from my core up through my body.

"Eric," I whisper as I come down from the high of my orgasm. His lips kiss my neck gently as he moves his hand out from beneath my shorts. I turn to face him. The first thing I notice is the tent in his shorts.

Staring at it, Eric whispers, "Not today, honey. This is all about you." He knows I'm not ready for his... him.

I wrap my arms around his neck and pull us together. It's a hug. An important hug.

When he says, "Thank you," softly in my ear, I pull back.

"I should be thanking you."

He shakes his head. His eyes are glossy. "You—" He chokes a little. "You trusted me, Violet. *Me.* You trusted *me.*"

I lean in and place a soft kiss on his lips. "Of course I trust you."

He sniffles as a tear slides down his handsome cheek. "I love you, Violet. Honest to God. I love you so much."

"Eric," I whisper. I lean in again and wrap him up tight in my arms. "I, I like you. A lot. I *could* love you. I'm scared, though."

"I know, Vi. I know. But I got you. I'll be here. Always. I'll show you; you can trust me with your heart, angel."

I believe him. But can I trust myself?

CHAPTER 26

Eric

She loves me.

Okay, those weren't her exact words; she said she *could* love me. I get why she's nervous and it's okay. I'll prove to her that she has no reason to be scared. Whatever it takes. No matter how long it takes, I'll prove it to her.

CHAPTER 27

VIOLET

Why do I feel like this?

Guilt.

I feel guilt. Guilt that didn't hit me until I watched Eric ride off on his motorcycle. Then it was sudden. The first thought in my head was: *What have I done?* That guy deserves someone who isn't a hot mess. Someone who isn't so confused.

I'm sure my self-help books would be giving me a standing ovation for letting Eric touch me like that. But what do they know? Okay, sure, they know things. Many of those writers have experienced the same thing as me and have come through on the other side. I don't know what I'm supposed to do, though. So, my solution? I spend the rest of my Sunday lying on my sofa. I can't seem to talk myself into crawling back into the same bed we just did things in. I'm trying to talk myself into getting up so I can change the sheets. I need to wash them, but maybe throwing them away would be better. The television is on, but I'm not watching anything. CB and Max are sound asleep next to me, and I think I saw Stella and Sherman sleeping under a sunny window together. I should check on Carl and the others in the spare bedroom, clean their homes, but moving seems so hard right now.

I hear my phone chime off in the distance. I'm not even sure where it is; probably still in my purse. I roll over on my couch and the scent hits me. *His* scent. He left it on the cushions of my couch. I press my nose in further and inhale.

He smells so good.

"No!" I raise my fist and punch the cushion as hard as I can and wince. My hand made contact with a stupid spring. Pushing myself up, I hold my fist out in front of my face. There's blood. "Of course there's blood." I can't do anything right.

Flopping back down, face first, onto the cushion, I spend an indeterminate amount of time sniffing my couch. Yeah, it's weird. Who cares? I sure don't. What does it matter? I'm broken.

I'm broken.

~

"Yo! Bitch. Wake up."

I'm lying mostly facedown on my sofa, so I can see the floor beside me perfectly. I force my eyes to open, but it's hard. It's like they're crusted shut. When I get the left one open slightly, I see feet. Feet in a pair of my favorite sandals. Keely, the dang thief.

"Wake the hell up. What's wrong with you? You sick? You were supposed to be at Dad's two hours ago."

"Dad?"

"Yeah, you remember him? He knocked up our mom?"

Our mom. I sigh and press my face back into the couch. I miss her. "I'm not coming." I've no desire to move from my spot.

"What's wrong?" Her voice has softened. "Are you sick?"

No. "Yes." Sick of my life. Sick of feeling like everything is wrong and nothing will ever get better. I'm sick of wanting more when I can't handle more.

"Oh, my poor bae," Keely coos. "Can I get you something? Is your stomach upset?"

No. "Yes. No, I don't need anything. My stomach is fine." Sort of. *Well, except for you to leave me alone so I can feel sorry for myself in peace.*

"Perhaps I should call the Palmer clan in to make you feel better."

I know my sister and that's an empty threat. She wants me to spill. "No. No one else." I push myself until I'm flat on my back.

"Ugh, you look like shit, twinny."

Twinny? That's a new one. "Gee, thanks."

"Serious. Do you need anything? Do you want me to take you to the urgent care place?" Keely's voice is soft. Something her voice never is.

"No." I sit up the rest of the way and have to wait a second, since I'm a little dizzy. I rub my eyes to get the crusty stuff out and then look at my sister. I should talk to her. I need to talk to someone. Probably a therapist. It's time. But, for now, Keely will have to do.

"Eric stayed overnight."

I half expect Keely to scream with joy at the news, but that's not what she does. Instead she makes no noise at all. She sits beside me, reaches her hand out, and takes mine in hers, asking softly, "What happened?"

I start with the dog park. I don't get into graphic detail about the morning, er, activities, but enough so she knows we didn't have intercourse. I even tell her what Eric said—about the love stuff. There's a long silence after I'm finished with my story.

Keely's kept my hand in hers the entire time, periodically squeezing my fingers and one or two times rubbing her thumb over my wrist as I talked. The silence is starting to worry me, so I finally ask, "Are you going to say anything?"

"Yes." She looks into my eyes. "You're depressed about it?"

Depressed? Sort of. "Guilty. I feel guilty, and I suppose that's making me feel depressed."

"You believe him? When he said the L word?"

I nod. "I do, even though the logical part of me thinks that's crazy."

"None of this has anything to do with logic. If it did, you wouldn't be on your couch like you were after it happened," Keely says. "Did he move too fast?"

I shake my head adamantly. "I asked him to, you know... and he kept asking me if I was sure."

"Good man." Keely finally smiles. "So, since logic has nothing to do with this, then it's all just bullshit in your head."

"Hey—" I attempt to defend myself but she's too fast.

"No, listen to me," she says, giving me a stern look. "You think you love him?"

I shrug, because I really don't know. "Maybe."

"Do you want me to tell you what I think, or do you want me to leave so you can wallow?"

Harsh. "Tell me what you think." I know I'm asking for trouble. Keely doesn't mince words.

"I think you have feelings for him. I'm not surprised he told you how he feels. We all see it when the two of you are in the same room. The man is gone for you."

I nod, trying to absorb her words.

"I think it's safe for you to believe him. I also think it's safe for you to have feelings for him, and I'm definitely sure it's good for you to have an orgasm."

"Keely!" I say, laughing. "Geesh."

"I've read some good books about victims of assault. One of them was all about feeling sexual again. The writer was a big advocate for self-love so you can connect with your own body, and then you can experience real love with someone else when the time is right."

"I've read things like that too."

"Tell me what part of last night do you feel guilty about?"

I already know the answer to this question, because it's been rolling around in my skull for hours. "You're going to think I'm insane."

"Nah. Tell me."

"I feel guilty because I don't think I should like it or even want it after Kyle."

Keely's eyes grow round, but then they return to normal. It's rather comical. "You're insane."

It catches me off guard, so I laugh. "Told you."

"You have as much right to a healthy sex life as anyone. Hell, *more* than anyone. Kyle raped you. You know rape isn't about sex. It's about power. That fucker already took so much from you. Don't let him take away your chance at happiness with a good man."

I've been on the verge of tears all day, but they just wouldn't fall. Now, with Keely's words, they're finally ready.

My "twinny" keeps going. "A word I kept reading was 'ownership.' You need to try to accept ownership of your sexual desires. Sex is more than just about getting your rocks off, Vi. It's about intimacy with a partner you care about. Feeling close to Eric in that way can make your relationship better. Do you feel like he's pressuring you?"

I shake my head frantically. "No. Absolutely not. It was all me. I just felt like a..."

"A what?"

My goodness. I'm ashamed to even say the word. But if I'm being honest... "A slut."

Keely turns from gentle to enraged in less than a second. "Are you fucking kidding me?" She pushes away from me until she's standing. One of her hands is on her hip, the other is pointing at my face. "Knock that shit off." Her voice softens. "You're nowhere near a slut, Violet." Keely's voice wobbles. "You deserve sex. Sex feels good. We women don't need to feel bad for wanting to feel good, for Christ's sake." She rubs her hands over her face. "I need you to repeat after me..."

I nod, because I can tell she's doing her best to say all the right things. I know she means what she's saying, though.

Keels places her hand over her heart. "I, Violet Palmer..."

I do the same. "I, Violet Palmer..."

"Do solemnly swear never to call myself a slut again. Not in my head, and not aloud."

I repeat the words. Words I'll do my best to heed.

Keely isn't done. With her hand still up her next line is, "I'll talk to Eric about how I'm feeling."

"Keely...."

"I said," she snaps, "I will talk to Eric about how I'm feeling."

Fine. "I will talk to Eric about how I'm feeling."

"Right now," she adds.

"Right now?" I squeak.

Keely searches the room until she spots my cell phone. "Here." She hands it to me. "Right now."

"Right now?"

"Now."

"Fine." I look up at her, half expecting her to leave the room. When she doesn't, I say, "Keely, come on. I'll do it but you need to step out of the room."

Sighing, she grumbles, "Okay." Pointing at my phone, she mutters, "Do it."

Without another word, I search for Eric's number and hit the green button.

It rings once before he answers with, "Hey, beautiful. This is a nice surprise."

"Hi," I croak. "How are you?"

"Good now. I was doing laundry and making my lunch for work tomorrow. You've saved me from the humdrum of my domestic life."

I giggle into the phone. "I'm glad." I find myself staring off into space, because I have no idea how to start this conversation.

"Violet? You there?"

"Yes." I look toward my kitchen. I know Keely's in there, probably eavesdropping because she's nosey like that. "Can I talk to you about, er, this morning?"

"This morning?" He pauses, then softly asks, "In your bed?"

"Yes."

"Are you regretting what we did?"

I blink a few times. Regret isn't the right word. "No."

I hear him sigh; it sounds like relief. "Good."

"I feel guilty."

There's a long silence on his end. "Guilty?"

"Can I just say everything and then you can talk after? This is hard for me."

"Of course, angel." God, he sounds so sweet.

So, I explain. I tell him why I feel guilty, and scared, and worried. I leave out the part about feeling like a slut, though, but I do tell him I don't feel like I deserve to like how it feels and I definitely don't want him to have to wait around for me to figure this all out. "I don't know when I'll be ready for, you know..."

"Intercourse?"

This is so embarrassing. "Yes."

"Violet. I love you. I've never told any other woman those three words. They mean something to me. You mean everything to me. If I have to wait a week, a year, hell, ten years, I'll wait. Honestly, I've never been happier just sleeping next to someone in my life. I slept better than I ever have. Plus, I woke up next to the sweetest, kindest, most beautiful girl in the world. I'd be completely content to do that for the rest of my life."

Oh, crap. Tears. I can't help it. He makes me so happy. I look up and see Keely wiping away at her cheeks. "Eric," I sob.

"Baby girl, don't cry."

I can't help it.

"Give me a chance, honey. Give *us* a chance. I promise I'll do what it takes so you feel safe with me—there's no pressure. You get to decide."

"That's not fair. You have needs."

"I need *you*, Violet. You make me happy. Hell, just hearing your sweet little voice over the phone makes me feel like I could conquer the world. The fact that you called me and not the other way around has made my year. Sex will happen when you're ready. I'm okay. Don't worry about me. Okay?"

My voice is all squeaky and hoarse. "Really?" It's hard to believe him. I saw his, er, pants this morning.

"Really. Now." He pauses. "Do you want company tonight? I'll bring dinner."

"No." I clear my throat. "Is it okay if I just have time to regroup?"

"Of course. Anything you need. I'll miss you, though. I'll worry that Max will start growling again. If he does, will you call me?"

I peek over at my sister. Her brows arch. "Yes."

"Promise? No matter what time? If he starts up, you'll call me?"

"Yes. Promise."

"Okay. Love you, Violet."

"Me too." I wish I could say it.

"Night, beautiful."

"Night."

I hang up and stare at my phone.

"Well?" Keely is so dang nosey.

I smirk at her. "Yeah?"

"What did he say?"

"I'll summarize." I sigh. "He's in this for the long term. He'll do whatever I need him to do."

Keely stares at me for a long time. All she's doing is blinking at me and it's starting to worry me. But, then she says something so very Keely, "If you don't marry him, I will."

That makes me crack the heck up. "Oh, yeah? What about Nick?"

"He'll understand."

I laugh some more.

Keely flops down next to me on the couch and wraps her arms around me. She kisses my cheek, then says in her softest voice, "I think you should try therapy again. It could help."

"I decided that too. I'll make an appointment at student counseling services at school this week."

"Promise?"

"Promise." So many promises today. I hope I can keep them all.

"I'm going to head out. I brought you leftovers from Dad's. They're in your fridge." She arches her brow. "Your empty fridge."

"I know. I need to get to the store."

"If your man is going to be over here a lot, you'll need to stock up. Those big ones eat a lot."

I laugh again. "Got it."

"Feed your man, honey." She winks.

"Will do."

I wave as she pulls out of my driveway. It's then I decide to take the boys for a walk. I look down at Max and CB. They've been so patient with me today. Bending down, I scratch both of them between their ears.

"My good boys," I coo. "Let's go for a walk."

Their tails go crazy wagging. Reaching for the leashes, I snap them in place, open the door, and follow them out. Taking in a deep breath of fresh air, I smile. A real one. "I'm going to be okay, fellas. I know I am."

CHAPTER 28

ERIC

I'm squatting down attempting to pull out the carburetor on a '74 Harley Shovelhead when I hear raised voices. Looking up, I see Molly and Sig Engel standing toe to toe. Molly's hands are jammed on her hips and her toe is tapping. I know that stance. I've been on the receiving end of it many times. She's pissed.

"Uh-oh," I say under my breath. Sig needs to learn if you mess with the bull, Molly in this case, you get her devil horns.

"No!" Molly shouts. "Stay the hell out of my office *and* my business."

"Jesus, Molls. Calm down."

Molls? I know I shouldn't be listening, but what the hell am I supposed to do? Sneak away?

"You shouldn't be up on a ladder like that, babe."

Babe? Oh, fuck.

"Don't call me, babe," Molly snaps. "I can be on a goddamn ladder if I want to."

"That's just ridiculous. You're just bein' stubborn, woman.

You're surrounded by men," he points his thumb at his own chest, "who can touch the goddamn ceiling without a ladder. Ask one of us. Ask *me*."

"Stubborn? A stubborn woman?" Molly is practically screeching like an owl. The sound isn't pretty.

Maybe I should have told Sig not to say shit like that to Molly. She doesn't put up with macho bullshit from us. She sure as hell isn't going to take it from the new guy.

"Molly." Sig tries to soften his voice. "I just don't want ya to fall. What if you broke somethin' or hit your head? Then what?"

"Jesus," Molly grumbles. "Go do your own damn job, Sig. It's none of your fucking business."

I watch Molly stomp back into the showroom, or as I like to call it, Keeton's brag room. The minute she's through the door, I barely hear Sig as he says, "Oh, *you're* my business, babe. You just don't know it yet."

Oh, hell no.

I blink at the closed door leading to the brag room and see Sig heading back to the other side of the shop to work on one of Keeton's custom bikes. I stare at the opening between our two shops, then back at the door Molly just went through.

"Shit." Sig wants my sister. My recently widowed sister.

That poor bastard.

As soon as I get home from work, I shower, put on some sweats and a T-shirt, and throw a frozen pizza into my oven. While that bakes, I grab my phone and call my girl. We've been talking every night since I stayed at her place last weekend. Sometimes we talk for a few minutes, and other times, like last night, we talk for over an hour. She told me about the cute shit the dogs had been doing. She also told me how sad she was two of her foster pets had found their forever home. At least that's what she called it. Her hamsters, Hammy and Sammy, found a place with a young family with a six-year-old boy who is allergic to both cats and dogs. It seems hamsters don't bother him at all. Violet sniffled as she talked about the little rodents, but she seemed sincerely happy for the kid. Me too.

The phone rings three times before she picks up, "Hey, Eric." She sounds sort of breathless.

"Did I catch you at a bad time?"

"No. I was out back setting up my new Adirondack chairs. I left my phone in the house."

"New chairs, huh?"

"Yeah. My dad built them for me."

I can hear the smile through the phone.

"Send me a picture."

"I will. They look perfect. He made them slightly smaller than you normally see at the stores, so they'll fit on my small patio. He also built me a matching table that sits between the two chairs. Now we can sit out there with our drinks and watch the sun set."

"That sounds nice." I smile. "Real nice, babe."

"I want to paint them a bright color and buy some flowers for my pots to match."

"I'll help ya paint. I enjoy that kind of stuff. I don't get to do it at my place."

"You do?" She sounds seriously surprised. "What about this weekend? We could grill or something since you left your grill here."

Ha! My plan worked. I plan to keep it there for the foreseeable future. It's the perfect excuse to eat at her place. "That sounds perfect. I'll bring the meat."

"Fine." She laughs. "Saturday?"

"Can we watch another one of the Hermione movies?" I'm getting into them; I can't help it.

"Sure." Her voice sounds like pure joy.

"Can't wait, darlin'."

"Darlin'? That's a new one."

"You like it?"

"Yeah. I like all your endearments."

"I'll keep that in mind."

I hear my timer beep. "Well, my frozen pizza's done. Call you when I get in bed. Sound good?"

"You don't have to."

"I want to. I like hearin' your voice right before I fall asleep."

"Me too, Eric."

"Great. Call you later, babe."

"Bye."

I hang up the phone and head to the kitchen. I'm gonna eat, watch a game for a while, then call her back. Not a bad night, if you ask me. The only thing that would be better was if I was at her place and there was spooning involved. Spooning is fucking awesome. Who knew?

Putting the entire pizza on a plate, I head back into my living room just as my phone chimes. Picking it up, I see a photo appear. Adirondack chairs and a small table. They're the perfect fit for her small brick patio. I type a response.

Me: Can't wait to kick back with you on one of those.

Violet: Me too.

CHAPTER 29

"What is it with these romantic, clever guys?" my friend Polly asks as we hide out in our cars waiting for Keely to drive past so she can fall into Nick's romantic proposal plan.

It's a good question. "No idea."

"So," she asks, looking at her fingernails. "You and Eric Gustafson?"

My inner eye roll is strong, but I keep that to myself and just shrug. "I guess." I don't want to look too excited about it. It's so new and, honestly, fragile. A shoe could drop and then it's over. But since Polly and Sadie are besties and we work together, it makes sense she'd know.

"You guess?" Polly's voice rings a little sarcastic.

We're both sitting in the front seat of my CR-V, so I slowly turn my head to look at her. "It's too soon to say anything else." Besides, if I talk about it too much, I'll jinx it. The last time we hung out together was at my house last Saturday. We painted my new chairs, had BBQ chicken along with some sides I made,

then we watched a movie. He didn't stay overnight because he
had to get up early the next day to babysit his niece, Maddy, so
his sister could attend a group therapy session for people who've
lost loved ones serving in the military.

I bet he's a wonderful uncle.

"Gotcha." She nods. "He's fucking gorgeous. Good work,
Red."

"I didn't do anything."

Polly snorts. "I know what you mean. Look at Cortland.
The guy was relentless and sort of rabid. I showed no interest,
but that didn't stop him." We both laugh at her use of the term
rabid. He was. And all because Polly wouldn't give him the time
of day. The poor guy didn't give up, though. He sent her gifts
practically every day and pursued her until she finally said yes
to a date. Now they're going strong.

I watch as several other cars pull into the lot. I see Lainie
and Keeton's car, followed by my dad's. Which reminds me, I
need to ask Dad when he's going to do the work on my floors.
I'm a little tired of tripping in my spare bedroom. I'll talk to him
tonight at Murphy's Pub, since I don't want to get out of my car
until Nick does his thing. Whenever that is. I'm not sure exactly
when this is all going down. We were given a rough time esti-
mate. The next car that slides into the lot belongs to Captain
Morgan. Polly must see him too, because she asks me, "What's
going on with the investigation?"

I take in a lungful of air. "I don't get briefed regularly, but I
heard the university clinic had no records of me coming in after
the assault."

"What?" Polly blinks at me. "Do they purge records or
something, you know, after a certain amount of time?"

"No. According to Agatha and Ian, there would have been
electronic files. They had others from around the same time on
the system. Mine was gone."

"Oh, Jesus," Polly says almost to herself. "That's terrible. It means it's a cover-up."

I shrug for the second time. "I guess."

"As you know," Polly looks at me, her head tilted to the side, "I watch a lot of true crime shit, right?"

I nod. She does. She's sort of addicted. Every morning we work together at the bakery, she tells us about some gross crime, like the one in Arizona a few years back where the guy murdered his wife, dismembered her, and buried all of her except her wedding ring finger, which he kept in his glove box. When they discovered it, her wedding ring was still on the finger. It's so disgusting it makes me shiver.

"Well, I wonder if it means they need to call in the FBI?"

"I don't know. They mentioned something about a task force a while back, but I have no clue what's going on. They don't tell me much."

I know Agent Banks mentioned that, but from the little I know, Nick is still working on it. He warned me that they were going to bring Kyle in for questioning in the next week. They just want to have everything worked out before they do it.

"So far, no one is saying it's a cover-up. At least not to me. Nick thinks it could just be one employee who was getting paid off. So, I...." Something catches my eyes on the street. "Ooh, there she is." I point to a light blue Honda pulling to a stop on the street in front of us, followed by a police cruiser with his lights flashing. "It's happening."

We watch in silence as Nick approaches the vehicle. I giggle to myself, watching Keely in her car. "She has no idea. She thinks he's out of town doing his school safety seminar."

"Ha!" Polly laughs. "I can see her lips moving. She's talking to herself."

We both laugh as Nick approaches the car. When he asks her to step to the rear of the car, my twin is pissed. That is until she turns to see him on one knee; then she turns into a blub-bering mess.

"Excellent proposal," says Polly with a beaming smile. "Excellent."

"Nick promised to film it for us so we can hear everything she says."

"Ten bucks says she was bitching about him pulling her over."

"I'm not taking that bet." I chuckle.

Keely turns our way. When she spots all of us, I see her happiness from here. *Good for you, twinny. Good for you.*

Dang, I'm stupidly happy for Keely.

A few days later, I receive a text from Eric.

Eric: Whatcha doing tonight?
Me: Nothing. I've got a late class.
Eric: Want me to stop over? Bring some food?
Me: My place is sort of a mess. Dad's working on my floors.

Dad's got tools and sample planks of wood lying about, mostly in the spare bedroom, but that's enough. He told me yesterday that there was more to the job than just nailing down the new planks. There was rot and some other things going on. He said he was going to need to pull everything up and fix the issue beneath the floor, then replace it with all new flooring. It's going to be expensive and take longer than a day to fix it all, which is why I've got tools and wood planks in my house. Sigh. I'll have to work extra hours at the bakery to pay him back. Sure, he'll insist on paying for it, but I'm not letting him do it. Not this time.

Eric: Why don't you come over to my place then?
Me: To your apartment?
Eric: Yeah. You've never been. We can order in.
Me: I won't get home until 7:30 or so.
Eric: Come then. That works.
Eric: We'll have a late dinner and watch something.
Me: ...
Eric: Please? I miss you.

I miss him too.

Me: What can I bring?
Eric: Just your beautiful self.

Awe, he's so sweet.

Me: What's your address?

I know where he lives. There aren't that many apartment complexes here in Page.

Eric: Whispering Sands Apt. 302 Sandhill Rd.
Me: I'll be there.
Eric: Can't wait.

When I knock on his door, I hold my breath.
Why am I so nervous?
The second it opens, I see a freshly showered Eric. I release

the breath I was holding. "Hi," I say, smiling, holding out my arms. "Cupcakes."

His smile is so big, I see a dimple I've never noticed before. Maybe it's because he's clean-shaven, or maybe he just really loves cupcakes.

"I told you to just bring yourself."

I shrug. "I had to stop at the shop anyway."

"Come on in." He holds the door open. "It's a bachelor pad, so don't judge." His laugh is nervous and sort of endearing.

I step into a short hallway. There's a coat hook on the left where he's got a leather jacket hanging. I'm tempted to lean in to get a whiff, but that's just weird. Moving forward, I step into the main room. It's open concept, as they say on those home shows. The galley kitchen is on the right, open to the small living and dining room. To my left is another short hallway that I assume leads to the bedroom and bathroom.

"Make yourself comfortable," Eric says, placing his palm on my lower back. "Let me get you something to drink. I've got lemonade, beer, wine, diet soda, and water."

"Lemonade, please."

"Have a seat. I'll grab that, and we can decide where we want to order from. I'm starving, so be thinkin' about it while I'm gone."

I honestly don't care where the food comes from. I'm just happy to be with him.

When he returns, he hands me my drink as he plops down next to me on the sofa. Reaching out, he picks up his cell. "What sounds good?"

I shrug. "You choose the place, then I'll tell you what I want."

"Well, there's Big Jim's BBQ. That place delivers."

I scrunch up my nose. I don't know why; I usually go along

with everything. I guess I don't feel like eating messy food in front of Eric yet.

"Mexican food? There are a couple good places close by."

"Sure. That sounds good."

I order a chicken quesadilla while Eric orders, well, everything. He must be hungry.

CHAPTER 30

Having Violet at my place was a little nerve-wracking. But the minute she stepped foot in here, I felt relief. I know it doesn't make sense, but none of this makes any sense. The thing is, I liked having her in my private space. I've only brought a couple chicks back here with me, and that was a while ago. The second I saw Violet, I knew that was never going to happen again.

After dinner, we cozied up on my giant sectional sofa. It's the biggest piece of furniture in my place, a necessity for a guy my size. Vi has had her head on my shoulder since opening credits, and my hand has been playing with her silky hair just as long. It's perfect.

"You like the movie?" I ask. I gave her the choice between three of my favorites. Well, okay, not my favorites. I like movies with explosions and car chases. I didn't think she'd be into that, so I chose a few from the second-tier favorites: *The Big Lebowski*, *Wedding Crashers*, and *Office Space*.

I was a little surprised she chose *Office Space*. She said she hadn't seen any of them, but I'm happy to report that she's been laughing right along with the movie. It's funny as shit, and it makes me glad I don't work in an office. When it's over, I run my hand up and down her arm. "You like it?"

"I did. I can't believe I've never seen that before. It was funny."

"It's going to be a classic someday."

"I can see that." She lifts her head from my chest, stretching her arms up above her head, just enough for her T-shirt to ride up. I catch a glimpse of pale, creamy skin. Skin I've touched before. Skin I hope to touch again someday soon.

After a big cat-like yawn, she stands. "I'd better go. I work at the bakery tomorrow. Early."

I peer at the clock; it's almost midnight.

"You could stay here."

"Nah, I need to let the dogs out. I stopped there on the way over and let them out, but they'll be chomping at the bit to go out again."

"Next time, bring them with you."

"But you can't have pets."

"I can have pet visitors." I wink. I'd like to tell her about my plans. About the nice piece of land I bought a few years ago. Land I haven't built on yet. Hell, I haven't even worked on a design. The time never felt right. It does now. She could help me. Maybe she'd even like the idea of living with me. Plenty of room for the dogs to run on five acres.

"All right," she says, interrupting my thoughts. "Talk to you later?" she asks shyly.

"Yeah, in about ten minutes. Call me when you get home so I know you're safe."

"Geesh, okay, Dad," she teases.

I move closer to her, place my palm on the back of her neck.

When she doesn't appear nervous, I kiss her softly. "Please don't ever call me Dad again, babe." I chuckle.

"Noted," she says, pulling my front door open.

"Call me when you get home. I mean it."

"Fine. Worrywart," she huffs. Turning away, she raises her right hand and wiggles her little fingers. "Bye."

"Night, baby."

I watch her walk to her car. I make sure she's behind the wheel and her motor is started before I wave again.

CHAPTER 31

VIOLET

I should probably be annoyed that Eric is insisting I call to let him know I'm home, but how can I be? He cares, and that's a really attractive feature about him. Not that he doesn't have other attractive features. Too many to count, actually.

I pull into my driveway and park underneath my carport. The minute I'm out of my car, I pull my phone out and hit Eric's number.

"You home, doll?"

"Just got out of my car. See? Safe and sound." Reaching into my purse, I feel around for my house keys. Once they're in hand, I slide the key into the lock and turn the knob, but it takes extra muscle to get the key all the way in. I should probably ask Dad to check it.

"You inside yet?" Eric asks with a chuckle. "I think we should talk until you're all snuggled up on your bed."

"Eric. I'm... that's weird."

"What's weird?" he asks instantly.

"Max and CB usually attack me at the door. Hang on, Eric." Pulling the phone away from my ear, I yell, "Max?" I hear nothing. "CB? Are you asleep, lazy boy?" Pulling the phone back to my ear, I say, "Hey, I need to go—"

"Babe. What's wrong? Where are the dogs?"

I hear a bark. It sounds like it's coming from one of the bedrooms. "Well, I heard a bark. They must have gotten themselves shut into one of the bedrooms." How they could do that, I have no idea, but CB is pretty crafty.

"I'll call you back." Before he can say another word, I hit the end button. I drop my purse next to the door and slide my phone into my back pocket. I have a feeling Eric will be calling me back soon, since I practically hung up on him. Sure enough, I feel my phone vibrate, but I ignore it for now. I need to see what the heck CB and Max are up to. In the hallway, I hear another bark.

"Where are you, little boogers?"

I step in front of the spare bedroom and reach for the knob when I feel it—searing pain on the right side of my face. The force of the blow causes me to fall forward, my face hitting the door.

It's then he screams. It's almost blood curdling.

"You fucking cunt!" I'm stunned. Frozen. This can't be happening. I turn my face slowly and see him. Kyle Maines is in my house.

My first reaction is to run, but he's blocking my exit to the living room. My only hope is to get into the spare bedroom and block the door. Ignoring the pain shooting across my face, I turn the knob and push the door open. Racing inside, I turn to push it closed, but I'm too late.

"You think you can get away from me, you fucking bitch?"

I shake my head, all while looking for a way to escape.

"I'm talking to you, you ugly cunt." He's breathing hard,

more like panting. "How dare you accuse me of rape? I did you a fucking favor. You wanted it as much as I did. Hell, you begged me for it."

He's delusional. "No. I didn't."

"How would you know? You were drunk. Drunk chicks always forget they wanted it."

"I'm pretty sure they don't."

I regret responding to him the minute his fist meets the left side of my face. It feels like my eye is popping out of the socket. The force is so great, I have to step back. I feel my foot catch on something, and I lose my balance, falling on my back in the middle of the floor. The room is small. I don't have much room to move with Carl's cage set up on my right and the turtle habitat on my left.

When I look up, Kyle has moved closer. He's standing over me, pointing. "I don't know why, all of a sudden, you're some poor victim. You're nothing but a slut. I've seen you with that biker dude."

I watch as he starts to unbuckle his belt.

"S-seen me?"

"Oh, yeah. I know all about you, Violet Palmer."

"Why?"

"Why?" He sneers repeating my question, but I barely hear his words. All I can hear is the sound of his zipper. The sound of the opening of his pants echoes in the room.

"I've seen him here."

He's seen him here? At my house?

"He's here a lot. Your pussy must still be as tight as the night I popped your cherry."

I stare in disbelief as he pushes his pants down past his hips and his penis pops out. He's hard as he begins to stroke himself. "Bet that biker asshole isn't as good as I was, huh, *Violet*?" The way he says my name will haunt me for my entire life. It's said with pure hatred.

He moves closer still.

"No! No, Kyle." I scoot back further until my back hits the wall. "Kyle. You don't have to do this."

"Shut the fuck up, cunt."

I hate that word. So, so much.

I feel his hands on my ankles and attempt to kick, but he's strong. Yanking on them, he pulls me away from the wall onto my back. He's on top of me before I can do anything, working frantically to get my jeans undone. Since he's distracted, I take the opportunity to hit and scratch at his face. That is until pushes himself up onto his knees and punches me in the face again, I see stars now and have to lie still for a second to get myself together. The taste of copper is on my tongue and I'm pretty sure one of my teeth is floating around in there. When I work it to the front of my mouth, I spit it out, hopefully getting blood on him.

He's got my pants undone but not down. I think about my kickboxing and the self-defense class that I took at the Y. The only thing I can think to do is bring my knee up to jam it into his junk. I close my eyes and conjure up the strength to do as much damage as possible. Using my hands, I push on his upper body all while bringing my knee up as far as I can. But he's stronger than me.

"Nice try, fat whore."

God, why me?

He's on top of me again. Pressing down hard. I'm tired. I want to give up. I let my right arm flop out to my side. When it lands, it makes contact with something hard and metal. A tool? One of my dad's tools. Using my fingers, I get a grip of some type of power tool in the shape of a gun. A drill? I don't even know if it's cordless or a plug-in type of tool. My luck, it's the wrong kind. Glancing at it, I see what it is. A nail gun. Since Kyle is distracted pushing my jeans down, I do the only thing I can right now. I lift it, push it into his upper arm, and press the trigger.

"Motherfucker!" he screams. He quickly grabs at his arm as blood seeps through his fingers.

Without another thought, I point the gun at his other arm and shoot. I miss. The second he reaches for it, I pull it away from him, aim, and shoot.

"Holy fucking hell!" he squeals.

I got him. I don't know what I hit, but at least it was something. I quickly move away from him and attempt to stand. He's there before I know it, trying to grab the nail gun from my hand. The gun goes off four or five more times in the struggle. When one of them hits my leg, I keep fighting. Using both hands, I do my best to point the gun back at him. Pressing the trigger as many times as I can, I shoot and shoot until he finally falls to the ground, clutching his exposed penis.

That's when I hear pounding footsteps and watch as the door to the spare room slams open. When I see him, the only word I say is, "Eric."

He rushes to my side. "Violet? You okay?"

I nod even though I know I'm probably pretty beat up. The truth is, I'm okay. "He t-tried to rape me again."

The next thing I know, Eric Gustafson has turned away from me and his big fist is making contact with the side of Kyle's head. The force of the hit causes Kyle's head to snap to the side. Placing his palm over the spot that Eric just punched, Kyle attempts to roll away from Eric, all while still clutching his genitals.

Eric looks at him, then back at me and the object in my hand. "You shoot him with a nail gun, babe?"

"Yes."

Eric stands over Kyle. He places his big booted foot on Kyle's neck. "You want to shoot him again? I'll hold him down."

"No. Please, no," whines Kyle.

There's a big part of me that would love to keep shooting. But I'm pretty sure that would come back and bite me on the butt. "No. We'd better call the police."

"No," Kyle whimpers. "Call an ambulance."

"No," I say matter-of-factly. "You can suffer."

"Fucking cunt," he spits.

"The fuck you say?" Eric snaps. He doesn't wait for a response before his big boot rises up, then stomps back down right on top of Eric's hands. Hard. The ones covering his junk.

I have the urge to giggle but I hold it in.

Kyle continues to complain, "Oh, Jesus. It's inside. Fuck. Goddamn, kill me. Please."

"All right," Eric says as he reaches into his back pocket. "Just remember, you asked for it." For a second, I think he's got a knife or something in there, but all he's got is his phone. I listen as he tells the police dispatcher that there's been an attack, the address, and to send help. He asks for Nick specifically. "Tell him we've got Kyle Maines."

Eric points down to Kyle. "You move, and *I'll* shoot you with the nail gun myself. I don't give a fuck what happens to me. You hear me?"

"Y-yes."

He removes the gun from my hand. My fingers are clamped so tightly around the handle, I have to force my hand open. Once he's got it, he places it on the desk behind me and wraps me up gently. I start to cry. It's coming from someplace deep and unnatural because I don't ever remember crying like that.

"Vi?" he whispers. "He hurt you?"

I know what he's asking. "He just hit me. He d-didn't rape me. I shot him before he could."

"Fuck, babe. You're kick-ass. I'm so proud of you." I hear him sniffle and feel his hand rub up and down my back. "You're fucking kick-ass."

You know what? *I am* fucking kick-ass. I shot that jerk right in the balls, and nothing has ever felt better. When I hear barking, I pull away from Eric. "Max and CB." I reach back and pick up the nail gun. Pointing it at Kyle, I say, "Don't move, fucker."

Eric's laugh hits me right in my heart. "It's the first time I've ever heard you cuss. Timing was perfect, beautiful." He nods toward the door.

I hand him the nail gun.

Eric chuckles, then points the gun down at Kyle. "You go. I'll keep an eye on this motherfucker."

"Jesus, God." Kyle is sobbing now.

Good.

I smile, then wince at the pain as I race out the door. The sound of whimpering is coming from my bedroom. I push the door open, and both of my little fellas race out and jump on my legs. It hurts, but I don't care. The minute I knew Kyle was in my house, I was worried he'd done something to my dogs. I feel around them to make sure they're not hurt. When CB tinkles on the floor, I coo. "Poor baby."

CHAPTER 32

Eric

Jesus. I've never been so terrified in my whole life. Terrified and fucking pissed off enough to kill someone. Namely Kyle Maines. I knew something was wrong. She'd just told me she'd let the dogs out before coming to my place. There was no reason they wouldn't be waiting for her at the door. My gut told me something was off. I also knew, thanks to my brother and Lainie, that they'd had Kyle Maines in for questioning yesterday.

So, with my suspicions rolling around in my head, I jumped on my bike and raced over to Vi's place. God, I'm so fucking glad I did.

Jesus.

I shiver thinking about what could have happened if I hadn't asked her to call me. Fuck. He could have killed her.

I stare down at the fucker and do something uncharacteristic for me. I stomp on his hands again.

"You cocksucker," Kyle squeaks.

Bending down, I know I've only got a minute or two before sirens start to sound.

"Hey, Kyle?" I ask, sort of nicely. He turns and blinks. I take that as a yes. "If I ever see you again, I'll fucking kill you, Kyle. Do you hear me? I've got some land. No one would ever look for your body way out there. Hell, I don't think anyone would even miss you. You get me?"

"My mom would miss me. You sick bastard," Kyle spits out.

"Me? *I'm* the sick bastard. *The rapist* is calling me sick?" I stand up again, and this time I place my booted foot on top of the nail that's sticking out of his arm. With consistent pressure, I push the nail in as far as it will go. The asshole screams like he's dying.

"Don't be a pussy," I mumble. "You'd better get used to tough love. Prison isn't for the meek." I move to his left, then I think to ask, "That your mommy out there in the Caddy waiting for you?" I noticed a fancy-ass SUV parked down the block. The license plate is burned into my brain.

He doesn't say a word. He merely stares at me. It's then I remember seeing the guy before. "You were at the convenience store a while back." It's not a question. I remember him asking me questions about my junk food—and about my girl. "You stalkin' her too?"

He doesn't respond. That's okay, I know it was him, and I know what he was up to. Placing my foot on a nail poking out above his right knee, I give it a little nudge with my foot. Okay, it was more of a hard nudge. "By the way...." He looks up at me. "Mommy Dearest took off the second I pulled into the driveway." I heard the V-8 engine roar past me as I was dismounting my bike. "Good thing I got her plate. Hard to miss a plate that says LT GOV. Shit. She must be as stupid as you are."

Kyle's about to say something, "She's not—"

That's when sirens start to sound. In seconds, I hear feet

stomping through the door. Cops are identifying themselves as they race around the place.

"In here!" I yell.

"Okay, Violet. Now that the captain is here, can you tell us what happened again? From the beginning?"

Violet sighs. She's exhausted. No wonder. It's almost four in the morning, and we're still in the emergency room at Lake Powell Medical Center. Her entire family descended on the place like locusts, doing their best to take care of their sister. They left an hour ago, leaving only Rob here. In addition to that, Violet's been x-rayed and examined from head to toe. There's an IV stuck in her arm feeding her antibiotics thanks to the nail they removed from her thigh. And her face. Fuck. Even though she's had ice on it for the last couple of hours, it's swollen and turning more black and blue every minute. Her tongue moves to the spot where most of her front tooth used to be. All that's left is a jagged stump. She looks like she went ten rounds with Ali.

"Yes," she answers Nick, her voice scratchy from talking.

I feel the need to stand up for her. "Can this be it, Nick? She's exhausted."

"Yeah. Sorry, Violet," Nick says, looking apologetic. "We need to hear it again while it's fresh in your mind."

"No worries, Nick. I'll tell you again."

And she does, starting from the moment she stepped out of her car to call me on the phone. My fists remain clenched at my sides when she gets to the part where Kyle hits her the first time. I want him dead, but the thought going through my head isn't vengeance. It's pride. I'm so goddamn proud of her. She was fucking fierce.

"Huh?"

Shit. I guess I said that aloud.

"What?" I blink at Violet then at Nick.

"You said 'fierce,'" she says, looking perplexed.

Keeping my eyes on her, I smile. "I was thinking how fierce you were. How proud I am of you."

"Oh." Violet's voice has softened. "Thank you." I can barely hear her. I can see emotion in her eyes, even though they're swollen nearly shut. "I'm glad you said that, Eric. For the first time in a long time, I *feel* like I was fierce. I wasn't the victim. I was the victor."

I gently slide my hand over hers. "Fucking fierce, babe."

"You ready to keep going, Violet?" asks Nick. "I know you want to get out of here."

I want her out of her. As soon as she's done with that IV, I'm taking my girl home.

Violet tells the story one more time with a few questions of her own. "How did he get the dogs locked in my bedroom?"

I know the answer to that one. "Dog treats. There was an empty bag of them torn open on your bedroom floor."

Violet's voice sounds shaky when she says, "He came prepared."

He certainly did.

When Nick steps out of the small alcove they call a room, I follow him. He's talking with Captain Morgan. Morgan takes off, and I call Nick over.

"Yeah?"

"Where is he?"

"Still in surgery, last I heard. We've got officers on him. As soon as he's released, we're taking him straight to jail." Nick pauses. "I guess I need to ask. Did you really stomp on his balls?"

"It was self-defense."

He arches his brow. "According to Maines, you exacerbated

the wounds."

"Exacerbated? I did no such thing. He was lunging for Violet. I did what I needed to do to protect her."

"There was a boot print on his arm."

"Self-defense. You heard Violet."

"Uh-huh." Nick doesn't sound convinced.

That can't be helped, I guess.

"You going to follow up on his mother?" I told Nick my side of things right after Violet went through her story for the first time. It included seeing him at the convenience store a couple weeks back.

"We're hoping some of Violet's neighbors saw something or, better yet, have surveillance cameras or even those video doorbells. We'll canvass the neighborhood first thing in the morning."

"Good."

"All right." Nick starts to leave.

"Why would his mother be there? She had to know what he was doing?"

Nick steps closer. "Between you and me?"

"Of course."

"He had boarding passes on his phone. The flight to Morroco was scheduled to leave first thing this morning. We've got someone checking to make sure Abernathy isn't fleeing too."

"Morocco? Why?"

"I was curious about that too. I looked it up. Morocco doesn't have an extradition treaty with the US."

"You think she'd risk it all for that worthless piece of shit?"

"A mother's love...." Nick rolls his eyes.

"Ten bucks she bought the ticket," I deadpan.

"I'm not going to take that bet, because there's no doubt in my mind. But, it's time to get the Feds involved. They have the resources needed to dig deeper into Frances Abernathy."

"Well, thanks, Nick. I know you got all of this started."

He winces. "I wish I'd had a unit on her at her place. I should have assumed he'd go after her. I feel like shit. Keely is pissed."

"She's just upset and worried. She'll be okay." Okay, I have no idea if she'll be okay. Thinking about it, I'm pissed off too. He should have had someone watching out for her. Well, maybe that's my own guilt at play. I should have been keeping a closer eye on her.

"Night, Eric. Call me if you need anything."

"Right. Night."

I turn to go back into Vi's room but stop when I see Rob in there with her. He's sitting on the bed, Violet wrapped up in his arms. Rob is an amazing father. I'd be happy to be *half* the father he is.

I move out to the waiting room while Rob and Violet have time together. After that, I'm taking her home with me. Violet doesn't know this, but I've taken care of her pets. Nick gave Keeton and Lainie permission to pick up all the animals before the house was completely taped off by the cops. By now, they should have already picked up Stella, Sherman, the dogs, Carl, Donatello, and Beatrix. If she's up to it, Violet and I will head over there tomorrow so she can check up on them. I know she'll worry even if they're safe and sound at Lainie's.

"She's all yours, son." Rob pats my shoulder. His hand stays put. I know he's got something to say. "No words, Eric. No words. You saved my baby girl. I'll always be indebted to you, son."

"She saved herself, Mr. Palmer. I got there after she'd already subdued him."

Rob gives me a knowing smile. "My girls are somethin', aren't they?"

I nod. "You did good, Mr. Palmer."

"Rob. Call me Rob." Rob pauses. "You're a good man. Almost good enough for my Violet." He winks. "*Almost.*"

"Yes, sir."

Rob clears his throat. "Eric? Can I ask you something?"

"Sure."

"What are your intentions?"

"My intentions? With Violet?"

Rob nods. His face is lined from worry. Years of taking care of five girls has taken a toll. "Of all my girls, she's always been most like her mother: soft, sweet, compassionate, and vulnerable." He points at me. "I'm concerned, and I believe I have a right to be."

"I see your point." I hesitate. I'm not sure how I can say this without sounding like a crazy person. "The moment I met Violet, I knew she was special. I couldn't stop thinking about her. The second time I saw her, my heart beat so hard I thought I was having a heart attack."

Rob gives me a knowing smile.

"I don't know if it was love at first sight, but I think it was. And since that first meeting, my feelings for her have only grown stronger. I'm scared shitless she's going to figure out I'm not good enough for her."

"You aren't," Rob deadpans. "But nobody is."

"I know." I release a small laugh. "I'm in this forever, if she'll have me. No matter if it takes her a year, five years, or ten years to be ready for us, I'll wait, sir."

Rob slaps his big palm on my shoulder. "You're her person."

I knew what he was saying. I'd heard Lainie say that to my brother. I don't even hesitate. "Yeah. She's my person too."

"Glad to hear it, son." He turns to leave. As he walks away, he says loud enough for me to hear, "And call me Rob."

"Will do."

CHAPTER 33

My body hurts, but nothing compared to my face. I'm so swollen I feel like the Stay Puft Marshmallow Man. Even after two full days of constant icing and taking anti-inflammatories every four to six hours, it's still swollen.

I slowly move off Eric's giant sofa and lumber into the bathroom. He went to work today at my insistence. I didn't want him to get into trouble with his brother, my brother-in-law, because he felt like he needed to hover. I promised him I would go no further than his kitchen today. I also told him Keely was going to come over and hang out with me for part of the day. I think my sisters secretly agreed to take turns staying with me.

I'd like to tell you that it bothers me, but it doesn't. I'd do the same thing if this happened to one of them. I'd want to be with them so I could help out and be confident they were really okay. I can endure all of their heavy-handedness because it's what family does. At least it's what my family does.

As I wait for Keely, I take a long, hot shower in the hopes

it'll soothe my achy muscles. Standing under the spray, I make a mental list of things I need to do before Keely comes over.

"Number one," I say aloud, "I need to contact my professors and probably the school to let them know I'll be out for a few more days." Finals are just around the corner, and I can't fall behind.

I feel my shoulders slump. *School.* Thinking about it depresses me. I don't enjoy it. Any of it. There are days I think I'd rather just work someplace. Like at Sadie Cakes Bakery. It's mindless work to sell cakes and treats, but it's fun because I get to spend time with Polly and my sister Sadie. Sadly, Sadie doesn't need another full-time employee. Maybe when the baby comes, but until then, what could I do? Staying in school is the smart thing to do. I need to get a real job after I graduate, whenever that is. If I keep taking electives that sound "fun" rather than taking my required classes, I'll never graduate.

Would that be so terrible?

I've made it my mission the last couple of years to finish what I started down at U of Southeast Arizona. I've always felt it was a goal I needed to achieve to help me heal. Now, I'm not so sure. Heck, even my new idea of going into counseling has lost its luster. While it would be rewarding to help other girls and women who have been sexually assaulted, I'm not sure my personality is right for that. No matter how hard I try or how old I get, I'm still painfully shy. How would that help anyone? What if a girl came to me with her story and I just sat there, frozen? She'd leave and maybe never get the help she needs. I know, I know, I'm exaggerating, sort of. There are great resources out there for people like me and my fictitious girl, but I'm not sure I should be one of those resources.

So, where does that leave me?

My shoulders slump further beneath the now chilly water. I turn off the tap and slowly dry myself off, dress, and pad back into Eric's living room. I look back at the kitchen, wondering if he's got anything good to eat. You know, like chocolate or ice cream or cake.

"Cake," I groan. "I'd love some cake."

Deciding to do a quick search in Eric's cupboards, I'm happily surprised when I find a bag of chocolate chips. "These'll do."

Tearing them open, I grab a handful and toss them in my mouth. But something's wrong. I quickly spit them back out into my hand and stare at the bag. Flipping it over, I read the expiration date: *July 2005*. I start to gag a little as I toss the entire pack into the trash. "2005?! What was he thinking?" I should probably go through his cupboards and toss out anything else that's over a decade old, but it's not my house. *His* things aren't *my* things.

With my appetite completely gone, I fill a cup with tap water and head back to the couch. I hope Keely gets here soon. I'm going stir-crazy. And, God, I miss my pets a lot. A *lot*, a lot. That's the precise moment I hear a bark at the door. Standing up fast, I use my hand and the arm of the sofa to steady myself.

Walking gingerly to the door, I peek out the peephole and see the top of Keely's head.

"Open up, bitch."

"Nice."

When I open the door, Max and CB go nuts. Max jumps first, hitting my sore leg wound. It's okay, I can take it. It's worth it if I get to see my little fellas. I step back, then bend to give them both rough scratches behind their ears.

"Oh, my goodness, I've missed you guys."

"You gonna let me in or what? I brought treats." Keely holds up two grocery bags.

"Treats?" I hope they aren't expired chocolate chips.

"I got you all your favorites, including but not limited to

Peanut M&Ms, fresh fruit, frozen yogurt, pretzels, Stouffer's macaroni and cheese, oh, and a salad."

"Oh, I love Stouffer's mac and cheese." It's the best. She brought some healthy things too, which I appreciate a lot. But right now, I need comfort food.

"I know. Now, move aside and let me put the yogurt in the freezer."

My stomach suddenly growls. "Yes, ma'am. Can I have the mac and cheese now?"

"I bought a big one so we could share."

"Awesome." I feel myself attempt a smile, but it's not happening. My face still hurts, and my broken tooth is wearing a hole in my tongue.

Keely looks at me and smiles, but I can tell it's forced. I know all of my twin's expressions, and this one says, *You look like shit, Violet.*

"You call about getting that tooth fixed?"

I don't have dental insurance. No matter what they decide to do, pull it or put a crown on it, it's going to be expensive. "No. I don't have that kind of cash."

Keely reaches into the purse she set on the counter and pulls out a white envelope.

"We knew you'd say that."

I pull up the flap and see a stack of money. "Geesh, how much is in here?"

"Three grand."

"Three thousand dollars?!" I screech.

Keely rolls her eyes. "Yeah. You need to get that tooth fixed, and you may need money for your hospital visit and ambulance ride."

"You don't have this kind of money, Keely."

"No. I don't, but collectively we do. Sadie's worked out your legal fund."

"My legal fund? Do I need one of those?"

"We all thought it'd be a good idea to be prepared since the asshole's mom is such a bigwig."

I nod slowly. I can see that now.

"Laura Ashbury told us she'd cover whatever you need for representation."

My eyes burn, but I refuse to cry at every piece of news, good or bad. "No," I whisper. Laura Ashbury is Charlie's grandmother. Charlie is going to marry my sister Sadie on Christmas Eve.

"Yes. Don't argue."

"Yes. I—"

"Be honest. If this sitch was reversed, would you fundraise for me?"

"Yes, of course, but—"

"Nuf said, sis. Get over it. We're helping. Step one, get that snaggletooth fixed."

"Snaggletooth? I don't think that's what you call this," I say, pointing to my jagged tooth.

"I looked it up. That's exactly what it is."

I sigh heavily. "Fine." I can't win with her. "I'll call tomorrow."

"Today." Keely pulls the phone out of her purse. "I've got Doc Olsen already cued up." She giggles. "I'm lying. I already called him. You have an appointment tomorrow morning at 8:00 A.M. Agatha will pick you up at seven forty-five to take you."

I attempt to arch my brow, but it hurts, so I stop. "Anything else, bossy?"

"Yeah, let's cook us up some cheesy goodness and watch *Real Housewives*."

Ugh, I hate that show. She loves it. "Sure. Which one?"

"Uh, duh." Keely rolls her eyes again. I swear her eyeballs are going to fall out. "*Atlaaaanta*. Is there any other?"

"Yes. There's Beverly Hills, New York—"

Keely holds up her palm. "Blasphemy. Now, go get comfy, I'll get this going."

I pretend to grumble, but, really, I'm pretty thrilled she's here. I'll even endure *Real Housewives* drama for her.

I'm awoken by a cool kiss on my lips and a soft voice in my ear. "Violet?"

I blink awake and see Eric standing over me with a brown paper bag in his hand.

"I brought you some soup."

"Yeah?" My stomach growls at the thought.

"Molly made it for you. She also sent rolls. She said they were soft to chew." He points at my mouth. "Because of your tooth."

"That was nice of her," I say, sitting up. And it was. I don't know Molly all that well, but she's checked on me several times since I got the stuffing beat out of me. She's also given me some useful intel on her little brother. Okay, not so useful, but it was funny intel. I may never tire of hearing about what a little rascal Eric used to be. "Remind me to send her a thank-you text later."

"Will do."

Eric places the bag on the table, then sits beside me. "How're you feeling?"

"Sore."

"I'll get you some pain reliever." He starts to stand, but I place my hand on his arm.

"I took some right before Keely left. I don't get another dose for a few hours."

"Right."

"Are you okay?" I ask, because he seems tentative. "What's wrong?"

Eric rubs his face. "I just heard."

"Heard what?"

"He was denied bail."

"Who...?" I blink a few times. Oh, wait. "Kyle?"

Eric nods. "Flight risk. He had a plane ticket to Morocco in his pocket."

"Wow. This is going to sound really pathetic, but the thought of him getting out never occurred to me. But, his mother—"

"Is under investigation. Didn't Keely tell you any of this?"

"No." I arch my brow. "She didn't." And I'm not sure how I feel about that. I don't like them keeping stuff from me. I look up at Eric. "I don't want stuff kept from me. I'm not some fragile flower."

"Well—" He chuckles. "—your name *is* Violet."

I don't laugh. Heck, I don't even smile. "I mean it, Eric."

His chuckle stops dead. "Got it." He holds his palm over his chest. "Never. It's why I came home and told you first thing."

"Oh, right." Crap, now I feel terrible. "Thank you."

"Do you want me to kick Keely's ass for you?"

Now I laugh. "You could try, but she's pretty scrappy for a shorty."

"I'm not scared. I've got you on my side, plus," he says, puffing out his chest, "I've got my eye on a new nail gun."

I chuckle, then say, "Good plan."

"Hey, let's eat, then let's go for a drive."

"A drive?" God, I'd love to. I'm getting stir-crazy.

"A drive and ice cream."

Be still my heart.

"Sure. Let's eat."

CHAPTER 34

ERIC

The evening air is cool for Arizona, so we've got the windows down in my pickup as we take the same route we would if we were going to Keeton's.

"Are we going to see my babies?" Vi asks, attempting a smile. It's awfully hard for her with all the puffiness.

"After. I want to show you something."

"Oh?" She looks at my profile. "Okay." I see her typing something out on her phone, then I hear a laugh, and more typing.

"What's up over there? You sound mischievous."

"No." She giggles. "I'm giving my sisters crap."

"Because they're treating you like a 'delicate flower'?"

"Yep." Violet types more. "You want me to read it to you?"

"Sure. If you want." I don't want to intrude on her private conversations, but, if she's willing....

"I wrote 'Ladies. I'm tired of you tiptoeing around me. I'm not going to fall apart hearing about Kyle Maines. You need to keep me in the loop. I deserve to know what's happening. I'm the one who will have to testify.'"

I hate thinking about her having to face that guy in the courtroom. "What'd they say?"

"Keely was first. She said 'B-i-t-c-h, I didn't want to upset you.' That's why I laughed. Keely is terrible. Then Lainie quickly followed that up with the same comment, minus the B word. Agatha hasn't responded yet."

I love how she spelled out the word bitch. She's so classy. I hear her phone chime again.

"Sadie apologized."

"What're you going to say now?"

"I just sent one that said, 'I love you guys. You're like family to me.'"

I chuckle, which turns into a laugh. "Good one."

Her phone dings once more.

"*Oh*, there's Agatha. She said, '*LIKE FAMILY!?*'" Violet looks at me and giggles. "She used all shouty caps."

I laugh because she's laughing and because, "I love your laugh."

"Yeah?" She looks surprised by my comment.

"Yeah. It's sort of tinkling."

"Tinkling?" Well, it's tinkling most of the time. Not this laugh, though. This one is deep and rumbly, coming from her chest. She laughs long and loud but winces. When she stops, she shakes her head, muttering.

"You in pain?"

"Yes. But I'll be okay. I took an anti-inflammatory at the ice-cream shop."

"Good." We ride in silence as we pass Keeton and Lainie's place. I pull my truck down the long dirt road toward the lot for the house I intend to build. She doesn't seem to mind that we've driven past her sister's house. I stop the truck in the middle of a large clearing. I did have the sense to have this part cleared of trees and rocks back when I purchased the place. I quickly move around to Violet's side of the truck and hold my hand out to help her down.

"Where are we?" she asks, looking around the clearing.

"My land." *Our* land.

"Your land?" Her voice sounds almost wistful. "It's beautiful here."

I know. "I bought this a few years ago. I want to build a house out here someday soon."

"You do?" She turns to face me. "You're so close to Keeton and Lainie's."

"Molly owns a piece of land about two miles down the road." I point east.

"I didn't know Molly lived out here."

"She doesn't. She and Adam planned to build a house out here, but...."

Violet's voice is barely a whisper. "I'm so sorry. That's so sad."

"It is. I hope she decides to do it someday. Adam wanted her to have a house out here close to Keeton."

"When are you going to build?"

"Soon. I've got the money sitting in an account just waiting for the right time." And for the right person to help me.

"You do?" Violet blinks a few times. "No. Don't answer that. It's none of my business."

What the fuck? I step toward her, wrapping my arms around her as gently as possible. Looking down at her, I gaze into her eyes. "Honey, I've been waiting for you to do this with me."

"That doesn't make any sense. We just met."

I shrug. "All I know is I never thought the time was right until the second I saw you at Keeton's place that day."

Violet's eyes look into mine, searching. "You really mean that, don't you?"

"I do. If I had one wish, it'd be for you and me to build a home out here together. Then we'd live here, have a few rug rats, and live happily ever after."

"That's more than one wish."

I'm not sure if she's joking. "It's one giant wish. I want you to be mine, Violet. I want you to be my girl, and sometime soon, my wife."

"Y-your wife?"

"I'm not asking today. It's too soon for you. You've had a lot happen recently. When I do propose, though, it'll be private and perfect."

"Oh, yeah?" Violet smiles up at me. Moving closer, her lips touch mine gently. "I wish I could really kiss you right now but...."

"We've got plenty of time for more kisses."

She rises up and touches my lips again. "I can't wait."

"So," I point to my left, "if we build something with two stories, we'll get a glimpse of Lake Powell over those trees."

"I love Lake Powell."

"Me too." I wrap my arm around her shoulder and bring her closer. "Can you picture it?"

"I can. I know exactly what I'd build here."

"You do?" I smile wide. "Tell me about it."

"Well, it has to be two stories, right?"

"Right."

"Well, while I like the more Southwest style homes, I don't think it'd work here."

"No?" I agree. I have a vision of something more rustic, like a log cabin.

"I see more of a log home."

No fucking way. I turn again to face her. "You read my

mind, honey." I bend down and kiss her lips. "You literally read my mind."

"Really?"

"When we get back to my place, I'll show you the stuff I've cut out of magazines over the past few years. You'll see."

"All right." Violet pulls in closer, bringing her arms around my waist. "I love you, Eric."

I barely hear it; it's said so softly and against my shirt. No matter how quiet she was, I'll never forget where we were when she said it for the first time, for real. On our land. "I love you too, Violet."

CHAPTER 35

VIOLET

It's been four weeks since Kyle broke into my place and got himself shot with the nail gun. The good news is, my face is pretty much back to normal. There are only tinges of yellow on the side he punched more than once, and my tooth is good as new after getting a crown. The tooth stuff wasn't fun, but at least I can smile now without feeling insecure. Besides that, lots has happened. For one, Polly and Cortland got married. It was a whirlwind romance. I mean, I knew Cortland was gaga for my friend, so I guess it makes sense they tied the knot.

Eric and I spent our first Thanksgiving together just a couple of days ago. Several families, all related to my sisters and Dad, congregated at Keeton and Lainie's home for a feast fit for a king. Lainie pulled out all the stops for us, making turkey, ham, and brisket along with so many sides it still makes my stomach hurt. Of course, Sadie provided the desserts. I helped with that, as usual.

Dad even showed up with Deb. No one acted surprised to

see her. We all just hugged her and welcomed her into the fold and that was that. Bam, Deb was in. Where that will lead, no one knows. But she's a really cool lady and one who makes my Dad smile—*and blush*. I couldn't help noticing her whispering things to him and then watched as the Palmer blush washed over his face. It was a tad uncomfortable, but that's okay. I can deal with my dad having a love life. I just don't want to hear anything about it. *Ever*.

A lot of stuff has happened related to Kyle in the last month too. In that short time, he had surgery to remove a number of nails from his body. Once he was released from the hospital, he was immediately taken into police custody, where he's been ever since because he was denied bail. No matter what Frances Abernathy tried, it failed. Not only that, all of her efforts only made her son's case more popular with the media, and not just newspapers and network news. Nope, there were paparazzi all over the place in Page. A few of them were camped out at my house, but Nick got rid of them lickety-split. However, I still have to keep an eye on my surroundings for lurkers.

When the news hit that Frances Abernathy's son was not only being charged with attempted rape and assault, but with rape stemming from an incident six years prior, women started coming forward with similar allegations. In four weeks, eight other women have contacted Nick's office. They referred them on to Agent Banks, who is heading up the task force on this case. I'd be interested to know how many of them were from the University of Southeast Arizona, and if that's the case, how many of them tried to go to the police. Either way, this investigation is going to get national attention if it hasn't already. Something I'm sure Frances Abernathy fears.

"You ready to go, Vi?"

I'm shaken out of my reflection by a hot guy in a pair of jeans that fit him in all the right places and a black tee that does the same. My man is gorgeous. And chivalrous. And sweet, kind, and patient. Almost a week after the attack, I was able to return to my house. I didn't go alone though. Eric insisted on staying with me. I wasn't about to argue with the man, since I wasn't keen on living alone right that minute. So, Eric packed up some of his things and moved in with me temporarily. That same day, I collected my animal family from Lainie and Keeton's and moved them all home. My goodness, I missed them so much.

Eric's been at my house for three weeks or so, and I've liked having him here. More than liked. I never gave having a boyfriend much thought, but the advantages far outweigh anything negative. The cuddling alone makes it worth it.

We still haven't taken our relationship past kissing. My mouth was so sore for the first ten days after Kyle's assault, kissing wasn't even possible. At least not anything other than a peck here and there. Once I healed, I found I really enjoyed spending time kissing him. We'd lie on the couch making out while a movie or television show played in the background. Before we fall asleep, there's always some hot kisses from Eric. He likes to spend extra time kissing my neck—a neck he calls elegant. After the kissing, I have found I fall asleep the fastest with my head on Eric's chest and with his hand cupping my bottom. He claims it's a perfect fit for his hand, and I find I don't mind it there at all.

In the morning—heck, I'm blushing just thinking about it— Eric is usually, how shall I say? He's aroused. We haven't addressed that part of things yet. Instead, Eric likes to kiss me slowly and passionately in the morning. It's a sort of lazy, dizzying kind of kissing—not like that's a bad thing. Morning kisses are my favorite so far.

I want to tell him I'm ready for more, but the second I attempt it, I freeze up. I'm scared to take the next step. Don't get me wrong; I'm not afraid of Eric. I'm afraid I'll freak out on him and turn into a crazy woman. That would break Eric's heart. I know the last thing he wants to do is scare me or hurt me in anyway.

I look over at him. He's waiting for me with the dogs leashed and sitting at his feet. I can do it. I can take this to the next level. I know I can. He's worth the risk. *We're* worth the risk.

"You ready?"

We're taking the dogs to the dog park today.

"You're in your head this morning," Eric says softly.

"I know. It's all good, though," I say, standing up from the rocking chair. Grabbing a light sweater, I step up to him. Moving up on my tiptoes, I press my lips to his. "I was thinking about us."

"Us?"

"Yes."

Be brave Violet. Say it.

"I was thinking I'm ready for us to be more..."

Say it!

I look up at him and can't help but feel so much love for this man. He's so freaking patient. "...intimate."

His brow arches, and it's so stupidly sexy. "Intimate?"

"Intimate." I look down at the floor and make eye contact with Max. He gives me the courage to continue. "I'd like to do more, um, things."

"Things?"

Now he's smirking, and I don't mind it one bit even though this is all very awkward.

"In bed."

"In bed?"

"Eric." I release a relieved laugh. "You don't make this all that easy."

He wraps his big arms around me, pulling me as close as I can get without climbing inside him. "Oh, I'll be easy."

"Ha ha!" Then I giggle. "You're terrible."

"I prefer naughty, but terrible works." He winks. "So, when will all of these 'more things' happen?"

Crap, he wants a timeline? "Tonight?"

"Tonight?"

"Yeah, we could try tonight. It's Saturday."

"It is." Eric leans down and gives me a soft kiss. "Honey. You know I love you and want you like crazy, but we don't need to do anything you don't want to do. We've got our whole lives to—"

I know where he's going with this. Interrupting him, I say, "I'm ready for more. I don't know what more *is* right this second, but I want to try."

Truth? I want to see him naked. Completely naked. I have yet to see that, since he's been extra careful not to strip down in front of me. He changes in the bathroom and never comes out without at least his boxer briefs on. It's a darn shame. A laugh escapes me.

A laugh that makes Eric's brows furrow. "What's so funny?"

"Nothing. I'm just surprised at my own thoughts sometimes." I shrug. It's true. I've just been waxing poetic about naked Eric. Something that never would have happened even six months ago.

"Mysterious." He nods. "I've got a very mysterious girlfriend."

I love the sound of that. *Girlfriend.*

CHAPTER 36

Eric

Fuck. She wants to be more *intimate?* Do more *things?*

I want that too, but the thought of her doing more than she's ready for scares the ever-lovin' shit out of me. I'll just make it clear she has to talk to me. She has to use her words to let me know what she wants or what she doesn't.

Violet and I spent the day doing very domestic things together. Things like grocery shopping, washing her car, working on her lawn, and going to the home improvement store to look at paint samples so we can repaint the spare bedroom. Things I never pictured myself doing with a chick, *ever.* But the thing is, I loved it. Every fucking minute of it. I mean, watching Violet pull eight million color swatches out and lay them all in a row so she can "narrow down" her choices was fucking priceless. In the end, she finally just asked me what I thought. I pointed to the one I figured was her favorite, a light purple color called Magical, since she kept going back to it. She must have picked that swatch up fifty times.

When I did, she gasped and looked at me like I'd just solved that pesky world peace problem, saying, "Oh, my gosh, I love that one too."

I shrugged. "It's my favorite." *She's* my favorite. Whatever she wants is okay with me.

When Violet gave me a little kiss, she said, "I love you, Eric."

I wrapped my arm around her and patted her sweet little ass. "Love you too, babe. Now, let's get this shit and go home. I'm starvin'." The fact I talked Violet into making her mom's lasagna again was playing havoc with my stomach, and this time she's making the sauce from scratch. Hell, thinking about it makes my stomach growl.

Violet pats my stomach and giggles. "I heard that."

"Can't get anything past you, can I?" I chuckle and pat her bottom again. I could do that all day long.

Grabbing the paint swatch, I head over to the paint mixing lady. "Two gallons."

"What finish?" asks the paint lady.

I look over at Violet so she can tell me what finish she wants.

"Um, satin." She looks at me. "Right?"

"Yeah." I have no fucking idea what satin even means, but I agree with her because I'm positive she knows. "Sounds good."

While the paint is mixing, we shop for brushes and other paint supplies that we'll need since we agreed to paint the room tomorrow. More domestic tasks. I can picture us doing this together in our new place. The one she helped me design. That night, after we got back from the lot, the two of us went through the pictures and magazine clippings I've been collecting for several years. When all was said and done, Violet's ideas synced perfectly with mine.

So, last week, we met with Keeton's architect and the general contractor he worked with to build his place. Martina Navarro does amazing work, and the fact that she and Violet hit it off was just a bonus. From the excitement in my girl's voice, I'd say she's going to enjoy working on this project, which is good, because she's a bit confused right now. She decided to take the next semester off from school. I don't blame her. This shit with Kyle is going to get out of hand soon, which will make focusing on classes harder than usual.

Yeah, word on the street (Nick Martelli told Violet) is that the Feds are going to indict Frances Abernathy for her hand in covering up Kyle's crimes. She'll be charged for everything from payoffs to blackmailing officials to doing whatever she could to shield her son from any trouble. She and the Chief of Police at the Tucson Police Department are both under investigation. Apparently, he and Abernathy were childhood friends and thick as thieves. The whole thing sickens me. I'm hopeful once Abernathy goes down, more women will come out with accusations. Guys like Maines don't stop until they're forced to, and the more women who come forward, the more time he'll get. Hopefully life.

We still don't know the deal with the university health center. Hopefully something will happen to explain all of the ways the system failed my girl, and with that, maybe it'll get fixed for the next woman.

CHAPTER 37

VIOLET

I had the *best* day today. Eric and I spent it doing really domestic things. I half expected him to start getting fidgety and doing that sighing thing my dad used to do whenever he spent too much time at the mall with his girls. We knew he'd reached his maximum overload on shopping when the sighing started. But Eric didn't do that. Sure, he looked bored a few times, but he was so patient with me, especially when I shopped for a new paint color for the spare bedroom. I knew I had to make some drastic changes to that room, thanks to the memories of Kyle's attack. How could I put my pets back in there? Animals are smart. They'd sense something was amiss.

Dad must have read my mind too, because as soon as the police tape was gone, he went in there and put down all new flooring. The original hardwood floor was dark and dingy looking. The new stuff is light and airy. It makes it seem like an entirely new room. Tomorrow, Eric and I will embark on our second home project; the first was painting the Adirondack chairs my dad built. We worked well as a team then and did it again today while shopping.

So now my lasagna with homemade sauce is in the oven. Eric's sitting out back in one of my chairs drinking a glass of lemonade. He grabbed a book from my shelf before he went out there and told me to hurry up so I can join him.

I pour myself an iced tea and grab a small salad I made and do just that.

"Hey," I say stepping down to my brick patio.

"Hey," he says back.

"Food's in the oven. Here." I hand him the salad. "I even layered your salad dressings for you."

"What?" he blinks, looking surprised. "It's pre-layered?"

I laugh because he looks sincerely surprised. "Yep."

"You're the best."

Reaching into my back pocket, I pull out a fork and napkin. "What can I say?" I shrug.

"You're a woman of many talents, babe."

"I know."

He looks surprised again. I guess I did sound pretty self-confident just then. Something he's not used to. Heck, I'm not used to it.

"So good," he says, taking his first bite.

I didn't eat much dinner. I couldn't. My stomach is filled with butterflies right now. The last thing I need is food to complicate that situation.

"You cooked. I'll do the dishes," says Eric, scooping up his last bite of pasta. "Food was amazing as usual, Vi."

I think Eric must feel the same nerves, because I noticed he didn't eat as much as he usually does.

I let him do the dishes. The kitchen's too small for both of us in there anyway. While he does that, I take the chance to freshen up in the bathroom. I brush my teeth and hair, pulling out the scrunchy I've got holding it on top of my head. I let it all fall down my back. I also decide to make some changes. Namely in the undergarment area. I wore a white cotton bra and panty set to do my errands. I feel like I need to change into something more, well, sexier. Not just for him. For me too, something my new therapist recommended. She told me not to think about the term sexy as something negative, but rather as something that makes us, me, feel good. Lingerie was her first suggestion. She was right; wearing pretty underwear for myself does make me feel more confident, even if Eric has no idea I've got it on beneath my clothes. Because sexy isn't about how *he* feels about it, it's about how *I* feel about it.

Once I finish up in the bathroom, I step out and find Eric sitting on the bed, his hands clasped in his lap. He looks up at me, and I'd swear he looks shy.

"Hey," I say, smiling.

"Hey."

I step over to him and stand between his legs. His hands immediately come up and rest on my hips. "You sure?" he asks softly.

"I'm sure."

"Tell me what to do."

"Me?" Oh, shoot. "You want me to tell you what to do?"

"You're in charge, angel. You're the boss."

Oh, my gosh.

"Okay." I reach for his hand and tug on it until he's standing. I move around him and sit in the seat he just vacated. "Will you take off your clothes?"

"My clothes?"

"All of them." That time it wasn't a question. I actually sounded rather sure of myself.

"You want me to strip for you, babe?"

I nod. Then I giggle. It can't be helped. "Yep."

Then something amazing happens. He does it. Slowly, ever so slowly, he reaches behind his head and starts to tug at his black T-shirt. As he pulls it up, it slowly reveals his stomach, then his pectorals. His nipples are dark and peaked. I look left and right at his arms. My goodness, the man has beautiful arms. The muscles are moving and flexing and it's a sight to behold.

When the shirt moves up and over his head, he holds it between a finger and his thumb, then drops it out to his side. My mouth is agape. Sure, I've seen him shirtless before and it's always impressive but couple that with the look he's got, the seductive one he's giving me right now, and my body feels charged.

Eric places his hands on the button of his cargo shorts. He pauses. "More?"

I don't even bother making eye contact. "More."

He slowly unbuttons and then unzips his shorts. They're loose on him, so they fall to the floor. Kicking them to the side, Eric stands with his hands on his narrow hips, right on the band of his gray briefs.

"More?" he asks again.

This time I look up. "Yes."

His thick fingers slip beneath the stretchy band of his boxer briefs. I watch as they begin to make the slow trek past his hips. His penis comes into view, and I gasp. That makes Eric stop moving. He's frozen in place.

"No. Don't stop." I look up to see concern all over his face. "Please?"

With a deep breath, he pushes his underwear the rest of the way down, kicking it off like he did the shorts. I take the time to gaze at him. Starting at his feet, I let my eyes move upward. When I get to his penis, I can't help noticing it's gotten longer and larger. It's pointing out toward me. I divert my eyes for a second, but then I move them back, starting at his stomach. I can see how hard he's breathing, and I notice his hands are shaking.

"Will you turn around?"

Releasing a nervous breath, Eric chuckles. "I feel like a piece of meat rotating on a spit."

"Oh." Shoot. I don't want that. "Never mind." I quickly stand and look left, then right, trying to figure out what I should do. "This was a bad idea. I'm sorry."

I move toward the door to give him some privacy, but he stops me. "No." His voice is soft. "I'm sorry, angel. I get it. You've never seen me completely naked."

Blinking, I blurt out, "I've never seen *any* man completely naked." I'm not counting what happened in my spare bedroom. His pants came down but that was it, thank goodness. I couldn't stand to see all of Kyle Maines.

"Shit," Eric mutters, running his fingers through his hair. "I fucked this up."

"No. You didn't. I should have explained instead of acting like some pervert."

"There's nothing perverted about wanting to see my body, honey. I want to see yours. I can't wait to see all of yours. I've just always been on the receiving end of a striptease."

"Oh." I look everywhere but at him. I'm not sure I like the sound of that. Does that mean he goes to strip places?

"I can read your mind, Vi. No, I don't frequent strip clubs." He nudges me backwards. "Sit. Let me finish the show."

"You sure?"

"Positive." He kisses me softly, then moves back to his original spot. "So, you wanted me to spin?"

I'm doing my best to keep myself from running away. I'm

humiliated. He says it's okay now, but I'm just—I don't feel comfortable with any of this anymore.

"Vi?"

I guess I didn't reply to him. I should probably say something. He's standing buck naked in my bedroom. I did that to him. I made him be naked. I'm sitting on the bed again. I'm fiddling and fidgeting, so I put my hands beneath my thighs to stop me from chewing my nails or worse. "You can get dressed."

"Huh?" Eric looks surprised.

"I don't know what I'm doing. I'm embarrassed. I didn't mean to demean you. I just...." Shoot, I'm crying. Not a lot. I'm not sobbing or anything, but the tears have started to run down my cheeks. It can't be helped.

"Babe." Eric takes two steps and is in front of me. Well, his penis is in front of me. I want to look away, but I can't. He's still a little stiff there. Not like he was, but somewhat.

I do my best not to stare. I look up at his face. "I ruined it. Let's not make this more awkward than it has to be. Okay?"

His big hands run through his hair, and a frustrated, gruff sound comes from his mouth. "Come on, Violet."

Uh-oh. He sounds mad.

"Don't cry. You're being ridiculous."

Ridiculous? That was probably not the right thing for him to say. With the courage I didn't know I had, I moved to my right to get away from the penis and stand. "I think you should go stay at your place."

"Why?" Eric sounds surprisingly whiny.

"I need some space. Time to regroup."

"The fuck does that mean?" He moves to the spot where his discarded shorts lie. Reaching down, he picks them up, stepping into one leg. He almost stumbles looking for the other leg hole. Once he's got them where he wants them, he pulls them up over his hips, hiding himself from me. It also means he's going without underwear. Interesting. "Violet?"

I stop staring at his shorts and look up at him. "What?"

"I'm not leaving."

Now what do I do? I wasn't kidding, I need some space. It's how I deal with things. Now that he's practically living with me, I don't have any alone time anymore unless he's at work, and when he's at work I'm usually at work, so that's not the same.

"Okay. I'm just going to go for a drive." I wonder how far away I can get before the sun goes down. Flagstaff?

"No. You're going to stay here and talk this out with me. It's what committed couples do when there's a conflict."

I can tell by the look on his face, he's angry.

"I need some space. You won't leave, so I will." I step around him and out of the bedroom and straight to my front door. Taking my purse in hand, I reach out for my fleece jacket and open the door, stepping out into a cool December evening.

"Violet." Eric sounds testy. "Don't just walk away. We need to talk."

I don't turn; I just keep walking. "I'll be back in an hour. Then we'll talk."

"No. Jesus. Violet?"

"Don't worry. We're good." *Or are we?* "I need to be alone."

CHAPTER 38

Eric

What the fuck just happened?

One minute I'm standing naked and semi-erect while my girl, looking fucking gorgeous, sits all prim and proper on the bed as she tells me to strip.

"I know what happened. I opened my goddamn mouth. Fuck!" I yell. It must have been too loud, because CB starts barking, and Stella, who was lounging on the couch, jumps up and scrambles out of the room.

I push the front door open and watch as her car drives off into the sunset, literally. I look down at Max sitting at my feet. "I fucked up, Max."

When he whimpers, I pick him up and take him with me into the bedroom. Lying on the bed, I place him beside me. I should talk about this to someone. I need advice. I'm not handling all of this with Violet the right way.

"Who should I call, Max?" He doesn't answer—he doesn't have to. I can read his mind. "Good idea."

Reaching over to the nightstand, I open the drawer and grab my phone. "Keely, it is."

"Hello?"

"Keely, hey."

"Who is this?"

"Eric."

"What?" she says loudly. "What's wrong? Is something wrong with Vi?"

"Calm down." Shit. Should I ask her? She may overreact. This could totally blow up in my face. But who else is there? Keely knows Violet better than anyone. "I need advice."

"Oh. Okay. What'd she do?"

"She left. Said she needed space."

"Okaaay. Can you back up there, buddy? What happened before that?"

Shit. "Earlier today, she told me she was ready to be more..." What word did she use again? Ah. "Intimate."

"Intimate. Okay. Big step for her. Go on."

"So, to start it off, she asked me to strip."

Keely bursts out laughing.

"It's not funny. She was upset."

"Upset. Why? What'd you do?"

"Nothing. I did it. I didn't realize she'd never seen a naked man before, so when she told me to spin, I told her I felt like a piece of meat rotating on a spit."

I heard Keely gasp, then she said, "Oh, shit."

"What?" Why does Keely's reaction cause chills to run down my spine?

"You embarrassed her. Didn't you?"

"No." Yes. "I didn't mean to. Shit. I didn't. I was just talking to her. I'm allowed to talk, right?" Now I'm getting pissed again. I do not understand women in general, and Violet specifically.

"She was opening up to you."

"Jesus, I *know*." I feel my eyes burn a little. It must be dusty. I'll clean up after I get off the phone. "She asked me to leave but I refused. That's when she said she was going for a drive."

There's silence on her end. It goes on so long I'm afraid she hung up.

"Keely?"

"Shh, I'm thinking."

So, I wait. And wait. After what feels like an hour, Keely finally speaks. "You're going to have to wait her out."

That's it? That's all I get from her. "Like wait for her here?" I'm confused.

"You're going to have to wait for her there. Plus, you'll need to wait until she's ready to talk about it. She's like an onion."

What the fuck does that mean? "Huh?"

"Not in the sense that she smells or she makes you cry, although, I believe I heard you sniffle a minute ago."

No comment.

"Violet's complicated."

"No shit."

"Vi's got layers. Some of those layers are sweet and kind while others are dark and scary."

Jesus.

"You won't really get all of her until you know about *all* the layers."

I'm sensing some bad news coming.

"She tell you about the assault? The first one?"

"Yes. Some. But I'm guessing not all."

"She'll tell you when she's ready. See? Onion."

"Violet is an onion."

"We're all onions. Lucky for you, Violet is a sweet Vidalia."

"You've lost me."

"That's okay. The trick is not to lose Violet."

I keep my mouth shut, hoping there's real advice coming.

"Make some popcorn, cue up one of her movies, and wait for her. She'll talk when she's ready."

Waiting for advice was the right thing to do. "Popcorn. Movie." Got it. Damn, I wish I had flowers. I wonder if any florists deliver at this time? I could make her a card. Or better yet, I could write her a letter. A *love* letter.

"Thanks, Keely."

"Welcome. Don't fuck it up."

I chuckle, then hang up. I've got shit to do.

CHAPTER 39

VIOLET

I was gone longer than an hour. I drove out to Lake Powell, to the spot where Ian proposed to Agatha, and parked my car. I was able to see the lake from my vantage point. It was quiet, probably because it's cold up here, much colder up here than it was at my place. I'm glad I grabbed my jacket.

I pushed my seat back so I could lie back and think. I ran through the events of the evening and winced when I recalled his words: "I feel like a piece of meat." Even thinking of the words makes me feel terrible. If the situation had been reversed, feeling like meat would have been the least of my worries.

After spending time alone, I decide running away was probably not the best way to handle things with Eric. When I pull up to my little house, Eric's motorcycle is there, but his truck is gone.

"He left." My shoulders slump. He did as I asked. He went home. My heart dropped in my chest. At least, that's what it feels like. He just did what I asked him to do, and that makes me feel like crap. Pushing the door to my car open, I step out slowly. With keys in hand, I unlock my door and am greeted by two furry friends, Max and CB. "Hey, guys." I sound pretty mopey, but that's how I feel.

Setting my purse near the door, I kick off my flats and walk through the living room on the way to my bedroom. I stop halfway through because of the folded piece of paper leaning on a bowl of popcorn. Handwritten on the paper is my name.

Oh, no. "He wrote me a note." I hesitate before picking it up. I'm scared of its contents. Well, scared isn't the right word. Terrified. But I have to do it. I need to hear him out. Picking it up, I slowly open it and read.

Violet,

I love you. Don't give up on me. I'm a dumbass. I say things without thinking sometimes. I know what we were doing was significant. I shouldn't have been so flippant.

I didn't mean to crowd you. I get what you meant by needing space. You have a right to that. But since you aren't here, I need to say what I need to say.

I didn't mean to make you feel embarrassed or upset. If I'm being honest, I'm not sure how to handle situations like this with you. You've been through two traumatic experiences in your young life and I haven't.

Unless you talk to me, tell me how you're feeling and what you expect from me, how are we going to make this work? By the same token, if I can't tell you how I'm feeling, how is that going to work?

My only answer for any of this is to tell you how much I love and admire you. You're the strongest person I've ever met. You're also the most beautiful, elegant, and sweetest woman I've ever known. You're smart and creative and curious and loyal. On top of all that, you're a little stubborn. That's not a bad thing. I like that side of you. No, I love that side of you.

You take care of everyone in your life, and I feel privileged to be one of those people. In the short time I've known you, you have treated me with love and respect. I can't believe how lucky I am. I hit the jackpot, and I'm not just talking about your cooking.

Please forgive me, angel. I need you, probably more than you need me.

I waited for you for an hour. When you didn't come home, I decided to head out. I'll be back, though. I'm not giving up. I won't ever give up on you, Violet, or on us.

I love you. Eric

"Wow," I whisper softly.

"Hey," says a deep voice behind me.

I jump at the sound. "Dang it, Eric." Placing my palm on my frantically beating heart, I laugh in relief. "Stop sneaking up on me."

"Sorry."

I look up at him and frown, because he's frowning. I need to change that. "Thank you for the letter."

"You're welcome," he says, holding out a bouquet of flowers. Not just any flowers. They're purple roses. "I got these for you." He looks nervous and his laugh reinforces that notion. "I can't believe the Page supermarket had purple roses, but they did."

I can't believe it either. "They're beautiful."

Holding out his other hand, I see he's got something else. "I got you this too."

It's the brand of my shampoo.

"I noticed you were almost out, so I bought you some more."

Honest to goodness, it's one of the most thoughtful things he could have done. I keep forgetting to buy more. Without thinking, I practically jump on top of him. He has to step back due to the force. With my legs wrapped around him and my face in his neck, I start to talk fast.

"I love you too, Eric. I'm sorry. I shouldn't have left. I should have just told you how I was feeling. I'm just not used to that. I'm a thinker. I needed to run through what happened. I won't do that again. If you want to hear what I'm thinking, I'll tell you."

"I want to hear, honey. If you don't talk to me, how will I know?"

Pulling back my head, I look into his steel-gray eyes. "Will you do the same?"

He whispers, "I will."

I kiss him. And kiss him, and kiss him some more. My tongue is in his mouth before he's got a chance to set down the flowers and shampoo. When his tongue meets mine, I feel him grow hard between us.

God, I want him.

Loosening my legs, I lower myself to the ground. Taking the shampoo from him, I place it on the coffee table. I do the same with the roses. "I'll put those in water later."

Taking his hand in mine, I pull him toward my bedroom.

"Okay," he says absently. I think I've got his undivided attention.

Once we cross into the room, I stop. "I'm sorry about earlier. I was really nervous, and when you said you felt like meat, I was embarrassed. I don't handle embarrassment well. I never have. I respect the fact that you told me how you were feeling. I didn't mean to make you feel that way."

I haven't been looking at him during my little speech, but I do now. "I just wanted to see you naked." I shrug. "You're gorgeous, and I wanted to see you."

Without another word, Eric reaches around me, wrapping me up in his arms. I'm lifted from the ground and moved to the bed.

"Sit," he says with a smile.

I sit.

Eric moves back to the spot he was in hours ago. He does the same as before; he reaches behind his back and slowly starts to remove his shirt.

"Eric. You don't—"

"Shh, baby. I've got you."

So I shush. He's got me.

When he's completely nude again, I can't help noticing how much bigger he is down there than he was earlier. And he was big then. When he slowly begins to turn, I gasp when I see his backside. It's breathtaking. Yes, I've seen his muscled back before. It ripples and moves as he works. I stared at it for a long time like the time he helped paint the new patio chairs weeks ago. But, couple that with his bottom? Oh, my goodness. His bottom is firm and round, plus he's got those little dimples right above each cheek. I want to kiss those.

"You like?" he asks, swaying his hips back and forth.

"Yes. I definitely like. You should walk around naked all the time." *Oh, shoot. I said that aloud, didn't I?* I press my palm against my mouth and start to giggle. I can't seem to stop.

"I'd be happy to as long as you do it with me."

Oh.

I watch as Eric starts to slowly walk toward me. "Your turn."

Oh. "Eric, I...." I feel my face heat. "I'm not ready for that." I point to the spot where he disrobed.

"I'll help." Eric pulls me up to my feet. Next, his hands move to my hips. "We'll do it together."

Okay. I lift my arms straight up into the air as he works my shirt slowly up past my chest, my head, arms, and then off, landing somewhere in the floor. Sliding his finger over the lace of my bra, the one I changed into earlier, he says, "Pretty."

"Thanks." I choke the word out.

My goodness. His eyes are mesmerizing with lids so hooded, I'd say he looked sleepy except for the fact that they're dilated so much, they've turned dark as night. The usual steely gray has changed to a charcoal hue.

His hands slide down my sides. His palms take their time moving around to my back and then to my stomach until they're at the band of my shorts. Before making another move, Eric looks into my eyes. "You sure?"

I nod.

"Words, Violet. I need words."

"Yes." I place my hands on the top of his to help him push my shorts down my legs. I kick them off until I'm standing in front of him in only my underwear.

"Matching panties," he groans. "Jesus, you're so fucking beautiful, Violet."

Thank you. The words don't come out. I place my hands on his upper arms and run them down to his wrists. Wrists that are shaking. "Eric? Are you okay? You're shaking."

"Nervous." He laughs. "And excited."

I can see he's excited. I look down at his penis, and it's now long and standing completely erect. I press myself to him and feel it between us. Moving to my tiptoes, I kiss him like I did before. Eric lets me. His hands are on my waist. They haven't moved. He's waiting, I guess.

Pulling back a little, I whisper. "I need for you to take over, Eric. Make love to me. If I need for you to stop, I'll tell you. Just don't be hesitant with me, please. I need your strength and your knowledge right now. Let me just feel."

Eric says nothing for what seems like a long time. Finally, he asks, "You're sure?"

"Positive."

Eric's hands move around me and up my back to my bra. He fiddles with it until I feel it loosen. He slowly pushes the straps down my arms until I'm revealed to him. My breasts are on the small side. I hope he likes that.

"Jesus," Eric groans. "Fucking perfect, Vi."

He kisses my lips, then my cheek and down my neck. He spends extra time there, which makes me squirm. His lips on my neck feel amazing. He kisses down my collarbone until he finally, finally gets to my breasts. Licking one, then the other, I squeak at the feeling. Eric pauses, so I place my palm on the back of his head, putting a little pressure on him to keep going.

I moan as he suckles me into his mouth. I can feel it down to my core. I press myself against him, wanting more. He moves to the other breast and does the same thing. His hand cups the lonely breast, squeezing gently, then his fingers slide over the tip, back and forth. I'm in sensation overload.

"Eric, don't stop."

But, he does. He's a cruel, cruel man. I forget about that when his fingers slide into the band of my underwear. He looks up at me but says nothing. I simply nod. He pushes them down all the way to the floor, and I step out of them.

I'm naked.

I'm completely nude in front of Eric Gustafson.

I look down, because Eric's on his knees in front of me. His hands reach around me until one hand is on each side of my bottom. Giving me a squeeze, he leans in and presses his nose over my front. He inhales, and I get the urge to pull away, but when he groans, I remain still.

"You're the most beautiful thing I've ever seen, Violet. Your skin is so soft. Your body is all womanly and curvy. I can't believe I get to be here with you."

If any other man had said that to me, I'd probably roll my eyes, but not with Eric. He means it. Every. Single. Word.

"Thank you." I say softly.

CHAPTER 40

Eric

"Thank you." Her voice is so soft, I barely hear her.

I kiss her below her belly button and let my lips move up, taking a moment to kiss and suck on her nipples again. She likes that. Standing, I lean down and kiss her lips softly. "Lie down, honey."

She sits on the bed, then scoots her body toward the center. Laying her head on her pillow, she watches as I reach for my jeans. Retrieving a condom, I hold it out in front of her. "Condom."

"Oh," she says nervously. "Good. I'm not on birth control."

I want to ask her if she wants kids someday, but that'll have to wait. My dick is so hard, it's painful. I've been leaking precum since the second I unhooked her bra. Moving up, I press her legs apart gently so I can move between them.

"Okay?" I ask.

"Yes." She smiles up at me and I see it all over her face. Trust.

Leaning down, I kiss her neck, a favorite spot, then up to her mouth. I kiss her upper lip and nibble on her bottom lip. Opening my mouth, I slide my tongue over hers until she opens to me. We've kissed a lot since I've lived with her. Every time is better than the last. Tonight is no exception, even though she's nervous as hell.

Reaching down, I gently slide my fingers through her. She's wet, but not enough. I want her to tell me she's ready. With the skill of years of too many one-night stands, I use my middle finger to coax her clit out from hiding. I feel her move her hips to the rhythm created by my hand. I move my finger to her center and slowly slide it inside. Jesus, she's tight. I don't say a word, though. Ordinarily I'm a talker during sex, but I'm afraid to say the wrong thing. Pumping the finger in and out, I use my thumb to press against her clit.

It's then that she finally speaks. She says breathlessly, "Eric."

My name has never sounded so good. "I feel you, honey. You gonna come on my fingers?"

"No. I want you. Now, Eric. Please?" Her voice sounds like a whimper.

Removing my hand, I reach for the condom, tear it open, and slide it down my shaft. Not gonna lie, I was about to lose it just from hearing her little sounds. Leaning back down, I kiss her softly. "You sure?"

"Yes. Geesh, Eric. Hurry."

I release a small laugh and obey. Using my hand, I line myself up to her and slowly begin to press inside.

Jesus. She's perfect.

"Okay?" I ask, holding back my need to thrust inside.

"Yes. More." Her hips move up and closer to me, essentially forcing more of me inside.

I press harder until I'm completely inside. I hold my breath for a second to keep myself from exploding. That is, until she says in a demanding tone, "You need to move, Eric. Please."

"As you wish, Vi. You're perfect." The words come out with a grunt. Moving faster with each stroke, I reach a pace that surprises even me. Violet is lifting her hips with each thrust until I feel her squeeze me so tightly, I have to stop.

"Eric," she breathes.

Once her grip on my cock loosens, I pull out and in again. I'd love to make her come again, but I'm only going to last a minute or two more. In and out I go a few more times. With one last thrust, I come, and I come hard.

"Oh, shit," I mumble. *Perfect.*

When my dick starts to soften, I look down at my girl. I can't believe how beautiful she is. Her hair is a wild mess around her head, like an auburn halo. I wish I could see it like that all day, every day. Her skin is flushed, and there's a sheen all over her. She's, in a word, breathtaking. "You okay?"

"Yeah." Her smile takes up her entire face from her eyes down to her mouth. "Never better."

Me neither. Never better.

CHAPTER 41

*V*IOLET

"You ready for the wedding?" asks Eric over breakfast.

My sister Sadie and her fiancé, Charlie, are getting married tomorrow. On Christmas Eve. "Yeah, you?"

"Yep. I pulled my suit out of the back of my closet. It's at the cleaners. I'll pick it up later today."

I take a moment to look at him. My goodness, the man is perfect dressed in plaid sleep pants and an old Gustafson Custom Motorcycles T-shirt. This one is white. Eric's got a bunch of the same shirt in a variety of colors. I've taken possession of a few of them myself. They're worn in perfectly, so they're soft to sleep in. They usually don't last long though; Eric and I, well, we like the sex. We've done it every night except for the few days last week I had my monthly bill (my period, in case you were curious). When that happened and I wasn't having cramps, I touched him. I made him ejaculate with my hands. It was thrilling. I haven't used my mouth on him yet, but he's used his mouth a lot. He likes to do it, and I'm not about to discourage him.

"You're blushing. What're you thinking about?"

I'm just about to take a sip of my coffee when he asks that.

"Nothing," I choke out.

"You sure?" Eric reaches out and runs his palm over my thigh. "Because I've seen that look before. Last night, to be exact."

"I was just thinking about Christmas."

"And my package?" His eyebrows move up and down.

"No." I laugh. "Perv."

"I'm not a pervert. I love you and your sexy body, and I think you love me and mine too." He looks almost affronted.

I turn away shyly, admitting, "It's true. I do."

"I know." Eric has moved closer until our lips are an inch apart. "You wanna?" He nods toward the opening between the kitchen and living room.

"We don't have to be anywhere..." I can't believe I'm contemplating this.

"I'm off work. You're off from the bakery."

"So, maybe we should get off together?" I blush hard after that unexpected statement from my own lips.

It doesn't faze Eric. "Exactly."

Eric stands, pulling me up with him. Then, before I can blink, he's got me in a fireman's hold and is stomping toward our bedroom.

"Eric!" I screech. "Your back."

"Shh, this is romantic."

I laugh, then stare at his pretty ass as it moves back and forth, back and forth. When he stops walking, I feel myself being lifted into the air and fall flat on my back onto the bed, bouncing a couple of times. I'm not able to protest, because Eric's reaching for my sleep shorts. I lift my hips to help, then I reach for my pajama top and pull it off as well. While I do that, Eric is out of his shirt and sleep pants, leaving us both very naked.

"Eric," I breathe. My goodness, he's a sight.

He reaches into the nightstand, pulling out a condom. I gaze as he tears open the wrapper and slips it on. I've helped him do that a few times. It's kind of erotic. I like helping.

Once it's on, Eric winks. "Time for something new." He leans forward, placing both of his hands on my waist. I laugh as he flips me over until I'm on my stomach. Blinking a few times, I stare at the top of my comforter. A sense of panic washes over me and I'm not sure why. When he starts to lift my hips up, it hits me.

"No." I shake my head. "No, no, no." I start to move my body, using my fingers to claw at the bed, attempting to escape. "No." I'm up on my knees now. "No."

I feel Eric's hands on me, and I know he's saying something, but I can't hear him. The room is loud, or maybe it's my ears. Everything sounds foggy. I feel him release me. *Move. Move. Move.* I'm off the bed and onto the floor on the other side in seconds. As fast as I can, I crawl to the corner next to my nightstand and wrap myself up in my arms, saying one more time, "No."

I've got my face buried in my arms. I'm not sure how long I'm there. When I feel a touch, I wince, but I lift my head and see Eric. He's blurry, but I can see he's got on pants again. When did he do that?

"Vi?" His voice is soft and tentative. "Say something, please?"

I blink until his face comes into better focus. He looks scared. My God, what did I do? "I'm sorry."

"What happened? What did I do?"

I stare into his concerned eyes and shake my head. "You didn't know."

"Know what?"

I stare more.

"Vi. Tell me."

"He...."

Eric's face changes then. From scared to something much more painful. Guilt. "Jesus, Violet. I'm so sorry."

I reach my hand out to his. "It's not your fault. You didn't know. Heck, *I* didn't know that would happen." I've put this off too long. I need to tell him. Everything.

Eric reaches out and grabs the comforter from the bed. Wrapping it around me, he sits in front of me on the floor so we're facing each other We sit in silence until I begin. "I was a freshman. It was my first party..."

He sits in complete silence, listening. I tell him what Kyle did, what he said, and everything afterward. Eric never stops me once. When I'm done, he's crying. I'm not talking a few tears running down his cheeks. No, he's crying so hard his shoulders are shaking, his hands are covering his face, and his head is in my lap. I run my fingers through his long hair and let him cry. I've never seen another person as vulnerable as Eric is right this minute. His anguish is palpable. And I feel responsible for that. Now it's not just me dealing with my past. It's both of us.

CHAPTER 42

ERIC

I have no words to explain how I feel right now. I'm overwhelmed by her story. Not just the story, but by the strength it's taken her to tell it. To me.

Don't get me wrong, I'm glad she did. But I've got regrets. Big ones. I should never have let that asshole make it out of Vi's house alive.

I'm still curled up in her lap like a child, but she doesn't care and neither do I. It was my instinct to go to her like this. She comforted me when I needed it the most. But now that I've stopped crying and I've wiped my tears, my hand is running up and down her bare leg. "I'm sorry you had to go through all that, Vi."

"Me too." Her fingers are still running through my hair. It relaxes me. "I should have told you sooner. I'm sorry I freaked out earlier."

"Me too, to all of that. If I'd known...."

"I know. I'm sorry. I never expected to react that way."

I sigh. "Let's not be sorry, okay? I never want us to be sorry. We'll learn from this like we have lots of other things."

"Like the fact that you hate mayo." She chuckles.

"Hate isn't a strong enough word."

"Yet, you like Ranch dressing."

He huffs. "It's not the same."

"Uh-huh." She snorts. "Just please stop throwing the mayo away. I like it, and it's expensive."

"Fine," I say, defeated.

"I love you, Eric."

"I love you too."

"Wanna take a nap? I'm exhausted."

"Will you still play with my hair?" Yeah, I sound like a pussy, but I don't give a fuck.

"Of course, babe."

I love it when she calls me babe.

CHAPTER 43

"To Sadie and Charlie," my dad says, raising his glass of bubbly.

Everyone else in Laura Ashbury's house repeats, "To Sadie and Charlie!"

The wedding was beautiful. The happy couple opted for something small in Laura's backyard. It was the perfect spot with a view of the breathtaking Arizona landscape as the backdrop. And since she didn't want to choose between her sisters, Polly stood up with her and Cortland with his big brother, Charlie. It made sense. Polly is her best friend and she's married to Cort.

I scan the large room full of Sadie and Charlie's family and friends. There's a lot of us squeezed into the space. I'm content hiding back in one of the corners. I like it because it enables me to people watch. I see Dad and Deb talking with Charlie's parents; Dad's arm is around Deb's waist. He's so happy. I may never get tired of seeing them together.

I locate the bride and groom next. They're getting ready to

cut the cake. Polly and I made it so she didn't have to. It's not as pretty as one of Sadie's cakes, but I insisted the bride should not make her own cake. Polly agreed.

As for the rest of it, Sadie stuck with traditional Christmas decorations for her ceremony. It made organizing the wedding so much easier, since Laura, Charlie's grandmother, had everything here. Laura even hired a professional decorator to set it up for the holiday.

I squish my nose up at the notion of hiring someone to do that job. I love decorating for Christmas, and it was even more fun this year with Eric's help. It turns out he loves Christmas too, and he even had some of his own decorations from his childhood in a box in his apartment—things he kept after his parents died. We spent an entire Sunday after Thanksgiving setting up the tree, decorating the house inside and out, and shopping for holiday collars and sweaters for Max, CB, Stella, and Sherman. Max and CB were thrilled. The cats? Not so much.

"You having fun?" asks Lainie as she sidles up next to me. Her pregnant belly is getting quite large, since she's due in less than two months.

"Yes. Are you?"

"If my feet didn't hurt so much and I didn't want to eat everything in sight, then I'd say yes." She chuckles.

I'm not able to reply, because Keely and Agatha move in next. "Hey, bitches," says Keely with a laugh. "How's it hangin'?"

I roll my eyes then laugh. Keely is so inappropriate, but I wouldn't change one hair on her head. "You having a good time, Keels?"

"Sure. I'm happy for my sister. If she weren't almost as big as Lainie, I'd say she was enjoying it too."

"Hey!" replies Lainie defensively. "Just you wait, Keely."

"No way. Not for a long time." Keely smirks. "Well, not for

a while, anyway. You can all make fun of me when I've got a baby-sized version of Nick Martelli inside me. I have a feeling he was a huge baby."

"You didn't ask him?" Lainie seems shocked.

"Nah. I'd rather be surprised."

"Well, Keeton was almost nine pounds."

I almost swallow my tongue at those words. I wonder how big Eric was.

Lainie laughs when she sees my expression. "According to Keeton, Eric was just over eight pounds. It was Molly who was the big one."

"Molly? She's tiny."

"She was over ten pounds."

"No," I gasp. I could never deliver a ten-pound baby. Who could?

My mind has wandered into the land of big babies with the last name Gustafson when I hear Agatha, "Hey, you're wearing Mom's locket."

Instinctively, I raise my hand and touch it. I've missed wearing it. When dad gave me my gift from mom on my sixteenth birthday, I just smiled. I knew it. I always played with that necklace. I'd sit on her lap and open and close it a million times. It was so pretty on her. She always promised me it would be mine someday.

Lainie looks confused. "I thought you said you lost it."

"No," Keely interrupts. "I told you it was in her jewelry box. The chain was broken."

"You are so nosey," I mutter.

Looking at each of my sisters, I say what I should have said months ago. "It was broken. It happened during the assault in college. I found the broken chain and the locket in my bra when I got home. It's been sitting in my jewelry box ever since. Well, until last week. I took the chain to a jeweler. He was able to fix it. Today is the first day I've worn it." I still don't know if I'll wear it every day, but for things like this, my sister's wedding, yes. It means my mom is here with me, with us.

"Shit," mutters Keely.

"Wow," says Agatha.

"Oh, honey," coos Lainie. "You're so brave, Vi."

"I know." I shrug. "I really am."

That makes them all laugh. I'm not sure why. I meant it. I arch my brow and give each of them the evil eye. "I *am* brave."

They all stop laughing.

"We know," Keely says suddenly. "We know. You're the bravest and strongest and prettiest one. We're all in awe of you. Never doubt that for one fucking second, Violet."

"Here, here," Agatha says with a raised glass. "Now, let's party, bitches." She turns to Lainie. "Oops, you can't. Sorry."

"Hey," Lainie whines as she walks away with the other two. "I can still have fun."

"Good luck with that," mocks Keely. "I'll have a beer for you. That's the kind of sister I am. I'm selfless like that."

"Bullshit," snaps Lainie.

Smiling at them as they walk away, I feel his arm slide around me, pulling me closer to his side. "You doin' okay?"

Since the thing yesterday, Eric must have asked me that question fifty times. "I'm great. How're you?"

"Good. Pretty wedding," he says, nodding at the room filled with family and friends.

"Beautiful."

Turning, he looks into my eyes. "What kind of wedding are we gonna have?"

I nearly choke at the question. "Huh?"

"I said," he smirks, "what kind of wedding are we gonna have?"

I'm speechless for a second until I turn the question around to him. "I'm not sure. What do you want?"

He shrugs. "Something small like this, except I want you to walk down an aisle on your dad's arm. I don't want to see your dress beforehand, because I want to get a glimpse of you when you start walking down the aisle, and I know the sight of you is gonna make me cry. I'll get to see what kind of dress you picked and the look on your face when you see me all gussied up in a tuxedo."

I feel my eyes get a little misty.

"I want you to have all of your sisters and as many friends as you want to stand up with you because you are loved, my sweet girl. All of these people will want to share that with you."

Crud. I'm crying.

"I want us to write our own vows, because I want everyone to know what you mean to me. I don't want to use someone else's words."

I sniffle. "Okay."

"And I want us to go on a dream honeymoon. Anywhere you want to go. Then, when we get back, I want us to build our dream home and start our family. I'm thinking three kids. What do you think about that?"

I sniffle, then laugh. "I think you've given this some thought."

"I wouldn't call it mere thoughts. It's more of an obsession."

"Well, it sounds perfect. Where do I sign up?"

"Patience, my sweet girl. Patience," he says as he kisses my forehead. "Let's give your sister her day. Then it's ours."

EPILOGUE

ONE YEAR LATER...

"Merry Christmas, Violet." Eric kisses me as he sits on the floor next to me as we sort through our gifts.

"Merry Christmas to you." I reach deep beneath the tree, looking for the first gift for him to open. Holding it out to him, I say, "Here, open this first."

Handing me my own gift, he says, "Then you open this first."

I nod at the long, slim rectangular box in his hand.

He tears at the paper like a savage. He did the same thing with his birthday gifts. It's kind of funny since I'm a "save the paper" kind of unwrapper.

As soon as he tosses the metallic paper aside, he rips open the box and stares. His mouth is moving, but no words are coming out.

"Eric?"

"Are you serious?" He finally speaks. I can't tell from his tone if it's a good thing or not.

"Yes?"

"Yes or no, Violet? You're either pregnant or you're not." He holds up the pregnancy test stick for me to see.

"Yes. I'm pregnant."

Before I can even blink once, Eric is up on his feet, lifting me off the ground.

"Are you fucking serious?" he screams. Wrapping me up in his arms, he squeezes me tight. "You mean it, Vi? We're pregnant?"

"Yes," I say with a giggle.

"You mean it?" He spins me around and around our new living room. Luckily, there's plenty of room for spinning since the place is huge—four times the size of my little house.

"I mean it. I just took the test yesterday. I'll need to go to the doctor to confirm it, but I'm 99 percent sure."

Eric kisses my neck, my cheek, my lips, then does it again. "The best Christmas present ever." He stops. "Second best. The first best was when you said 'yes' to my proposal last Christmas. This is a very close second."

I close my eyes, remembering last Christmas morning. We did what we're doing right now. We woke up and sat on the floor beside the tree. We exchanged gifts. I can't remember what they were, but I know his were thoughtful.

When I thought we were finished, Eric reached into the limbs of the tree and pulled out a small, square box.

"Violet?" he asked, hesitantly. "I meant what I said yesterday. We gave your sister her day, now it's ours."

I remember him popping open the box and me gasping. Inside sat the prettiest little diamond ring I've ever seen. It was a rectangular cut diamond set in white gold and on either side of the diamond were two smaller purple stones that he informed me were amethyst, but he preferred to call them violet stones.

No matter what they're called, I love it.

"I'm glad," I say, wrapping my arms around him. "I'm guessing I'm not very far along. I haven't felt sick or anything."

He sets me on the ground, but his hands are still on me. His palm is now over my stomach. "The doctor will be able to tell, right?" he asks absently as he rubs a hand over my belly. "Our child is here." Eric's voice is soft.

I place mine over his. "It is."

Looking into my eyes, he smiles. "You've made me so happy. Since the second I met you, I knew you were my girl. I can't believe how lucky I am."

"Me too, Eric." And I mean that. He's stood by me during all of the good and the bad. In the last year, there's been more of the latter, thanks to Kyle Maines and his evil mother. I believe that's *almost* all behind us now. Unless there's an appeal.

Two months ago, Kyle was convicted on six counts of rape in the first degree. A lot more than six women came forward, but the state's attorney only felt confident that he'd get a conviction on six; mine wasn't one of them. The only good part about that was I didn't have to testify. At the insistence of his father, now divorced from Frances Abernathy, Kyle pled guilty to the assault at my house, which means that crime didn't make it to trial. I had the option to sue him for damages in civil court but chose not to. I wanted it to be over. *Finally.* Knowing Kyle will be spending years behind bars is enough for me.

As for the former lieutenant governor, she was indicted in federal court for her role in the conspiracy to cover up her son's crimes. She and the Tucson Chief of Police have both been charged, since she played a role in hiring him, her old school friend. Convenient, considering the chief was hired the same year Kyle started at the university. Which means she knew. She knew about Kyle. She knew he was a predator. It's despicable.

Anyway, she along with several Tucson police detectives were charged in connection with the rapes at the U of SE

Arizona. She also bribed a number of people, including two staff members at the university health center. It was enough money to pay their tuition and fees. I can see why they'd be tempted. Unfortunately, it looks like they'll be charged too, eventually.

I've learned a lot about all of this legal stuff, like the fact that it takes charges longer to be brought forward in federal cases than state crimes. I think the FBI wants to make sure they convict Abernathy, so they're taking their time. Her trial is supposed to be coming up in the next few months. I'll cross my fingers she gets lots of time behind bars to think about what she's done.

I'm jogged out of my thoughts by Eric's voice. "We going to tell your dad today?"

Dad and Deb are coming over for brunch later. Since everyone else is home with their little families, I invited the two of them over.

I guess an update on my dad's love life is in order. Deb is now living in Page. We were all a little surprised when she told us she was opening a second shop up here. But I guess her moving up here makes more sense than Dad moving far away from his daughters and grandchildren. So Deb bought a piece of land next to Gustafson Custom Motorcycles, which means it won't be long until there will be a custom auto shop next to Keeton's place.

I thought Eric would have been upset with the competition, but according to him Deb is like a sister. He's happy to support her choice to set up shop here. I was relieved because it meant that this thing between Deb and Dad is going strong. So strong, she's adding a spot for a woodworking shop in her new building. Dad will still do his carpentry work like he usually does, but he's planning on going part-time soon. Then he'll have more time to do what he wants—build furniture.

He'll be successful too. He did all of the finish work on our place, plus he designed and built the beautiful kitchen and bath-room cabinetry. Actually, our entire home is perfect. There are large floor-to-ceiling windows that span two levels, all facing Lake Powell, which you can see perfectly from the upper level; the level that houses three bedrooms and two baths. Downstairs is the kitchen, dining and family room all in one. It's also where our master bedroom and bath are located. An office, laundry room, and a second full bath are also downstairs. There's enough space for both sides of our family to congregate, but not so big we could host a wedding here.

Which reminds me. I scan the room and lay eyes on the photograph that hangs in the dining area. Actually, it's one of many photos. Photos of our wedding, of Aggie's wedding, of my niece, Rachel Montgomery Gustafson. It's fitting that the first-born girl be named after our mom. Lainie was hysterical with happy tears when we all agreed it was the right thing to do. And next to that is a picture of my nephew, Finnigan Robert Ashbury, born last April 11, a week later than expected. I'm pretty sure Sadie tried to bribe her obstetrician to do whatever it took to deliver earlier, but Charlie, being a doctor himself, talked her off the ledge.

It won't be long until Aggie and Ian's little addition is added to the wall. She's due next month. We already know it's a girl to be named Lily. As for Keely? She's happily married to Nick with no plans to "get knocked up" anytime soon. I think Nick's ready, but they'll have to work that out together. No way am I getting involved with any of that. Keely told us all to mind our own business. So that's what I'm doing even though, now, I wish she'd decide it was time. I'd love for our kids to grow up together. Selfish, I know.

As I continue to peruse our photos, I smile when I see the one of Eric when he was about eight. My goodness, he was a beautiful boy even then. If he'd lived in Page then, I probably would have loved him back in middle school. There are lots of pictures of the Gustafson clan on our walls, and I never tire of looking at them.

But my favorite picture is the one of us at our wedding. We did it exactly like Eric described. We married in the same church as Lainie and Eric. I wore my mom's wedding dress, since I was the only one who was tall enough to wear it. Keely thought I should change it, have it altered so it was different for my wedding, but I disagreed. I wore it just like she did. I paired it with her locket, which made it perfect. I carried purple roses down the aisle in one hand while the other held on to my father's arm. Eric was breathtaking in his black tux and purple bow tie.

The minute he saw me, he cried, which made me cry, which made my dad cry, and then it made my sisters cry. You get the idea. It wasn't pretty, but it was perfect. Then came the vows. I framed them and have them hanging next to the picture. I thought Eric would cringe that I framed his words and hung them in our dining room, but he just smiled and blushed a little bit. He was proud of his vows, and so was I.

Violet, the day I met you, my life changed. In one second, I knew. I knew it when my heart started beating double time when I looked into your eyes. I knew it when you surprised us all with your "that's what she said" joke.

Then, on the night we stole Andrew's BBQ grill and it happened all over again, I knew it wasn't a fluke—that there was something special about you, something that couldn't be explained.

Before you I never believed in love at first sight. But, I'm here to tell you—to tell you all here today—that it's real. The love of my life appeared out of nowhere like an

*angel. The only credit I'll take for any of this is believing
it could happen and going for it. If I hadn't, I know I'd
walk this earth missing out on the best part of me.*
        You.

Oh, my goodness. Rereading it makes me cry all over again. He's so wonderful. Sure, he's not perfect. He leaves his dirty socks everywhere. *Literally* everywhere. I find them in sofa cushions, behind the toilet, in the pantry, and so on. He blames the dogs, but that just isn't possible. Besides, Max has never been fond of socks. CB? Well, maybe. It doesn't matter. I love them all, so even if they do like to leave socks everywhere, I'll pick them up happily because they're my boys.

Speaking of our furry family, we officially adopted CB and Carl the one-winged parrot. I couldn't bear the thought of them having any other forever home than ours. We still foster pets. It can't be helped. We love them, and now that we have some land, I hope to foster chickens and other outdoor animals. I'll just need to talk it over with Eric. Or maybe I'll just surprise him someday.

"Hey," Eric says behind me. "Whatcha writing?"

"Our epilogue."

"Our epilogue? Why?" He places his hand on my stomach. "We're just getting started."

~

If you'd like to read more about The Palmer Sisters, be sure to check out Molly: The Palmer Sisters Book 7.

Molly Gustafson Barone never pictured her life turning out like this— as a single mom to a three-

year-old daughter. But that's what
happens when your husband, the love of
her life, runs off and dies in Afghanistan.
Sometimes life throws you a curve-ball
that slams you right in the head. The only
good thing to come out of all that pain?
Madalyn—the small piece of Adam that
lives on and the only person she'll ever
need. Maybe...

Sigmund "Sig" Engel is a man
on a mission. After leaving the service, he found himself in the
sleepy little town of Page, Arizona, working at a custom bike
shop. Fate isn't what brought him to her. It was a promise he
made to a fallen brother and a decision that may just change his
life forever.

Help

If you or anyone you know has been a victim of sexual assault, there are a number of National organizations who are here to help as well as local organizations in your area. Here are links to just a few.

You are not alone.

～

RAINN'S MISSION

RAINN (Rape, Abuse & Incest National Network) is the nation's largest anti-sexual violence organization. RAINN created and operates the National Sexual Assault Hotline

800.656.HOPE, **online.rainn.org**

in partnership with more than 1,000 local sexual assault service providers across the country and operates the DoD Safe Helpline for the Department of Defense. RAINN also carries out programs to prevent sexual violence, help survivors, and ensure that perpetrators are brought to justice.

NSVRC (National Sexual Violence Resource Center)

The National Sexual Violence Resource Center (NSVRC) is the leading nonprofit in providing information and tools to prevent and respond to sexual violence. NSVRC translates research and trends into best practices that help individuals, communities and service providers achieve real and lasting change. The center also works with the media to promote informed reporting. Every April, NSVRC leads Sexual Assault Awareness Month (SAAM), a campaign to educate and engage the public in addressing this widespread issue. NSVRC is also one of the three founding organizations of Raliance, a national, collaborative initiative dedicated to ending sexual violence in one generation.

717-909-0710 PHONE 717-909-0714 FAX
717-909-0715 TTY
877-739-3895 TOLL-FREE

More links:

The National Center for Victims of Crime
Joyful Heart Foundation
Feminist Majority Foundation
CDC: The Centers for Disease Control and Prevention

ACKNOWLEDGMENTS

Thank you to Hot Tree Editing for editing this book from start to finish.

And an extra special thank you to Becky at Hot Tree Promotions for your advice, expertise, and your positivity.

And for my beta readers. Thank you so much for your time and feedback!

ALSO BY KAYT MILLER

Bedhead

Redhead

Deadhead

FarmBoy

Game Changer

One of a Kind

The Virginia Chronicles

Our of the Blue: The Flynns Book One

Mick'sology: The Flynns Book Two

Vested Interest: The Flynns Book Three

The Importance of Being Ernie: The Flynns Book Four

The Importance of Being Kennedy's: The Flynns Book Five

Quirky Girl: The Flynns Book Six

The Art of the Game

Lainie: The Palmer Sisters Book 1

Agatha: The Palmer Sisters Book 2

Sadie: The Palmer Sisters Book 3

Cortland: The Palmer Sisters Book 4

Keely: The Palmer Sisters Book 5

Violet: The Palmer Sisters Book 6

Molly: The Palmer Sisters Book 7

The Portrait Painter

Hopeful Romantic (Link coming soon.)

Thanks to Margie Dill (Link coming soon.)

ABOUT THE AUTHOR

How did it all start? Well, I love reading and one day I was searching for a book. A book about a certain type of woman and a specific kind of man and I couldn't find it so, I wrote it. I called it Game Changer and it couldn't have been a more appropriate title. It changed my life in many ways. While my real job is teaching young people, my fun job is conjuring up characters and situations to write about.

My goal, as a writer, is to write stories that relate to all of us, to make readers laugh and maybe cry sometimes. I hope my readers can escape into a fantasy, one that's actually possible. Sure, some of the stories could be dubbed "Insta-love" stories but that's okay. I fell in love with my husband pretty damn fast and with my daughter the second I saw her. So, it's a thing, I swear.

Please Follow Me on these social media sites. Following on BookBub to learn about special book deals.

I love hearing from you!

Thank you so much for reading Violet and Eric's story! When I start a story, it begins with an outline, notes, and lots of crazy thoughts running through my head. When I actually start writing, the characters take over, leading me through the story like they're holding my hand—guiding me. The process is exciting and cathartic. With that said, I hope you enjoy the story.

If you did, please go to my website, www.kaytmiller.com, and join my newsletter so you can be the first to know what's coming up next. And...

Please, leave a review!

No matter how you feel about the book, please leave a review. Reviews are important to authors and other readers. I, for one, read them and sure, it takes me a week or two to get over the bad ones, but it's how we learn, right? Seriously, I've gained great insight in this process through your eyes. So, post on Amazon or Goodreads. You can also contact me via my Website, or in an email if you've really got to vent. ;)

Chapter 1
Molly

"Happy birthday dear Madalyn, happy birthday to you."

I'm singing along by my mind is on other things.

I can't believe our little girl is three, Adam. She's so much like you. She may look like me but everything that makes her a special little person is all you, Adam. God, I wish you were here.

I do my best to shake off my thoughts. As soon as the song ends, we all clap. I take the opportunity to look around the extra-large table we've got set up at Gustafson Custom Motorcycles, more specifically in Keeton's showroom, or brag room, as my little brother Eric calls it. It fits. Ordinarily, the room is filled with my big brother's awards, framed magazine covers in which he's featured, and one or two custom motorcycles.

But not today. No, today almost everything has been cleared out to make room for my baby girl's third birthday party. We needed space since our family has blown up in the last couple of years to ten times the amount we were when my Maddy was born.

I see my brother, Eric, first. He's holding his son, Oliver, who is just six months old. His wife, the sweetest person on earth, Violet is cooing at her baby next to him. I smile because I'm happy for them. My brother is a great guy and an even better father. I'm so proud of him I could burst.

I search the crowd for Keeton, the oldest in our family. When I spot him, he's on the floor in the play area they set up when their little girl, Rachel, was old enough to come to the shop now and then. Now she's two and a handful. Not only that, she's got her daddy wrapped around her pretty little finger. Example. Keeton, my big-bad biker brother is wearing dark jeans, a black t-shirt, leather biker boots, and a tiara. No joke. A tiara. That's what he does for his girl. Or I guess I should say girls. His wife is Lainie. She's wonderful and sweet and amazing and Violet's older sister. It doesn't seem possible that one family could produce two such genuinely kind people but it turns out, it produced five. Well, correction. Keely is an acquired taste but she's still funny as hell and cool. I like her spunkiness.

I blink when I realize I've been staring at my brother playing with Rachel. I watch as Lainie moves closer with her palm on her stomach. She's pregnant again, due sometime in the spring. My brother has it all. He really does. And he doesn't take it for granted. Neither of my brothers do. They know how fragile and unpredictable life can be. One minute you're happily married awaiting the birth of your child, and BAM, the next thing you know your husband is dead a week before her birth.

I sigh. I can't start that kind of thinking. Not today — of all days. Adam died three years ago in Afghanistan. He died doing what he loved—serving his country. Granted, he was getting out so he could be here with me and Maddy, but he loved his job.

Shit. My eyes burn a little bit but, goddamn it, I'm not

going to get all maudlin on Maddy's big day. We've been planning this party for weeks. Her theme is based on her favorite Disney character. No, it's not a princess. It's a horse. Maximus from the move Tangled. She loves that horse and I don't blame her. He was hilarious. So, yeah, Sadie made her an amazing cake shaped like a horse, the walls are decorated in Tangled gear we bought at a party store, and she's never been happier. It could also be because she's surrounded by cousins, friends, aunts and uncles. She's a social butterfly so the attention she's getting today, along with too many presents, and way too much sugar, is making her vibrate with giddiness.

"Hey, Molls."

I look over at another one of the Palmer sisters, Agatha. "Hey." I peek down at the little one on her hip. "Hey, there Lily," I say in my mom voice. "You're getting so big."

"And stinky." Agatha pinches her nose with her free hand. "Mind if I use your office to change her?"

"Actually," I say as Lily holds onto my finger. "We've set up Lainie's office as a make-shift changing area. It's even stocked up with diapers, wipes, and a rocker."

"Oh, my gosh. You're amazing." Agatha says with a huge smile. "Thanks."

"No problem." And it's not. It was actually Keeton's idea. Not only do we have the babies I've already mentioned, we've also got Sadie and Charlies little guy, Finn. He's nearly two as well. He and Rachel were born only a couple months apart. In addition to that, Polly and Cortland Ashbury have a newborn, Keely is pregnant due in July. There's one other person with similar news but I promised to keep that a secret until she's further along.

"Mama," says my girl from her booster seat. She's completely covered in cake. Head-to-toe in cake.

"Yes, birthday girl?" I reach out and swipe some frosting from her cheek and put it in my mouth. "Mm, yummy."

"Mama," she giggles. "Don't eat my face."

I will never tire of hearing that giggle. Is there anything better than a child's laughter? No. I laugh as I reach for another taste. "But, you're so delicious."

"Mommy. No!" she says in her demanding voice. A voice I remember hearing a lot from her father. Don't get me wrong, my Adam was bossy as all get out, but he was the love of my life and I was his. He did everything he could to make me happy.

Everything but live, I guess.

"Okay, boo. I won't eat your face. Are you ready to open presents?"

"Yeah!" she shouts at the top of her little lungs.

"Let's go get cleaned up." I brought a second outfit for her to wear for precisely this reason. Cake is her Kryptonite.

"Okay." She hops down from her chair, places her gooey, cake covered hand in mine, and off we go to the make-shift baby room.

Chapter 2
Sig

If you'd told me, ten years ago, that I'd be standing around at a kiddy party with a local cop and a retired FBI agent, I'd have punched you in the throat for being a fucking idiot. Me and cops have never seen eye to eye on shit. Hell, the reason I joined the Army was because I *had* to. As a juvenile delinquent, and a repeat offender, it was my only option. Well, not my *only* option. I could have gone to jail instead but they gave me a choice and I jumped at the Army option. Little did I know the Army would be the hardest thing I've ever done. And I'm not just talking physically.

So, yeah, here I am at a kiddy party standing around with guys I'd easily call my friends. If my father could see this shit, he'd probably roll over at the sight. Not only do the pack of us do stuff like this together but we fish, play poker, and hang out to watch a game now and then. So, yeah, they're my friends and they have been for the past couple of years; ever since I moved to this sleepy little town.

And I've needed them.

When I left the service, I felt sort of empty inside; like part of me was gone. Hell, the minute I changed out of my army fatigues for the last time, I felt like I'd lost a limb. That is until I came here. I walked into Gustafson Custom Motorcycles and met Keeton, a man I'd heard a great deal about, shook his hand, and suddenly felt better.

Hell, I'm not going to get into all that bullshit now. I'll save that for another day. No, today is about princess Maddy. I don't say that all bitchy either. She *is* a princess. She's, hands down, the prettiest little girl I've ever seen. And sweet? Damn, she's a sweetheart. And funny. The little girl cracks me up daily with all of her silly questions and completely uninhibited observations. For instance, Maddy has informed me multiple times that I'm too tall, too hairy, and I need to smile more. Yeah, she's highly critical of me. She takes after her mama in that regard, that's for sure.

Speaking of her mama, I scan the room in search of her. I don't have to look far; she's over talking to her daughter. I watch as she swipes frosting from her kid's cheek and places it in her mouth. Maddy laughs which makes Molly smile. Not something that happens all that often.

"So, what'd you get my niece?" asks Eric Gustafson as he slaps me on my back.

"Drum set."

"Damn, what're they going to do with two of those?" snickers Eric.

"One at your place?" I smirk.

"Or at yours. You live right next door to her, she hangs at your place more than she does mine, it makes more sense to put it there."

He's right. Maddy hangs out at my place every now and then so Molly can do girl shit. I'm not her regular babysitter by any means but I'm there if she needs me.

"Well," I chuckle. "Lucky for you, I wasn't an asshole. You'll have to wait and see what I got her."

I actually made her something. A wooden doll bed for her favorite toy. It rocks like a cradle. I carved the doll's name, Dolly, in the headboard and had a local seamstress woman make the bedding for it. I hope she likes it.

Eric turns just as his wife, Violet, steps up holding their baby boy. "Time to open gifts, guys. Can you all come over to the table?"

"Sure thing, honey." Eric says softly reaching his arms out toward his baby. "Let me have my boy."

Violet raises him gently and places him in Eric's arms. They both stare at their kid and I can't help but feel a pang of jealousy. I want that. I want *all* that.

www.ingramcontent.com/pod-product-compliance
Lightning Source LLC
Chambersburg PA
CBHW051652180726
48284CB00006B/1974